Macgregor's Bargain

by
Rowena Williamson

Copyright © 2012 Rowena Williamson
All rights reserved.

ISBN: 1466499524
ISBN 13: 9781466499522

Acknowledgements

This book took many years and the help of many people.

My dear friend, literary agent Andrea Hurst, has pushed me, pulled me, and formed Just Write at the Pier for budding writers. Her unselfish work with all of us has made a difference in our lives. Author Bharti Kirchner has generously helped me bring this book to its present state. Thanks, Bharti. Audrey Mackaman, friend and editor is also a Scottish Deerhound lover

The members of Whidbey Writers Group, all of them fine writers and editors, have helped me over the years.

Mare Chapman, a writer herself, has been a cheerleader and travel companion.

I thank my sons Andrew and Philip, cover artist for *MacGregor's Bargain*, and my daughter in law, Sara, for the joy and love they've given me.

And to the memory of Phil, who jumped up and cheered when I won my first award for this book.

MACGREGOR'S BARGAIN

Chapter One

July 1744

Anne Drummond turned toward the deerhound Bard as he growled and walked to the east facing window. Anne's heart thudded against her stays and she knew the great hound sensed her fear. Anne began to follow him as her maid Fiona said, "Hold still, or I'll never get this lace right."

"They must be coming. Bard senses them," Anne said. "Hurry, go downstairs, see what he looks like, and come back! Take Bard with you. Let me be alone for a moment to gather myself."

Fiona nodded and stood, arms crossed. "You look beautiful."

Anne gave an unladylike snort. "Go!"

As she turned back to the window, she saw horsemen coming through the screen of trees that marked the road from Fort William.

"The bridegroom cometh," she muttered, trying to pick out the man who was her betrothed.

After the door shut, she looked again at the horsemen nearing Castle Caorann. Four-no five men, looking around as they rode, no one really leading.

She clasped her hands and wished she could pray. She promised herself she would show no emotion, no fear that would delight her grandfather who hated her for disgracing him, and according to him, the entire Drummond clan.

She hoped this man, this member of the proscribed MacGregors, would not be too odious. But she was afraid, and she must be sure that MacGregor and her grandfather would never know.

And as far as the stranger went, the man who had come to marry her, she would meet him calmly, and hope that her dreams were wrong, that he would not lead her people into war.

* * *

Two deerhounds, tall as ponies, burst through the open doors of Castle Caorann. Like gray shadows, they circled the nervous horses. As Niall MacGregor dismounted and slapped the dust from his clothes, he noticed an old man standing in the doorway.

"Ye've come at last. I thought mayhap the British warships had captured you. I am Alasdair Drummond."

MacGregor bowed. "Niall MacGregor. Your servant, sir. The winds were not in our favor. I bring you greetings from Lord John Drummond in France."

He followed Alasdair Drummond through past the open ironbound door into the great hall of Caorann Castle.

"Fiona, send the trollop down!" Drummond bellowed.

A red haired girl, dust cloth in hand, fled up the staircase followed by one of the deerhounds that had come in with the men; the other hound stayed at Drummond's side.

MacGregor, walking behind his host, looked around the great hall that would be his after his marriage to Drummond's granddaughter.In spite of the August heat outside, the ancient gray stones held the chill of winters past. Dust motes drifted in the sunlight from high windows, and his eye caught the movement of a tattered battle flag, so old the colors were shades of gray, hanging on the wall next to a crossed pair of claymores.

Drummond led the way into a room lined with bookshelves, casement windows opened to an enclosed garden. Sunlight fell softly on late roses, their scent coming to MacGregor on a breeze from Loch Laggan. The hound followed them in and went to lie in front of the fireplace.

From a table near the door Alasdair Drummond took a decanter of whisky, pouring each of them a sizable drink. MacGregor examined the grandfather of his betrothed as he took his glass.

The old man grinned slyly. "Our secret. The tax man has yet to find where we make our whisky. Fine, is it not?"

MacGregor nodded, inhaling the scent of peat smoke in the whisky.

Drummond was just short of six feet, his belly hanging over the belt of his trews, his yellowed, old fashioned wig askew. The old man's red nose and cheeks showed years of raw Highland weather, and, MacGregor suspected, a great deal of whisky. Drummond peered at him through a thicket of gray eyebrows.

The two men raised their glasses, toasting exiled King James Stuart, away in Rome.

"Shall we discuss our contract?" MacGregor asked.

Alasdair Drummond guffawed. "Yes, the land comes first, then the wench. I have over a thousand acres of land, the peninsula where Castle Caorann sits and to the top of the hill above. Two more bits toward Loch Linnhe. Thirty families, the people tilling runrig fields and giving a share to me. And over a hundred men to fight for the Prince."

Drummond drained his glass and poured more. "I have a good factor. He is a bit soft on our people at times, but honest, and he keeps a good tally of our animals." The old man eyed Niall. "I hold not more than 100 pounds a year, but few debts. Did Perth tell you I have more money? Well he lied," he said.

He poured more whisky in his own glass, added a bit to MacGregor's "You received her miniature?"

Niall had the small painting in his bag: a girl of eighteen, rather plain, with a strong face and heavy lidded, almond shaped eyes. He nodded.

"You were told, I'm sure, of her bein' caught in the sheets with the Duke of Perth's youngest brother? I kept her locked up here to make sure she wasn't breeding." Drummond nudged the deerhound with his toe. "It's easier lookin' after this kind of bitch when she's in heat." Then Drummond laughed at his joke.

MacGregor eyed him. What sort of man would talk of his own kin that way? He turned to the door as he heard a rustle of skirts. A young woman in a yellow satin gown with narrow hoops, white lace at the sleeves and a lace scarf at the modest neckline, walked in and curtseyed. He wondered if she had heard the old man.

Anne Drummond was nearly as tall as her grandfather, whom she passed as if he weren't there. The hound that had trotted up the stairs now pressed against her, and Niall saw her hand clutching the rough pelt, her knuckles white. The lace scarf at her bosom trembled as if her heart beat hard, but her steady look gave nothing away. Her hair, nearly the same chestnut color as her eyes, was bound in a net at the nape of her neck, a few tendrils escaping.

"Well, MacGregor, do ye still want her after seein' her? She's no bargain, but the land will be yours."

The girl stood silently, merely watching MacGregor as he gazed at her.

"Well, Mistress, do you speak? Have you agreed to our marriage?" MacGregor asked.

She opened her mouth, then shut it and cleared her throat. Before she could speak her grandfather gave a bark of laughter.

"I have heard from the Duke of Perth, girl," said Drummond, "and young Hugh his brother will wed at Hogmanay. And you and your bridegroom will be there to wish him well."

Anne Drummond swallowed and bit her lip.

"Ah, news to ye. Ye didn't think Perth would wed his heir to you? Not after seein' you act the strumpet."

Looking directly at Niall MacGregor, Anne Drummond said, "Sir, I have agreed to the marriage." Her husky voice quavered but her face was a calm mask.

The old man gave a disgusted snort, slammed down his glass and told MacGregor, "She's yours then. I have things to see to." He motioned to his hound and they left the room, Drummond calling over his shoulder, "I'll be nearby when you're through here. D'ye wish a chaperone, lass, tae keep yer reputation intact?" His booming laughter followed him into the hall.

In the silence that followed after, MacGregor looked around. "A pleasant room."

"It is part of the original tower, 300 years or more, when our family first came here. All the rest was added over the years, first the addition in front, then years later the back wing."

She walked to the window, the hound following. MacGregor caught a scent of lavender as she passed him.

"My father built the walled garden for my mother." When she turned back to him, sunlight shown for a moment on her face.

"A fine library. Do you read?" he asked.

"I read. I have done a great deal of reading this past twelvemonth."

Her hound stretched out with a noisy sigh, laying his head on one of her feet. She seemed nervous, looking at MacGregor then away, her hands clasped tightly together.

Anne Drummond cleared her throat; when she spoke, her words seemed rehearsed. "Master MacGregor, I am not averse to our marriage, if you have no very bad habits save your support of King James Stuart. I dislike the Stuarts as much as I do the Hanovers. The Stuarts tried in 1715 to take the throne and failed, to the sorrow of many widows left behind. The Hanovers are cold and cruel, and they will take revenge." He interrupted. "I work for the Stuart cause. For two years I have been with Prince Charles in Italy and France. Before that, I was in the court of King James in Rome. I will continue my work. The Stuarts will be on the Scottish throne within a year."

As if he hadn't spoken, Anne said, "I could not make a more advantageous marriage now because of my disgrace. The Duke of Perth has chosen you, and as he is chief of our clan, I honor his wish, although I do have the right to refuse ." She turned again, looking out at the garden. " But this is my land and they are my people. They depend on me, not on my grandfather."

He moved so he could see her expression.

Anne raised her chin and said coolly, "In all honesty I must tell you that I still love Hugh Drummond. But as I will be responsible for the people of Caorann after my grandfather's death, I can only hope that your plans do not endanger this clan."

"Ah. In all honesty. Well, as long as I don't find a cuckoo in my nest, I suppose I shall be able to make do with what you offer. But I warn you, Madam, I will make sure that you do not threaten the Jacobite cause."

He saw a brief flare of anger on her face. Then she nodded. "Good, then. We agree. Come, Bard."

The hound stood, stretched and yawned. Anne curtseyed to MacGregor and left the room, the hound stalking after her, with one look over his shoulder at Niall.

MacGregor watched Anne Drummond go, then turned around, examining the room. A comfortable room it was, and the little he had seen of the land and castle showed everything well kept. He finished his drink and wandered around the library, examining the books. The girl might be a problem. He hoped she would be more biddable after their marriage, but he knew Highland women held their own with their men.

This opportunity to raise men for the Stuarts' cause meant when the Jacobites won the battle to come, and King James was on Scotland's throne, the MacGregor clan would not be proscribed, they could once more own land, could marry and bury their dead in churchyards. That was why he had come; this would be the holding of MacGregors in the future, Drummonds be damned.

He rubbed the auburn stubble on his face. He would wash and shave before the guests came.

A fine bargain, he thought.

Chapter Two

In the great hall, Anne Drummond stopped at one of the massive fireplaces, where a peat fire blazed to ward off the castle's chill, even in summer. She breathed deeply, willing herself to be calm, waiting until her hands stopped shaking, then looked around.

Up in the minstrel's gallery shadows hung, seeming to separate and move, and Anne shivered. Bard leaned against her, his nose pressed against her hand. She patted him.

"Come, Bard."

They walked through the great hall to the kitchen downstairs at the back of the castle, Anne planning today's menu, anything to keep her mind off the future.

"Oona," she called, as she walked down the steps to the kitchen.

"Mistress?" The old cook came to the door, wiping her large red hands on her apron. "I'm fixing sommat for the lads just come."

"Dinner will have to be late, perhaps four of the clock. Grandfather has sent along the loch for people to meet MacGregor, but it will take time for them to gather." She frowned, counting guests. "The joint of venison will do, but make sure of extras - a mutton broth, perhaps. Do we have enough fish? Shall you send the lads down to the loch to catch more? Then that will do, with garden greens, and a pudding, with some berries. And will you tell Jane I need to see her?"

Oona nodded. "Aye. Dinner will be ready by four. The joint is already on the spit. Mistress Jane is down the cellar. I'll send a boy down for her."

Anne and Bard walked through the kitchen, where women were busy at the stove and hearth, then out into the sunny day. Wind smelling of wildness and heather blew off the loch and caused her skirts to billow around her ankles. The kitchen yard with its tidy garden ended at a gate to the stable yard on the castle's west side. She saw four men leading pack horses toward the stables while a small man, his red hair turning gray, watched them.

"Iain," she called.

Iain, her grandfather's factor, held a large, nervous gray stallion. The horse twitched its ears as it swung its hindquarters around. Iain grinned and nodded at Anne.

"Iain, is that MacGregor's horse?"

She walked toward the horse till it shied at her windblown skirts. She stopped, admiring the beautiful beast.

"Aye; he's fine, isn't he?" Iain said, as he patted the silky hide. The factor was in his fifties, his red hair going gray.

Anne nodded and looked at the four strangers who were eyeing her with undisguised curiosity. She spoke to the nearest.

"I am Anne Drummond. MacGregor's belongings can go into his room. Go into the kitchen and someone will show you the way. The cook is preparing food for you."

The man bowed to Anne. "I'm his cousin Calum. This one is my wee brother Davey," he gestured toward a youth who stood taller than he. "And yonder are our cousins Will and his brother Murdo. The great dour one is Hamish."

Will and Murdo nodded as Hamish took packs off one horse.

Anne turned her attention to Calum. He did look a great deal like Niall MacGregor, tall, with the same dark auburn hair, though much friendlier.

"Should you need anything, please let Iain know. Guests are coming to hear the news from France. Will you and the others join us?"

"I will get our men settled now." He bowed again and took the stallion from Iain, then joined the other MacGregors as they led the horses into the stables. Hamish carried the packs toward the castle.

Anne called after him. "Are those MacGregor's?"

At the man's nod, she said, " Tell the housekeeper you are to put MacGregor's packs in the new wing."

"Iain," Anne asked, watching him go, "what do you think of MacGregor?"

"I'll tell you true, this one's not come begging. Their horses are all beauties. The men are a fine lot, and well spoken too."

Anne said, "MacGregor has money, and men for King James's cause. Grandfather will do well from this. He'd marry me to the devil if there was a profit."

Iain looked down and said nothing, but she saw his smile.

"With all the guests arriving, I must see to rooms, in case they stay the night."

Iain nodded. "There is still room in the stable block for their clansmen."

Anne turned to walk back to the castle, the gray stone walls rising above her, Loch Laggan beyond, shining pewter in the sunlight. She thought of her grandaunt Seana's house in Edinburgh, and laughter and parties...and Hugh Drummond, her own distant cousin, with his slim body and his brown hair and eyes so like her own, and his sweet words to her. Hugh, the reason she was sent back in disgrace to Castle Caorann.

She sighed as she went around to the front of the castle. From here, she could see the small island in the center of the loch where her parents were buried. The ruined chapel stood stark and white against the background of trees on the far side of Loch Laggan.

As she entered the courtyard she looked up and for a moment she thought she saw a figure in a window of her own tower room. She shivered, then shook her head.

Wild fancies I'm having-a curtain moving, most like.

Anne pushed open the heavy oak doors, entering the great hall. The housekeeper swept past her carrying a load of clean linen, her heels clicking on the stone floor.

Macgregor's Bargain

"Jane. I asked for you."

The housekeeper halted and waited for Anne to speak, her heavy brows drawn together, black hair pulled tightly under her cap.

"Did you put MacGregor in the room across from Grandfather's?"

" I pointed the way to the man with packs. D'ye not think it too grand for a MacGregor?"

Anne studied the woman. "I think not. He doesn't come from a cow byre in Balquidder. Besides, if they stay up half the night carousing, they won't disturb me. And make sure at least three other rooms are set up in case other guests wish to stay."

Jane nodded grimly. "As you wish."

Anne made a face at the retreating poker-stiff back. Jane had made her disapproval plain since Anne's return from Edinburgh. She had been housekeeper and in virtual control of daily life at Castle Caorann for years, and showed her displeasure at taking orders from Anne.

On her way up the stairs, and along the back corridor in the new wing of the castle, added by her great grandfather, girls were airing rooms, the scent of lavender in the air from clean linen. Narrow recessed windows showed a view of the sunlit loch.

Autumn was near. Anne had noticed red rowan berries during her ride today through the harvested barley fields. The Drummond people were coming back from the shielings in the hills where they had spent the summer caring for cattle and sheep. Anne remembered summer days of her childhood up in the high meadows. As the cattle fattened on the lush grass, sheep were sheared and wool spun, cheese and butter made for the winter.

In the best guest room in the new wing, the bed was hung with curtains made during her mother's life by Loch Laggan women. The green and brown embroidery on the ivory colored curtains matched the rug that lay next to the bed. This back wing had been decorated by her father. Anne could not remember him, nor her mother. Both of them lay in their graves on the burial island out in the loch. With a finger she traced the intertwined patterns.

She went to the window and looked south along Loch Laggan, at the brilliant reds and golds of bracken and rowan, at the purple of heather.

MacGregor's men had left his cases in the room, and as she turned from the window she paused for a moment, looking down at them, thinking of marriage to this stranger.

"Are my belongings so fascinating, mistress?"

MacGregor's voice, deep and mocking, spun Anne around to face him. She smoothed down the front of her gown. Bard moved in front of Anne and leaned against her, staring at the interloper. Though MacGregor was well dressed in doeskin breeches and a green coat and buff waistcoat, his clothes were travel stained. A coppery beard was just beginning to show, redder than his hair. He was tall, his face lean with a long nose, a little flattened at the bridge. His wide mouth curled at the corners now as he watched her.

"No, sir. I was lost in thought, and knew not what I was looking at."

MacGregor walked past Anne to look out the open casement.

"A fine view, mistress. A fine room for so humble a guest."

She lowered her eyes as he turned, so he might not read them. *He mocks me*, she thought.

"Indeed, sir, you are my grandfather's guest as well as my betrothed, and any guest would be treated so."

"Tell me, do you like the life here? It must be dull for a maid as young as you. Do you not miss the balls and music in Edinburgh?"

Her jaw tightened, but she did not look up. Was there undue emphasis placed on the word *maid?*

"I fear, sir, though I have lived in Edinburgh and enjoyed it mightily, I am not traveled enough to feel as comfortable anywhere as I do here, in my own home. I would not be happy to leave Loch Laggan for long. We here are tied to our land."

She finally raised her head to look sideways at him, to see the effect of her words on a landless, proscribed MacGregor. He was examining her in a way that made her uncomfortable. She curtseyed and left the room, head high, the great hound pacing behind her.

Macgregor's Bargain

Along the corridor to her room, Anne stopped to look first down into the shadows of the minstrel's gallery, then beyond it into the great hall. Servants still scurried around, and she heard her grandfather's voice roaring at someone.

She climbed the stairs to her own room, the one she loved best. The round room in the east tower above the library held one large casement window looking south east over the loch, to the mountains and the glen that led down to the headland on which the castle sat. Another window near the fireplace faced north and west with a view along the loch, the blue Grampian Mountains rising above the quiet water The sun was still high in the sky, but westering. Nearly two months since midsummer, and the days had shortened. As Anne began to disrobe, she strolled to the east window. The rose garden below her was filled with shadow. Something moved: a bending of stems as if a breeze caught the last blooms. Petals scattered.

Anne pulled the window shut and turned, frowning. This room, this haven of peace, seemed disturbed now, as though it were a pond into which someone had thrown a stone, leaving ripples of unquiet behind. There was a restlessness here, outside herself. Bard sensed it too and roamed the room, looking into corners, staring at the bed, before he settled himself on the hearthrug. She turned again, feeling the weight of someone behind her. It was not the first time she had felt this. And as always, when she turned, there was no one.

Was it her mother, dead since she was an infant? As a child, she had often been comforted in the night by this sense. But today there was a different feeling, one of foreboding . It must have come with those men, the MacGregors. She shuddered.

Anne heard footsteps, a high voice humming just outside the door, and Fiona came in carrying Anne's newly pressed gown. Fiona had inherited her father Iain's red hair and freckles, and her mother Morag's brown eyes. Barely coming to Anne's shoulder, she had to raise high the full gown she carried so it wouldn't brush the floor.

Fiona helped Anne out of her yellow morning gown, and into a chemise and corset. She tied the first petticoat around Anne's waist. Anne's gown, made of apricot brocade over a pale green

Macgregor's Bargain

satin petticoat, was one from Edinburgh days, in the latest fashion. Its square neckline showed the long smooth line of her neck, and her breasts, pushed up by her corset, threatened to burst from their confinement. The sleeves of the gown were tight to below her elbows, then billowed out in layers of lace.

As she fussed the ruffles on Anne's sleeves, Anne frowned.

"Does it not look well?"

Anne shivered. "Yes, I just had an odd fancy." Then she examined her reflection, turning from side to side. "Do I look like an Edinburgh lady?"

"Perhaps you might be wearing the fichu?" Fiona waved a bit of transparent lace. "These are country folk here, and that gown shows a bit too much bosom."

Anne shook her head. "I think, Fiona, I might as well dress to please myself. They have their own opinions of me."

She sat down at her dressing table and Fiona brushed out Anne's hair, then pinned it up and teased a few curls loose. She stood back and admired her work.

Anne rose, grinned, and made a sweeping curtsey, her skirts and petticoats billowing out. "I think the green shawl, too, Fiona, for the chill on the stairs."

Anne walked down the broad stone stairs as Niall MacGregor appeared at the door of the library and looked up. Head to one side, she looked just as steadily back at him, and then continued downstairs, holding her gown from the rough stone, faithful Bard padding behind.

MacGregor moved aside to allow her into the room.

Bard went to lie in front of the fire near the other deerhound. Alasdair Drummond sat near the dogs, his brown satin breeches, green velvet coat and lace neckpiece at odds with his coarse face, and his red waistcoat straining against its gold buttons.

Niall MacGregor, on the other hand, looked as if he wore satin and velvet every day. He had changed into black satin breeches and coat, with an embroidered white waistcoat. His hazel eyes flicked over Anne in an admiring, impersonal way, before he again spoke to her grandfather, carrying on a conversation that had begun before her entrance.

"France is a good place to be now. So much seems to be happening so quickly. The attitude toward the English is very poor indeed, which is all to the good of Scotland. The French will do all they can to help our cause. They are afraid of Hanover ambitions in Europe, and the Flanders War."

"And well they should be, sir. Those damned Germans want to rule all Europe!" Alasdair Drummond poured a large glass of brandy and downed half of it in one gulp as he stared at Anne's bare bosom. "Now the wench is here, let us speak of the betrothal. Castle Caorann has no heir save Anne. Anne's mother and father were poor specimens, both of them, leaving just her. As a MacGregor, with no land, but money and men, you will do right well with this match ."

Anne saw MacGregor's face tighten as Drummond continued.

He hawked and spat toward the fireplace, missing it and startling Bard, then glared at his granddaughter. "I give you to Niall MacGregor, and good riddance. He'll sire some sons on you, and they'll take the name of Drummond since MacGregors can't hold land, being proscribed."

Again Anne watched MacGregor's eyes grow cold. She knew the proscription of the MacGregors as outlaws meant more than not holding land; they could not sign their names on any legal paper. MacGregor would probably use his mother's name as his uncle Rob Roy had done, and his and Anne's children would be christened Drummonds.

"I hope there'll be no lack of Drummonds at Castle Caorann. And the mighty Duke of Perth, Lord James Drummond, will have no cause to take this castle for his brother Hugh."

MacGregor said nothing, simply sat watching the old man and twirling the brandy in his glass

Drummond said grimly. "I wish you luck, sir. The trollop is not only too free with her favors; she has a nasty tongue on her, and too many other unladylike airs. If you think she could do with a good beating, I'll gladly lend you my crop." He stood up, peering beyond the rose garden wall. "My guests come, MacGregor. They will want to hear your news." He strode out into the great hall.

MacGregor went to a table by the mullioned windows and poured brandy from the heavy decanter. He looked at her. "I appreciate your honesty earlier today, when you spoke your mind."

She nodded. "I do hold honor highly, sir. But I do love Hugh, and he loves me, whatever must happen."

MacGregor shook his head. "I doubt not that you were loved. I only doubt that love was the kind that poets write of. A randy young man will promise much to a maid, and, if she is unused to the ways of men, it can go hard for her. As for Hugh Drummond, he must be either very cruel or very weak, to make the maid who loves him suffer so."

His eyes drifted down to the low neckline of her gown.

She caught his look, and wished she had added the fichu.

He grinned. "I admire your gown, my lady. I had no thought of seeing such among Highlanders."

"You won't, sir," she retorted. "I wore this because my grandfather hates it, it reminds him of my shame. If you don't like it, I will not wear it again."

"Indeed, I think you should. I have no objection to men eyeing my wife's tits, as long as I'm the one who holds them."

Her eyes widened, her face turned red. "Surely, sir, that is no way to talk to one you hardly know."

He laughed softly. "I did embarrass you. So you're not quite the shameless hussy of your grandfather's reports." He bowed, and left the room, shutting the door behind him.

Anne stared after him, hearing her grandfather welcoming the first guests. She sank into a chair, her hand over her eyes, feeling the dull hopelessness in which she had wandered this past year. And now this man, come from over the water, would wed her because he wanted land and status in Scotland. It was a good bargain, for him and for her. She must accept this. She could expect nothing more. But what was to come, after? The dark fear she had felt earlier still lay in the back of her mind.

I will not cry she thought. Loch Laggan must be kept safe through what was to come. She must be strong for her clan.

She sighed, and looked in the tiny mirror tied at her waist by a ribbon, to make sure traces of tears did not show, then went to greet her guests.

Chapter Three

The MacPhersons, the Munros, the MacTavishes, neighbors from around Loch Laggan, came to hear the news from France. Others from farther away would come in the next days for news of the King over the water. They gathered in the great hall, as servants busied themselves at the long table set below the minstrel's gallery.

Anne had known all of them since childhood, but she knew they were thinking of her disgrace on this, her first appearance since her year of seclusion. Gavin Munro beamed at her as his eyes rested on her bosom. His wife Agnes, taller than he, her imposing figure clad in a gray gown that resembled tarnished armor, and seemed as invulnerable, pulled him along after nodding grimly at Anne.

Lucy Robertson greeted her with kisses on both cheeks. An Edinburgh native who had known Anne for years, she was married to Anne's childhood friend Alan MacPherson.

"I think your dress is lovely," she said with a conspiratorial smile. "Does your grandfather approve? Did he tell you I've called, many times? And so has Alan. Does this mean you're out of Purgatory?" She giggled behind her fan.

Anne smiled back at her. "Yes, I am out of Purgatory and no, Grandfather told me nothing. He tried to make me believe that everyone shunned me. But I knew you and Alan better than that."

Across the room, Alan stood next to Alasdair Drummond, listening to some interminable story. When he caught her eye he slowly shut one eyelid in a wink.

Katherine MacTavish swooped down on them, decked out in a purple gown many years out of date the froth of lace at her enormous bosom reminding Anne of the curl of a wave in front of a man of war. She kissed Anne, who curtseyed, then turned her attention to Lucy.

"Now, then, my dear, you must tell me all that has gone on in Edinburgh. It's been well over a year since I last was there. Is that lovely dress of yours the latest style?"

"I think Anne's is, but most cannot wear that style. It calls for a near perfect form, and more height that I have." Lucy said sweetly to Mistress MacTavish as she continued, "And I daresay that society, or some parts of it, would shock you. Ladies of fashion now drink, and swear, and naught is said if a married lady entertains a gentleman not her husband in her boudoir. And all the time the city fathers refuse to allow harmless plays and such entertainments. 'Tis a most upside down sort of place."

Katherine MacTavish's eyebrows threatened to climb up to her wig. Her fan swished briskly. "Ah, I feel much safer here in the Highlands, surrounded by decent folk. And Anne, Loch Laggan lands have done well this summer, have they not? Our own crofters have benefitted from the mild summer. Now I must speak to dear Alan. I have not see him since Lucy and he were wed." She swept off toward Alan and Alaisdair Drummond

Lucy and Anne wandered close to the fireplace, its flames casting light and shadow across them.

"Is it true," Anne asked, "that Edinburgh is becoming.."

"Oh, indeed," Lucy replied. "My father is quite concerned about the crowd my brother sees, and he's very careful that my younger sister not be caught up by someone who...oh, dear."

"Might ruin her? Did he hold me up as an example?"

"Yes."

"Please don't be embarrassed, Lucy. What happened, happened, and my grandfather has finally found a way to save his honor, and to pay me back for my humiliation of him."

"Alan says your grandfather...Oh, my, I do seem to be even more stupid than usual."

"I know very well what Alan would have to say about my grandfather."

A movement at the arched doorway caught Anne's eyes. Niall MacGregor stood looking around him. She noticed he was taller than any man in the room, and he carried himself as if Castle Caorann already belonged to him.

"Oh, my dear, who is that man?"

"That," said Anne, amused in spite of herself, "is Niall MacGregor, my bridegroom and my grandfather's revenge."

Lucy stared at her, her blue eyes round. "Well, and do you approve of him?"

"Grandfather has bound me to it, and I have agreed, and we will marry as soon as banns are read."

MacGregor joined Anne's grandfather and Alan. Drummond spoke to Alan, the two younger men bowed to each other, then Alan's turned to look at Anne. He bowed to MacGregor again and made his way to Lucy and Anne. He dropped a kiss on Anne's cheek.

"This past year's been so long. I have missed you," Alan said. "And now it seems you're soon to be wed."

Anne nodded. "And I missed you, and I am so sorry that I missed your wedding. It is heartening that you thought of me. My grandfather would have me believe that the whole world had turned against me." She rested her hand on his arm. "And yes, I have agreed to the marriage."

"Ah, well, I hope you know we will always be for you. As for our wedding, I am sorry too. But will you stand godmother for our infant?" He grinned widely, his ruddy face glowing.

"Oh, such news. Of course I will, and gladly. When is the cherub due?"

"Not for six months yet. We haven't told anyone else. You're the first," Lucy said.

Macgregor's Bargain

"Well, I am honored."

Alan looked down at her, all his laughter gone. "Your grandfather says you'll wed yon MacGregor in just three weeks."

"Ah, yes, but he's not just any MacGregor. He has a great deal of money and men, and, in addition, the ear of the King over the water, or at least the Prince. This was too great a plum for my grandfather to turn away. And he seldom gets the worst of a bargain, as well you know, even when what he has to trade is rather damaged." Anne shot a disdainful look at her grandfather.

She noticed Niall MacGregor watching her, then he strode the three of them.

He bowed to Lucy as they were introduced. "Your servant, Ma'am. Anne, your grandfather bids us go supper."

Back straight, her hand atop MacGregor's, she led the way, and took her seat at the far end of the long table. Her grandfather, with clumsy gallantry, led Lucy to sit beside him. Alan sat next to Lucy, while Anne faced the prospect of having Donald Munro on one side of her, MacGregor on the other.

"Still, don't you think the old ways were best, when ladies ate separately?" Agnes Munro's shrill voice grated on Anne's ears.

"Nay, Mistress Munro, I much prefer that men and women dine together. It makes for much more interesting conversation." Anne smiled winningly at her.

Anne drew back as Donald Munro peered down her bodice. He reminded her of a ferret, with his beady black eyes and pointed nose.

Anne asked MacGregor, "And what news of the French court, sir? I'm sure Mistress Munro would be much enthralled to hear that they are even more licentious than ever."

"Indeed, some may think so. I think, Mistress Anne, that you might enjoy it. There is beautiful music being composed these days, and there are many plays and operas and, er, other entertainments." He turned his smile on the lady to his right. "Some of the plays are a bit suggestive, Madam, but then titillation has always been exciting, hasn't it?"

To Anne's astonishment, Agnes Munro giggled like a schoolgirl and tapped Niall's arm with her fan. "La, sir, you are a rogue. I should die of embarrassment."

Macgregor's Bargain

MacGregor grinned at Mistress Munro, then at Anne, and she smiled back at him before turning back to see to her other guests. The table gleamed with candlelight, reflecting from crystal, and satins and jewels that her guests wore. It formed a pool of light below the dark shadow that rose to the high ceiling above the minstrel's gallery.

Anne watched to make sure servants passed courses as they should: soup, and a savory pie of hare, a saddle of venison, salmon from the loch, and capercaillie, and greens from the herb garden. She drank a good deal more wine than usual, and ate very little. As the puddings were passed, and the apple tart, she sighed.

"You do well as lady of the manor, Mistress." Niall MacGregor looked at her over the top of his goblet.

"Thank you, sir, I have been lady of the manor most of my life, so I've had time to learn my lessons carefully."

Her grandfather stood, and Anne felt her heart began to pound. She hoped he would not remind the guests why his granddaughter was marrying beneath her station.

"In a few moments, when the ladies retire, Niall MacGregor will tell us all the news, and the plans our King is making. First, I will announce the betrothal of my granddaughter Anne to Niall MacGregor. Three weeks from now, after the banns have been read, they will wed. MacGregor, as my grandson by marriage, brings with him his troop of men from France, and guns and ammunition to help us when the rising takes place. He will join the Drummond clan. A toast, ladies and gentlemen, to King James Stuart and his son Prince Charles, and may the Hanover usurper turn tail and run back to Germany where he belongs!"

There was a roar from the men at the table and everyone stood to toast the King over the water. In the minstrel's gallery Iain's oldest son Dughal tuned his pipes.

Then Alasdair Drummond looked down the table. "And to my granddaughter Anne and her marriage to Niall MacGregor." In a perfunctory manner he raised his goblet to the two people at the other end of the table, as people along its sides raised their glasses to Anne and Niall.

Macgregor's Bargain

The first strains of a *pibroach* made everyone look up at the piper, and the men began banging on the table.

Anne rose and led the ladies into the library.

Lucy linked arms with her and murmured, "I'm sure MacGregor won't be as bad as your grandfather. And you'll have more freedom."

"I will, I know, but I do not have the freedom to marry the man I love."

Lucy looked contrite. " I am sorry, dear. But now, I haven't heard you play your harp for so long. Do play for us."

And Anne did, the clarsach, as always, giving her joy.

Drummond poured whisky all around, and the men sat back, the land holders from around the loch, Niall MacGregor, and his cousin Calum, the MacGregors. Above them in the minstrel's gallery Dougal played a pibroch, his skill making the men pause, look up at him and smile, some of them keeping time to the tune.

"Now, then, tell us how it goes, and how many men from France will join us. And when will the Prince come?" Drummond's voice broke in.

Niall looked around the table. "Soon, I hope sir, but English ships are always there. That is a great difficulty. Already some of our guns have been returned to France because the ships could not get past the English. As far as men: we have Scots who have been in France since the '15 and they and their sons will join us and we have been promised French troops and Irish mercenaries. We can hope that the French will continue to engage the English forces in the Lowlands." He stopped and drank, his brows drawing together. "King Louis of France has not been forthcoming with more than promises as yet, and some are urging Prince Charles to wait for more assurances. The Duke of Perth has been most persuasive in urging that invasion begin as soon as possible. As you know his brother John stays near the Prince." He looked around the table assessing the clan leaders, wondering if they would be able to bring enough men to win against the English might. "But it is up to you gentlemen to make sure that the Highlands will rise when Prince Charles comes. Others will urge Borderers and

Jacobites in England. My own people here tell me of lairds who say they will not bring their clans to the fight, remembering their harsh treatment after the '15. Clans such as the Campbells and others who will always side with the Hanovers." He paused at the burst of angry voices that followed his words.

"Those damned Campbells have always been traitors. I know the MacDonalds and Camerons will be with us, and the clans from the Isles," MacTavish blustered.

Francis MacPherson, Alan's father, cleared his throat, his calm voice stating what they all knew. "We must have money, more money. Money will buy arms, money will buy soldiers. Many of us are still poor from the '15. Nearly thirty years, and we are still repairing the damage done to our lands by the Sassenach."

Niall lifted his glass. "The French are promising gold. As to clans here, I leave most of that to you. Runners are being sent the length and breadth of Scotland, and into England, to gauge the strength of our supporters. Our best hope is to have Catholic English come with us. I can promise you that within a year Prince Charles Edward Stuart will land on Scottish soil. And we must be ready to fight, and to win. And I will tell you, gentlemen, we do have men in high places in London to bring information about the Hanover plans."

Those around the table exchanged glances. Niall did not tell them that there were others, in Paris and Edinburgh, who were watching the Stuarts. That was his business, and from what he had seen and heard, he wondered if he could count on these men to keep Jacobite plans to themselves. This would be a different kind of war, and he could not be sure how untrained Highlanders would fight it.

When the men finally appeared in a cloud of whisky fumes Anne was still playing, and the ladies' chatter had all but ceased.

Niall came to Anne's side as she sat fingering her clarsach.

"Ah, it's you who play. I saw this clarsach earlier."

Anne nodded as she played. "And you, sir?"

"A bit, but on the lute or the guitar. Perhaps we shall play a duet, one day." There was something in his voice that made her blush.

A clock in the hall struck ten. Lucy and Alan prepared to leave with the Munros.

Anne drew Lucy aside. "Will you be my attendant? As a dear friend from Edinburgh days, it would mean much to me."

Lucy nodded, her sweet face lighting up. "Oh, I should love to. Shall I come, let's see, the day after tomorrow? We haven't long to plan."

Anne caught her hand, realizing how much she had missed the company of friends. "Yes, do." Then, in a louder voice, "But don't bring Alan. I remember he tore my best dress when I was eight, and I got spanked for it."

She was rewarded by his loud laughter. Anne hugged him, then hugged Lucy. "Alan doesn't deserve anyone half so nice as you, but how fortunate I feel that he did find you."

After the others left Anne, carrying two lamps, escorted Katherine MacTavish to the bedroom that had been prepared for her and her husband Robert.

"I am sure that the men will stay up most of the night. I do hope you'll sleep well here. This wing is quieter than the old rooms." Anne handed Katherine one of the lamps.

Katherine lingered at the door. "Anne, since you are motherless, I do hope you will call on me should you need advice or help."

Anne, surprised, said, "Thank you. I shall do that. I hope you find the room comfortable. Would you like me to send Fiona to help you ready for bed? She is in my room just now, I am sure."

"Yes, thank you, Anne." The older woman said good night to her and entered the bedchamber. Anne blew out a gusty sigh as she made her way back to her tower room. *Three weeks! I must send a message to Aunt Seana.*

Chapter Four

Anne woke as the sun first struck the windows of her room. She planned her day as she lay among her pillows. The MacTavishes would probably leave early, unless the men chose to hunt. The weather was good, and the Loch Laggan hounds were eager for a long stag run. A message to Aunt Seana must go off immediately. Iain's older sons would be delighted to race each other to Edinburgh.

Grandfather would be so relieved to get her off his hands, he was sure to allow Grand Aunt Seana to come for the wedding. She had been held to blame for Anne's escapade, as Anne had been at Seana's in Edinburgh for her introduction to society.

But the other wedding... her Hugh, married also, no happier than she. She sat up. But she would see him, at Christmas time, short months away. And, though all the world might be at Castle Drummond, they would look at each other, and she would know that, though they were forced to marry others, their own love for each other would not die. She sighed and bit her lip.

Luckily, as Anne remembered the night with Hugh, the mating part didn't last long, and if MacGregor got her with child quickly, the whole thing would be over soon. She could happily handle such a bit of nuisance for the rewards it brought. Her people and land would be safe for her own heirs and she would run the estate and see that the people of Loch Laggan were well cared for. MacGregor would probably always be away with his men, fighting someone.

Anne climbed from the bed and rang for Fiona, reaching for her riding clothes. As Fiona opened the door, Anne heard the sound of voices rising from the great hall.

"Is everyone down already? Are they eating??

Fiona rolled her eyes. "They eat as if they hadn't had that enormous meal last evening. And there are some ill looking men this morning. They reek of spirits. The MacTavishes left at dawn. Mistress MacTavish asked that you not be disturbed."

Dressed in a skirt that came to her ankles, a loose shirt and riding boots, Anne, followed by Bard, went down the stairs and into the great hall. The ruins of their early meal cluttered the table as the last of the guests made their preparations to leave. Alasdair Drummond's voice thundered over the chatter.

"We'll be by soon to call on you. This time we will make sure the Germans on the English throne are routed. Niall tells me they don't even speak English, let alone the Gaelic."

After Anne had bid her guests goodbye and returned to the table, Jane deposited a plate of bannocks and porridge in front of her.

"Jane, I need more gowns. I want you to send to Inverness and have Mrs. Simmons come with fabrics that are suitable. Tell her she and her helpers will stay here, and do impress we'll be more than generous. I'll need several new gowns, and, of course, something for my wedding..."

Anne saw Jane look up and nod grimly. Without turning, she knew it was MacGregor.

"...something suitable, in black, or purple."

"Mourning, Anne? Don't you think that's a bit heavy handed?"

Arch and coy, imitating ladies she had seen in Edinburgh, she simpered at him over her shoulder. "Oh, la, sir, you did startle me.

Surely, it isn't fitting for a groom to discuss his bride's trousseau with her."

He sat opposite her, and motioned for Jane to leave them. Anne watched the Jane's stiff back as the housekeeper retreated to the kitchen.

"No, for you, it should be gold, or russet, or green, the colors of the earth."

She snorted, salted her porridge and scooped up a spoonful.

"What does a man do to get breakfast here?"

"Well, you do not insult the housekeeper by waving her away like a common kitchen maid. And you ring, and hope she hasn't told everyone in the kitchen they are not to serve you." She took a large bite of her bread and grinned at him, showing a childish gap between her two front teeth and called over her shoulder, "The MacGregor awaits his food!"

Meg, one of the youngest kitchen helpers, ran through kitchen door and deposited a bowl of porridge in front of MacGregor, and retreated.

"I wonder what Jane told them about you? Poor wee Meggie looked terrified." Amused, Anne finished her meal and stood up.

MacGregor raised his brows. "I often affect young maids so."

Anne fairly raced from the room, out the front door, into the courtyard, round to the stables. MacGregor did make her nervous. She was unsure how to behave to a betrothed who was more a business partner.

There would be no sweet words whispered, no hasty kisses, being courted by MacGregor.

The Drummond horses had been augmented by those of MacGregor and his men, who were busy grooming their charges. She watched for a moment as two men tried to control the big gray.

As she walked toward them, she heard Calum MacGregor say, "This devil will never calm down. Why Niall picked him..."

Looking over his shoulder as Anne approached, he warned, "Lady, please, come no nearer..."

Macgregor's Bargain

The horse reared, pulling back on his rope, forcing the men to dodge his hooves. Anne paused, standing quietly as they brought the horse down again.

"How long has MacGregor had the horse?"

"Not long; he bought him in Inverness. He seemed a likely stud, and Niall's had no trouble with him."

"What's his name?"

"Iolair."

The horse snorted.

"Eagle," she murmured, and moved closer, softly repeating his name. This time the horse stood quiet, and she touched his jaw. He snorted again, but softly, and nudged her with his head.

Calum MacGregor said, "You have the way, Mistress Anne."

The other man, she recognized as Calum's brother Davey, still holding fast to the rope, nodded. "Aye, she does that."

She thought that though they were MacGregors, they were nice men. "So, you've just come over with MacGregor?"

The hulking red-haired David grinned at her. "We've been in France these past years. Our brother Rab and our cousin Dughall are still there with Niall's men. And some who came over from France with us have gone to their own homes for a bit."

She nodded. "Are you being made comfortable? The rooms in the stable block aren't the best, and we do have room in the castle."

"Och, we prefer them. We like being near our horses. We've been made comfortable. Iain's been a good host, and the food's the best we've had since leaving France."

They were really quite charming. "Should you need anything, tell Iain."

Iain had come to stand beside her, and she took his arm and led him away.

"Please treat these men as you would our clan."

He nodded, and looked down to kick a dirt clod. "They're fine sorts and are loyal to your betrothed. I've seen worse men than these MacGregors."

"Come then, Iain, I'd like to ride Vixen today. Will you saddle her?"

• 28 •

Macgregor's Bargain

They strolled into the dark of the stable.

"Aye. Lass..."

"Yes?"

Awkwardly, his expression tender, he said, "If ye need me, or any of us, we're your men. Ye may choose to wed, but should you have trouble, we'll be there."

Yes, you would, wouldn't you? Anne thought. She patted his hand. "I know, my friend."

Iain saddled and bridled Vixen. Anne stroked her nose and spoke softly to her.

Leaving the stable, Iain following with the pretty little sorrel mare, Anne saw the MacGregor men saddling Iolair.

The stallion snorted as the mare walked sedately by him, and the men held him tightly. Beyond them, Anne saw Niall MacGregor walking from the castle.

She put her foot in Iain's cupped hands and vaulted into the side saddle, giving the watchers just a glimpse of boot-clad ankle as she swept her skirts around. Tapping Vixen gently with her reins, she trotted toward the narrow neck of land that connected the castle with the mainland. Bard loped along ahead of them.

Anne needed desperately to be alone, to be away from people to sort her thoughts, and she headed for a small glen up the mountainside, her refuge since childhood. The mare, sensing her urgency, bounded up the slope, along a wide, coffee-colored burn, on a path hardly more than a deer trail.

In the late August warmth red rowan berries glowed among the dark needles of the pine trees. The path crossed a smaller burn, with grassy spot beside it, a huge granite boulder in its center, and a stillness broken by birdcalls and the rush of the burn. High above, a waterfall traced silver threads down the steep mountainside

Pulling up beside the rock, Anne dismounted and tied Vixen to a rowan tree. She walked down to the burn and scooped up a handful of water, and drank, then wiped her face with her icy wet hand. She sat on the soft thick grass and leaned against the sun-warmed rock. Bard, after following a scent along the burn, came back and flopped down beside her, his head on her lap. Anne stroked him absently, looking down the hillside at Castle Caorann and the stables and cottages that surrounded it like chicks around a protecting hen. The castle's odd shape showed from here: its one tall tower, a newer part half surrounding it, then her great grandfather's addition.

I should have brought a book, she thought. She often had, but then she didn't usually leave home so precipitously. So soon, she would be MacGregor's wife. Would she be able to help the people here? Would her grandfather insist on taking all the men and boys to fight? Bard winced as the thought caused her to tighten her hand into a fist in his fur. She wouldn't let it happen. They would go off, her grandfather and MacGregor, to fight their war, and she would remain, to do the really important work.

Vixen snorted, and Anne looked in the direction the mare had turned her head, ears pricked. She expected to see MacGregor, but a hare hopped past, and she relaxed. The soft air lulled her, and she leaned back against the rock and dozed.

Suddenly, she felt cold, so cold, so fearful that she sprang to her feet, startling Bard. The mare jumped at her sudden movement, then went back to her grazing. Anne looked around, bewildered. The sun still shone, and yet... Puzzled, she shivered, and felt her heart racing. Then, just as quickly as it had come on her, the chill passed. She frowned, wondering, then shrugged. *A bit of a dream, no more.*

Chapter Five

A week later Alasdair Drummond rode with Niall and Calum to the Munros' manor house farther down the shores of Loch Laggan.

"The man Munro can't keep a thought in his wee head but for the hunting," grumbled Drummond. "One day he's hot to fight for the Prince, the next he's grizzling about how he can't leave his lands in his factor's care. He has only maybe 20 men of fighting age."

Calum rode up beside Niall. He pointed to Munro and an elderly man coming toward them through the stubble of a barley field.

"That's his factor," Drummond said. "Jamie Munro. He's a fair hand in a fight, but getting old. Keeps the crofters in hand." They dismounted as Munro walked up to them, carrying a musket nearly as tall as he was.

"Ah, you've come at a good time. We've worked right hard. Come then and share a dram or two?

Indeed, both Munro and his man were sweating in the mild air, though judging from the hares dangling from their belts and the grins on their faces, the work had been much enjoyed.

Inside the house, Munro led them back to a small dark room used as his study. He propped his gun against a wall and sent Jamie off with the hares, then poured whisky for them and motioned for them to sit.

"Now then, what news?"

Niall spoke. "I have had word from the north where I sent some of my men. The MacDonalds and Camerons but wait for the call to arms. The English continue to try to stop French ships from leaving harbor, but some of the French government men are supplying our cause with money and guns, and will send soldiers when the time comes."

Alasdair Drummond said, "Forbye, we must make sure our own people are ready. Munro, how many men do you have?"

Munro hesitated "I have thirty able-bodied men and boys over fourteen and under sixty. But some remember 1715 and say they will not fight for the Stuarts, who'll just run back to France or Italy, as King James did then, and leave us to face the wrath of the redcoats."

"By God, man!" Drummond thundered. " We had ten thousand men in '15, and this time we will have thousands more! Tell them they are our clan, and they will fight, or you'll burn their thatch and they'll have no homes to stay and cower in! We will have our rightful king on Britain's throne!"

Munro gulped his whisky and nodded. "Aye, well, they will follow me when the Prince comes, I have no doubt."

MacGregor said, "I assure you, sir, that Prince Charles is a different sort than King James. He has the power to bring men to his side, and he is a warrior. He has a keen mind. He has already proved himself in battle in Italy. I have men bringing in enough arms to see us to victory, and we must not fail the Stuarts."

Munro tutted."Ah, I know, I know, man, but some of the Protestant lairds fear that Stuarts, being Catholic, will make them bow to the Pope. After all, that is the reason the Protestant Hanover is on the throne now, Britons would not have a Catholic monarch. And those who are Church of Scotland will be hard put to follow a Papist."

"Catholic or Church of Scotland," Niall said, "we are talking of our land now, of our home that the English see as theirs. We are Scots, whatever our religion, and the Stuarts, not the Hanovers, are direct heirs to the crown of Britain. My God, the King of England speaks German and hates to live in his own realm!"

"Be that as it may," said Munro, then flinched at Drummond's glare.

They rode back along Loch Laggan, the sun catching ripples on the loch, the mountains purple with heather, and beyond, distant blue mountains to the west.

Calum said to Niall, "I've never seen a bonnier place, I think."

Niall nodded. People bringing cattle and sheep down from the shielings where they had spent the summer in the high hills, waved at the horsemen, and moved their stock and small children out of the way. They looked stronger, healthier, Niall noted, than in other countries-and many clans people he'd seen in Scotland.

Drummond glanced over the cattle, his expression more pleasant than usual. "They're a fine lot, these black cows. They're well fattened. We'll have plenty of food for the winter, and for our Prince if he comes before next harvest."

Tenants' black houses clustered on the shore of the loch. The houses were built of stone, thatched in heather, the roofs held in place by cords looped over them, stones at the ends to protect them from the gales that blew down the loch. They had no windows, no chimneys. Blue peat smoke wafted out through thatch and open doorways.

Peace lasted only until they reached the castle and saw horses being unpacked in the stable yard.

"God damn," Alasdair Drummond growled."That besom standing by her horse is my sister Seana. How the hell did she get here so soon? I have always thought she was a witch."

And indeed, there stood Seana Drummond, his widowed younger sister, tall, thin where he was rotund, his harsh facial features turned pleasant in hers. She walked toward him, Drummond's deerhound prancing beside her.

Macgregor's Bargain

The men dismounted and Drummond motioned for young Fergus to take the horses.

"Well, brother, will you not welcome me? I've come to help the bride prepare for her wedding."

"'Twould be a different wedding if you'd done you duty in Edinburgh, and not let Anne run off and play the whore."

Seana turned her back on her brother and looked at MacGregor, then at Calum. "And which of you young men is the groom?"

Niall said, "I have that privilege, Madam." He gave a courtly bow and raised her gloved hand to his lips.

"I am his cousin Calum, Ma'am." Calum grinned and bowed.

Drummond still stood glaring at his sister, so Niall offered his arm and led Seana toward the castle. As they reached the front door, it burst open and Anne hurled herself at her aunt.

"Oh, my dear! I am that glad to see you." Anne kissed her great aunt on both cheeks and then pulled her indoors, without a glance at MacGregor. "Come, you must see my new gown patterns. Grandfather was so glad to get rid of me that I will have lovely new things that he bought without a murmur."

MacGregor stood looking after the two women. It was the first time, he thought, that he had seen anything like animation on Anne's face.

In the following days Anne saw little of MacGregor, except at mealtimes. He and her grandfather seemed to be forever riding out hunting or discussing the Jacobite cause in Drummond's study. He would smile at her absently at dinner and occasionally he gave her a measuring look, which caused her great discomfort.

The dressmakers from Inverness slept in servants' quarters above the kitchen and Anne, taking advantage of her grandfather's temporary generosity, had ordered six new gowns. If she was to attend Hugh's wedding in the winter, she would be dressed better than the bride, she thought, and she gave a great deal more care to those clothes than to her own wedding attire.

Lucy came often, helping Anne pick fabrics for her wedding dress, all palest green and silver lace. Under Lucy's direction, the seamstresses made lawn nightgowns, with lace trimming as fine as spider webs.

Lucy held up a piece of rose silk, so sheer her hand showed through, and grinned.

"This, I think, for the wedding night?"

Anne shuddered. "You do have an odd sense of humor, Lucy. You know how it'll be for me."

Lucy looked contrite, then said, "He's a fine looking man, Anne, and I have seen him look at you like..."

"I know how he looks at me. D'you think that'll make it the easier?"

"Anne, bedding can be good, you know. He's a likely man. You may find you can enjoy him, if you but open your wee tight mind."

Anne threw a pillow at Lucy. "I'll have the damned gown made, then, and I'll wear it, though I might as well wear serge. The man has no more caring for me than I for him. I'm just a brood mare, and though I can smile at you now, I dread sharing my wedding night with him."

Lucy, her face softening, hugged Anne, and smoothed her hair. "I know, my dear, I know."

Drummonds and MacGregors went hunting day after day, and fished the loch, to fill the larders for all the coming guests.

Anne discussed each meal with Oona, determined that she would show everyone that she was a suitable chatelaine for Caorann Castle. No guest would go hungry, nor sleep in a musty bed, nor have an unfilled glass. The pipes would play, and musicians were coming for the dancing.

As she stood in the wine cellar, surrounded by kegs and casks and bottles, Anne frowned. Perhaps it would help a bit if the bride got a bit fou', and the groom found himself with a limp bed partner.

Guests began arriving early on the day before the wedding- Lucy and Alan first, to help Anne, who seemed to become paler as the day wore on. Niall, courtly and charming, flirted with Lucy and discussed war and politics with Sir James Drummond, Duke of Perth.

Sir James bestowed a dry kiss on Anne's cheek, called her kinswoman, and seemed to forget her as he talked to Alaisdair Drummond and Niall.

Anne spent her day seeing to the preparing of meals, greeting guests, trying to think about the moment, not tomorrow. Thirty guests sat down to dinner at three in the afternoon, and Anne watched wearily as course followed course and voices grew louder as glasses were filled again and again. She looked up at the ceiling of the great hall, its beams blackened by age and centuries of smoke. How many brides had sat so, waiting for a marriage to a stranger? It all seemed to be happening a distance away from her.

After the tables had been cleared, the room readied for dancing, Anne sat watching the musicians warm up. Dear Aunt Seana plopped down beside her, her cap askew on her gray curls.

"You should try to look more cheerful, sweeting."She fanned herself and looked at Lucy and Alan, then toward the punch table where Niall MacGregor stood with Anne's grandfather and Sir James. It was obvious that they were more intent on their business than on Niall's wedding party.

"What do you suppose they're talking about?" Seana asked.

Anne sighed, disgusted. "What they've been talking about since MacGregor came. The King over the water, and Prince Charles, and how much gold and soldiers the French will give, and how they're going to make the Sassenachs bow down to the Stuarts."

Seana sighed, too."They never learn, the men, do they? Seems they should have learned from the '15, with your own grandfather getting wounded, and my dear David killed. King James sailed away when he saw he couldn't win, and he left his Highlanders worse off than before, with their few weapons hidden in their thatch because the English wouldn't allow them guns even for hunting. But then your Niall is a leader in this, so you must be hearing a great deal."

"I don't talk to him about it anymore. I told him what I think. Auntie, I'm afraid. I agreed to this, but now..."

Concerned, her aunt asked, "Why, child? D'ye think he'll beat you. or misuse you?"

Anne shook her head, studying Seana's face. How could features so like her grandfather's, look so much kinder?

"Nay, I think not. He said he doesn't beat women. But he pays little attention to me. Not like Hugh..."

"Enough then." At once her aunt's face took on more resemblance to Alasdair's. "If he's not as hare-brained as Hugh Drummond, so much the better. Perhaps he'll keep you from doing something as stupid as you did, running off like some silly servant girl."

If they had been found just a night earlier, Anne thought, she would still have been a maid. But, then, it would have made no difference. The moment she had slipped from her aunt's house, she had been lost. Anne jumped as Niall's brown hand grazed her bare shoulder. She saw the heavy ring on one finger, a wildcat etched in gold, with an emerald eye. His hand was gentle, but she held still, willing him to take it away.

"Seana Drummond," he said, "I haven't seen you dance this evening. Will you dance with me?"

Anne watched her aunt preen. "Ah, Niall, now how did you know I am so fond of reels?"

He laughed as he bowed before her, and reached for her hand. "Why by your feet tapping, my lady."

He pulled her to her feet, bowed briefly to Anne, and led Seana away, the old lady giggling girlishly at something he whispered into her ear.

At the end of the reel, sweating and breathing hard, Alan and Lucy halted in front of Anne, and Lucy dropped into the chair next to her. Alan held out his hand to Anne.

"Come then, you used to be the lightest dancer in the world. Show me if you still are." And he whirled her away, the wide skirts of her yellow satin gown billowing around her. She saw MacGregor look at her briefly, before she became involved in the whirling pattern of the reel. Suddenly he was beside her, and Alan clasped Seana's hands as Niall held Anne's. They raised hands and came close together, and his eyes flickered a little. She dropped her lashes and pulled back, and Alan held her again as they moved to another part of the room.

The noise level rose in the great hall, as the drink went round. Men who had kept themselves a little separate from MacGregor

Macgregor's Bargain

now treated him as long lost kin, and Anne, shocked, saw Alan MacPherson fling an arm around MacGregor and lead him to the center of the room. He motioned Padraig, Alasdair Drummond's piper, to him, and waved a hand to silence the musicians.

"Now, then, man, you've been in France these long years. Can you still dance like a Highlander?"

Niall laughed, throwing his head back, his voice booming over the crowd. "Does a Highlander ever forget?"

Alasdair Drummond came forward with his sword still in its sheath, pulled it, and laid sword and sheath on the floor to form a cross. Anne walked near, not believing her eyes. Her grandfather was laughing, in fact so was almost everyone. She saw young Seonaid MacKintyre lean slightly toward Niall, looking up at him through long black lashes. Niall grinned down at her, and pinched her chin.

Lucy stood beside Anne, clasping her hand, laughing with excitement.

The bagpipes wailed from the minstrel's gallery, and Alan, his coat and shoes cast aside, walked to one of the vees formed by sword and sheath, and danced around the cross, never touching scabbard nor sword, arms raised, feet flying, always controlled. He danced aside and MacGregor jumped in, his coat discarded, clad now in tight breeches, shirt, stockings, the silver embroidery on his vest gleaming. His dance was smooth and structured, but he leaped higher, his feet moved faster, till, covered in a sheen of sweat, he stopped and made deep bow. The crowd roared approval, and his smile encompassed all the people in the room. He met Anne's stare, and his grin widened. She turned away and walked to the punch bowl.

She felt him behind her as she poured herself a cup of punch. "You didn't seem impressed, Anne."

"I doubt you were trying to impress me, sir. And I doubt it matters what I think."

The fiddles began again, and he took her arm. "Walk with me to get my shoes, then dance with me. It would look passing strange if the bride and groom do not dance at least once at their own party."

"Well, it's a passing strange courtship, isn't it, MacGregor?"

She sipped her punch, then gulped half of it.

He pulled the mug from her lips, laughing, and took a drink.

"'Tis potent. It would be a shame to be sick at your own wedding, Anne. Mayhap you should use a little discretion"

She looked around. The only people watching them were far enough away to give them privacy, but they were watching. She leaned closer, smiling sweetly. It wouldn't do to let anyone think she was a less than delighted bride. "Ah, but I am not known for my discretion."

Then, his arm around her, Niall MacGregor led Anne into the dance. He was good, and when he swung her off her feet he did it easily, his hands firm and not hard about her waist. His eyes kindled a bit as she slid back down against him, and she swung back hastily, and into another's arms.

The late supper she had planned was as sumptuous as she could make it. There were roasted grouse, a whole lamb, salmon from the loch, crabs and oysters from the west coast. Anne had overseen everything, and Seana, doing a final critique, announced she was sure all was as fine as the best of Edinburgh hostesses could do. Jane, the housekeeper, snorted.

Niall seemed determined to stay near her the rest of the night, whether to keep an eye on her behavior, or to play the eager bridegroom, she knew not. He filled her plate for her, and found her a place to sit near the MacPhersons. She shut her eyes and leaned back as Niall carried on an animated conversation with Lucy and Alan, as if Anne's silence were most natural. The food tasted good, and though she thought she would be unable to eat, she found she was ravenous.

Anne stood. "I'm sure the party will go on for hours, Lucy, but I must rest." She turned to MacGregor and fluttered her lashes as she had seen the MacKintyre girl do. "I must look lovely for my wedding."

She walked away, weaving among her guests, urging them to eat and drink, accepting their compliments.

She took Seana's hand and pulled her along. "Auntie, please come with me."

Macgregor's Bargain

When they reached the quiet of her room, Fiona helped her unlace her bodice and underskirt while Anne went over details for tomorrow with her aunt. The green wedding gown and its silver underskirt hung on a form in the corner. Fiona helped her into a long white nightdress, and she sat while the girl brushed her hair and braided it.

Then, wrapped in a shawl, she sat with her aunt near the fire.

"You were giggling like a girl. You were flirting with MacGregor."

Her aunt chuckled. "He has the way with him, you know. And he has wit, as you do. I'll wager he spent few nights alone, in France." Seana frowned and said, "Anne, you don't need me to tell you about men, and such..."

Anne laughed. "D'you remember that men and such put me in the position I am? I know what to expect."

Humor returned to her aunt's dark eyes. "Aye, well, you might find it a bit different. Hugh was but a green boy. Niall is twenty-six or twenty seven, with, I suspect, enough experience for three men. Forebye, he likes his women, does Niall MacGregor, and it shows all over him. He may show you a few things that shock you..."

"Another word and I'll run away." Anne put her hands over her ears, her face scarlet.

Seana raised her hand. "I promise, not another word."

Soon the older woman, seeing her niece's drowsiness, kissed her goodnight and sent her to bed.

Chapter Six

Anne stood in the center of the sunlit room, hearing the wind blowing hard against the windows. Bard lay by the fireplace, watching as Lucy, Seana and Fiona fussed with her dress and her hair.

She examined herself critically in her mirror. The dress. Was it too pale? Her skin looked a bit dark, especially her face, from all the times she had ridden without a hat. Her unpowdered hair was pulled high on her crown, close on the sides of her head, with clusters of curls on top, tendrils coiling on her neck, and three curls hanging over one shoulder. The women gartered pale green silk stockings at her knees, and she slipped her feet into high heeled satin slippers. Carefully, Lucy placed a silver lace veil over Anne's hair as Seana dotted rouge on her cheeks and lips.

The image in the mirror smiled. The glossy chestnut hair shone through the silver lace. Her eyes glowed between kohl-darkened lashes.

She thought she looked almost virginal; but then that was what she was.

Anne's grandfather, resplendent in satin breeches, a silver waistcoat controlling his girth, a velvet coat with silver buttons making him look nobler than his wont, thumped into the room.

"The bridegroom waits, lass. Quit delaying."

Anne glared at him. "I had hoped the bridegroom had come to his senses, and escaped to France, or at least to his kin in Balquidder."

"Now, Anne, don't make your grandfather angry. His face is already scarlet with the effort of keeping his belly in." Seana looked pleasantly at her brother.

Drummond frowned, and motioned for his granddaughter to walk from the room, which she did with difficulty. Her gown, close in front and back, spread nearly four feet across, and she had to slip sideways through the door.

The Loch Laggan Drummonds, as was true with many Highland families, had never succumbed to the blandishments of John Knox. They remained Catholic. Their religious views were not strong, but they managed to bring in a priest to serve in the chapel for christenings, weddings and burials, and sometimes on holy days. The chapel had been built in the west wing several hundred years before, and though Alasdair Drummond's father Dughall had spent a great deal of money renovating the main part of the castle, the chapel was still small, dark and cold. Today, though, the press of people and many candles heated it. Anne hoped she wouldn't faint. Her stays felt too tight.

As she walked beside her grandfather, she saw Iain and Morag standing with their sons.

Niall, clad in dark blue satin with a silver embroidered vest, stood at the altar, his cousin Calum by his side. The two could have been brothers. Although, Anne thought, Calum's hazel eyes seemed to dance with laughter while Niall's face was somber.

Demurely, she looked down, seeing her green satin slippers peek from beneath her gown with each step.

Of the ceremony, Anne remembered little: kneeling, standing, sitting, automatically murmuring responses, until Niall's brown hand reached for hers, and placed a heavy gold ring on her finger. Then he leaned forward and briefly touched her lips with his own.

Seana had overseen the laying out of the wedding feast. Anne sat beside her husband and ate, unaware of the taste of her food. She drank goblets of wine, and later she danced, first with her husband, then with his cousin, then, it seemed, with every man in the room.

She stood with Niall and James Drummond as Perth asked, "Now, then, what do you do? I'm sure you've no time to work the land here. How soon do you plan to be away to France?"

Niall shrugged. "The Prince sends word that, though there are still some problems, he is optimistic. I must wait, as we all must. Anne and I will go to Edinburgh to find what support we have. I have a house there that I bought long ago, and I haven't seen it since I've been back."

The day spun slowly away, and candles and lamps were lit against the growing dark. Anne sat and stared at the supper table laden with food. Appetites were hearty and no one seemed to notice that she ate nothing.

The guests rose from the table, rowdy as all the wine and punch could make them, began to watch the couple. Then, after the table was moved back, so the dancing could begin, Anne saw Gavin Munro whisper something to Robert MacTavish, and the two men looked at her with broad grins.

Pigs, she thought.

The two great fireplaces cast flares of light and shadow up into the high ceiling, and candles wavered with the movement of the dancers.

Niall leaned toward Anne and murmured, "It's late. I think..."

"I'm not ready to leave yet." Her cheeks felt hot, and she looked toward Calum MacGregor. He held out his hand to pull her into a reel.

Then Niall was there, grabbing her hand, as he led her away from his laughing cousin.

"It won't do, for me to carry you over my shoulder. I'd probably suffocate under all those yards of skirt. Why not collect Seana and Lucy, and act the proper bride?"

"Because, as you well know, I'm not a proper bride."

Ignoring her jibe, he steered her toward Lucy and looked for Seana, who galloped by just then with Perth. At MacGregor's gesture, Seana broke away and joined Anne and Lucy.

Macgregor's Bargain

With shouts of encouragement sounding behind them, Lucy, Seana and Anne made for the stairs. Feeling she couldn't breath deeply enough, Anne stopped halfway up, her heart beating furiously.

"Oh, Seana," she whispered.

Her aunt put an arm around her, and Lucy took her hand, and they went into the room that had been Anne's all her life, now to be shared with a stranger.

Fiona, tears in her eyes, began unlacing Anne's gown.

"Fiona, stop it. It's Anne's wedding, not her funeral." Seana poured wine for the four of them.

"To you, my dear. I hope your marriage, in spite of its beginnings, proves to be a good one, and that you fill this old pile of rocks with many bonny bairns."

Standing in her chemise, Anne drank her wine and watched Fiona shake out her pink silk nightdress and sacque.

They took off her chemise and pulled her nightdress over her head, tying three ribbons at her breast. She drew the sacque on, and sat at her small dressing table, watching in the mirror as Fiona pulled the pins from her hair and began to brush it.

Seana took a small vial from her reticule. "Here, my dear."

She pulled out the stopper and touched it to Anne's shoulders and hair. The odor of sandalwood rose around her. She felt her stomach lurch, and wondered if she would be sick.

Anne turned her head as she heard voices roar from downstairs.

Lucy said, "He comes now," and made for the door.

Quickly, Seana kissed Anne as the door opened, and Niall, surrounded by laughing men, was pushed inside. He, too, was laughing, wine from his goblet spilling onto the floor.

Anne stood up, forgetful of her revealing clothing. Niall halted in mid laugh and looked to either side of him, at the openmouthed stares of his cousins and Alan.

"Madam," he bowed, then shoved the men out, Seana, Lucy and Fiona trailing them, and shut the door. He leaned against it, ignoring the shouts and ribald comments coming from the other side, as he looked at her.

The curtains had been drawn, the fire crackled in the hearth, and the candlelight, making her hair shine red, lit up the robe she wore, turning it to flame, outlining her legs through the sheer layers. The shouts and laughter outside died away, and they stared at each other.

He looked very large, standing in the half-light by the door. His mouth was set in a stern line, his cheekbones cast shadows on the lower part of his face; his eyes, too, were shadowed. As he walked toward her, his lips turned up in a half smile.

"You look bewitching," he said. "I'll wager every man who saw you will be rutting tonight." She turned away from him, and sat in the chair closest to the fire. He followed, and sat across from her, and waited. "Would you care for more wine?"

He shook his head. He stood and walked to her and pulled her to her feet. She drew in her breath and looked up at him. Could he see her heart beating?

He raised his hand and drew one finger along her jaw, down the small cleft in her chin. "Don't tremble, lass, I'll not hurt you."

Anne shut her eyes and swallowed hard.

Niall grinned. "You don't believe me? Did it hurt you, with wee Hughie?"

"Don't call him that." She pulled away from him and her sacque fell open. She saw his eyes flare as they swept her body.

Swiftly, she threw the robe aside, and tore the ribbons of her gown free, letting it settle in a pool around her feet.

"Is this what you want, MacGregor? Shall I climb on the bed now, and spread my legs?"

He had taken a step toward her, and now he halted.

"For God's sake, pick up one of those enticing things and wrap yourself. I've no intention of raping you." His laughter came welling up as she bent, red faced, to pick up her nightdress and sacque, and put them on. "Christ, you do have a sense of the dramatic, don't you? I'm surprised you haven't thrown yourself off some cliff for the loss of your great love." He moved a little closer. "You are a work of art, though, lass."

Macgregor's Bargain

His hand, when he touched her shoulder, was gentle. He slid his hand down to hers, and led her to her dressing table and sat her down.

"Stay there."

Niall left the room, and she heard him calling for Calum, who answered. There followed a burst of laughter from downstairs. She waited, not moving, until he came back carrying a leather purse.

"I brought a bride-gift. I did not realize how well it would suit you, as I had only seen the miniature your grandfather sent. Shut you eyes."

Anne felt something, heavy and cold, settle around her neck and between her breasts, in the vee of her sacque. She flinched. Then she opened her eyes and looked at the barbaric necklace. The gold links were large, intertwined, holding a silver disc, strange animals and vines encircling a gold stone. Her eyes met his in the mirror.

"It's beautiful," she admitted, and raised a hand to stroke it.

"It has been in my family for more years than anyone knows, and I've carried it with me from Scotland to France and back again. It suits you well."

"Why?" She realized, too late, that the question sounded coy, as if she searched for a compliment.

He didn't seem to notice. "It needs a strong woman, doesn't it? It carries a bit of history with it, and it wouldn't suit a court lady, simpering and fawning. It probably belonged to some pagan who could cut off men's heads with her own sword, as could you, I'm sure."

He grinned at her black glare.

"Now, then, let me take it off."

"But I want to wear it.."

"For what we do now, Madam, you wear nothing."

He stepped away, taking her hand, leading her to the bed. He sat on it, pulling her down to sit by him. She avoided his eyes.

"Anne, I will not rush you. I believe you know little more than you did as a virgin." He cupped her chin and turned her toward him. 'Before I do anything, I want to ask some questions. Will you answer me honestly?"

Macgregor's Bargain

She nodded, still looking away from him.

"Did he hurt you? Did you bleed?"

"Yes," she whispered.

"And then?"

"Then he went to sleep."

"That is all?"

Anne nodded.

Niall bent and kissed her gently, then ran his tongue over her lips. He drew away and said, "Now I will show you what pleasure is."

Something was wrong, Anne thought, her eyes still shut, her mind befogged by more than the lassitude of sleep. She frowned. A nightmare? No. She felt no fear: more the knowledge of something amiss. She heard the fire crackle and the clatter of a dish.

"Fiona?"

A man's voice. "Not Fiona. Today I'm your lady's maid."

She sat upright, covers slipping to her waist. She pushed back her tangled hair and squinted across the room. The bed curtains had been pulled back. The light, except near the fire, was gray. It was cloudy out, then.

Niall said, "Good morning, Anne."

Her eyes opened wide as she remembered. She pulled up the coverlet.

He grinned. "Is there a part of you left to hide? I doubt it."

"Where is Fiona?"

"Probably hovering downstairs, listening for sounds of distress. Of course," his grin widened, "she could have heard some screams last night."

She stared at him, as her memories of last night struck her. What had she done? He went to her armoire and pulled out a demure robe and tossed it on the bed.

"Would you like me to turn away? It's a bit late for modesty." He shrugged and walked back to the fire. "Your chocolate is here. Jane will bring food soon, you may want to be clothed."

Hastily Anne stood and pulled the robe around her, buttoning and tying the waist. She pushed her tousled hair from her face as she thrust her feet into slippers. She winced a little.

▪ 47 ▪

Macgregor's Bargain

He went to her dressing table and picked up her brush.

"Come. Come on, lass. I won't bite you - for a while."

She crossed the room and sat down. Gently, with a large comb and a brush, he smoothed the tangles from her hair. She avoided his eyes in the mirror, buttoning her sacque to the throat.

"D'ye braid this now? I'm not much at tidying up hair."

She pushed his hand away and coiled her hair into one thick braid. Then, before she could get away, he pulled her to her feet and gave her a smacking kiss on the cheek.

"You look very young this morning. Except, of course, there's a bit of the wanton about the mouth. It's a little fuller, I think."

She pulled away from him and went to the table by the fire, pouring chocolate into small eggshell thin cups.

"You don't talk much in the mornings, do you, lass?"

She cleared her throat. "What..what happened...it changes nothing, you know."

That ironic grin again. She wanted to throw the cup at him.

"I think it changed you, a bit."

"You know what I mean. I still love Hugh..."

With a few quick strides he was beside her, taking the cup carefully from her hands and setting on the table. Then he sat on the sofa, pulling her onto his lap. She sat stiffly.

"Now hear me. You should have better manners that to talk about your lover to your bridegroom, but I'll ignore that. You are my wife now. Mine." She tried to pull away, and he pulled her back. "We don't love each other. But you're a clever lass and if you use a bit of judgment, we can learn to live together amicably. D'ye think I won't lust after another woman? But you will carry my heir to Loch Laggan. That, I'm sure you've heard, is the burden of being a woman and there's naught you can do about it. Last night you came to enjoy the getting of an heir, if I am not mistaken."

Her face scarlet, eyes flashing, she managed to free her hand and cracked him soundly across the face. He stood up, frowning and she tumbled to the floor in a flurry of white ruffles and blue ribbons.

Niall leaned over and pulled her to her feet, his good humor restored.

"I always thought lasses with soft brown hair and gentle brown eyes were quiet little things, small thrushes to be held gently and cared for. But in you lurks a redhead." He grinned. "Yes, I'm sure, somewhere in Scotland, there's a girl with red, red hair and green eyes, and the disposition of a saint."

"You're mad, " Anne muttered, and reached for her chocolate.

At a soft knock on the door, she looked toward it and called, "Open."

Jane, eyes cast down, led Iain's youngest son Fergus into the room. He carried an enormous tray laden with food.

"Thank you, Jane," said Niall. "That will be fine. Just set it on the table in the corner."

She nodded, still not looking at them. Fergus, blushing, gave Anne a timid smile.

"We'll care for ourselves. Tell Hamish I'll need him later in the morning, not before."

Jane shut the door quietly as the two went out.

Anne asked, "What is amiss with Jane? She was ever ready to let her own opinion be known. I never saw her so quiet."

Niall led her to the table. "I had a wee word with her about the importance of being polite to one's master and mistress."

Anne raised her brows, impressed in spite of herself, and then, smelling the odor of hot food, realized how hungry she was. Another knock on the door, and Fergus walked in, holding two bottles of wine and a jug of ale. Niall nodded to him and the boy laid his burden on the table and scurried out.

She reached for an apple and took a large bite, the juices dribbling down her chin. She licked her lips and caught MacGregor's eye. Whoever had arranged their tray must have thought they would need nourishment, she thought, for it was laden with salmon, a partridge, oatmeal and bannocks, and pudding with thick cream. She tore off part of the bird and added it to the pile on her plate. She spooned a large lump of oatmeal into her mouth, and poured ale into her goblet.

He shook his head, grinning. "If that is the way you ate in Edinburgh, they must have thought you a savage."

Macgregor's Bargain

She carried her plate back to the fire, curling into a chair. "I used my manners there. Since its only you here, what does it matter?"

He nodded. "A reasonable thought." His own plate was no less full than hers. He poured a glass of claret and joined her, sitting across from her, watching her in amusement.

Anne frowned. "Why is so much I do funny to you? I don't like it."

"Well, then, I hope you get used to it. For you do amuse me, very much."

She asked, "Why?"

"I think of you, a wee bairn, bellowing like your grandfather. You should have been a forlorn little waif, with your parents dead and your grandfather a callous old bore, and Jane bent on keeping you under her thumb, but instead you must have fought them. I like that. I like spirit." He laughed and shook his head. "Had you been a man, Anne Drummond, you would have led an army. You would fight with the best of them, and the Stuarts would have a champion, indeed."

Anne drank her ale. "I think not, Niall MacGregor. The Stuarts would not have a champion in me."

His face grew serious. "You don't favor the German Hanovers?"

She shook her head. "No, I don't favor them. I don't favor any kings. But the Hanovers will win. I know it. In the '15 they won. I don't like to hear Grandfather and our friends, and you encouraging them, talking about the Stuarts coming back. The Stuarts are foreign now, too, you know." She frowned and looked at the fire, stretching her legs toward the warmth. "They probably can't speak English any better than the Hanovers, let alone the Gaelic. The Stuarts will not come back, and Loch Laggan may lose everything. We in the Highlands live on dreams. I hate the Sassenachs as much as anyone, but our hopes for the Stuarts are the ones who'll ruin us."

His long legs crossed, chin on hand, he pondered what she had said, and when he spoke, there was genuine interest in his voice. "What's your reasoning, lass?"

50

"D'ye really want to know? I've thought a great deal about it, but Grandfather says women don't think right. And I…I know things."

He motioned for her to continue, and leaned his head back, his plate forgotten at his feet.

"It's not the English who'll urge our men to war. It's men like you and my grandfather. And when they go to war, they'll lose everything. Their lands, their money, their rights, what little they have now." Anne pointed her fork at Niall. "Your clan has been proscribed; you've had to use your mother's name, I'll wager, buying that house in Edinburgh, as well as on our marriage papers. Think what it would be like if all Scotland was proscribed. We couldn't wed, or be buried, or own land. The English were cruel last time, in 1715, and the times before. Next time, what will they take from us? Our lands, our clans. They took most of our weapons after the '15. This time they'll do that, and leave the men dead and the women and bairns weeping and hungry. There'll not be enough men left in Scotland to sire another generation of strong sons to fight another war." She drew a deep breath as she reached for her ale. "Why do you talk to us about the King over the water, and the French helping us, when they'll only promise, and give nothing?"

He rose to pour himself more wine. "You speak well, Anne, and I doubt not your argument is fair. But I think we can do it. Prince Charles is not like his father. He can raise men to his side, he can demand, and get, loyalty. If he has some good advisors, he has the makings of a leader." MacGregor stopped and frowned. "What do you mean, you know things?"

She sighed and drank her ale. "My mother, they say, had the Sight, and Morag, Iain's wife, Fiona's mother, who knew her well, says Mother passed it on to me."

MacGregor shook his head. "I would need more than that to change my mind. You may have the Sight, but can you tell me how well it has served you?"

Anne looked down and shook her head. "It isn't like that. It is that sometime I feel very cold, as if there are things around me I should be seeing, or hearing. And then again I see people that shouldn't be there."

Macgregor's Bargain

"Then I will wait until I have evidence." Lightly, he said, as he poured more ale for her, "Perhaps we should think of things we do agree on. Let's see..." with an exaggerated leer, he indicated the bed.

She stood up and backed away, but not quickly enough. He pulled her into his arms and buried his face in the soft curve of her shoulder.

Niall gently bit the back of her neck and Anne shivered. "Shall I continue with my instruction? Last night you seemed a willing pupil."

He cupped her chin, turning her face up to his, moving his lips against hers. She stood rigid, willing herself to stillness, not allowing herself to push against him, trying not to remember the way she had felt last night. But her lips parted.

Chapter Seven

It was past noon. Niall MacGregor stood by the bed looking down at his bride. Chestnut hair tangled on the pillow, Anne slept on her stomach, one bare arm hanging over the side. He stretched. The night and morning had proved to be more enjoyable than he could have hoped.

She's a likely lass, though I hope I can make her keep her opinions to herself. Damn women who think.

Niall heard soft knock on the door. He opened it to find Hamish holding a letter.

Hamish whispered, "I was told you'd want to shave. And a courier is waiting in the kitchen for an answer."

Niall looked over his shoulder at Anne, still asleep, and sighed. "Best be getting to work," he told his cousin. "Let us return to my room."

An hour later, as Niall walked down the stairs he heard Alasdair Drummond's voice, and a quieter response from another man. Drummond and the Duke of Perth emerged from the library, and when they saw Niall they stopped.

"I thought we'd not see you for another day or two," Drummond said, grinning salaciously. "Did you find your bride acceptable?"

Perth, too, seemed interested in Niall's answer.

Niall looked at Perth. "Acceptable, yes. But now we must plan a bit. A courier brought me a message from France. I'm sure your brother in Paris has also been keeping you informed, my lord. Shall we go into your study, sir?"

The three men settled themselves around Drummond's desk.

Niall began."My news is not good. The English have some excellent spies, and some of them seem to be very close to Prince Charles. One of Walpole's agents has brought the entire plan of a French invasion of England to the Hanovers. I think they knew it as soon as it was conceived. At the same time King Louis is using the Stuart claim to the throne to frighten England, he is ignoring Prince Charles."

Perth coughed into his handkerchief and examined the blood on it. "My brother John in France says the Scots who have been there since the '15 have found Irish ready to fight with us. Indeed, he says Prince Charles is surrounded by them."

"Aye," Niall agreed, "but I am not so sure that is a good thing. Some of them encourage him in drinking and sporting."

"Well," blustered Drummond, "and that sets him apart from his father, who prays too much. Prince Charles is a real man, after the wenches and the wine."

Niall frowned, and his words cut across Drummond's laughter. He spoke coldly, one phrase at a time. "But you miss my point. King Louis is ignoring the Prince. The Jacobites in England are hesitating. Some Scots who have been in France since the '15 are not eager to fight again unless…,"he held up his hand, cutting red-faced Drummond off. "Unless we have a guarantee of more French money and arms. Have you heard of the Protestant winds? No? Well, they are our worst enemy, after the English. How many ships have been blown back to France because of them? Or have been blown into the range of English cannon?" Niall turned to Perth. "You and your brother stand strong, I know, and think this is the time to fight. I am here to find how many will stand with us. Munro? MacTavish? Both of them are full of doubt. Old Lord Lovat in the east will go with the one he thinks will win. And the Calvinist Borderers fear the Pope more than they hate the English.

Besides, they have done well since the '15. Their cattle and crops are safer than they have ever been."

Perth and Drummond exchanged glances. Perth said ominously, "Do you not want the Stuarts to come?"

Exasperated, Niall answered, "Of course I do. That is what I am here for. Have I not been working to bring them back for eight years? But it is my responsibility to make sure when they come, they are supported by enough men to take the throne. Gentlemen, we Scots can learn from the English. They do not go wildly ahead. They plan."

Alasdair Drummond, his face scarlet, bellowed, "Aye, and a Scot can beat any five Sassenachs!"

Niall laughed. "You are right, of course, so we must have at least one fifth as many Jacobites to fight them."

The two others shook their heads at his humor and Niall left them to find Calum. His cousin sat in the stable cleaning harness.

"Well, Coz, how went the wedding night? God, man, what is that mark on your neck?"He burst out laughing.

Niall grinned. "The lady kept me amused, and I'll tell you no more. I have work for you. Take Davey and ride out. Go south and west. Send someone up to Sutherland. I want to know what people are saying about the Stuarts, what they've heard, gossip, anything. You should enjoy that, I know, because taverns are the best place to learn the lay of the land. Mayhap you will find a wench or two to ease your jealousy." He clapped Calum on the shoulder. "Now I get back to my bride. I am sure she is missing me."

Calum laughed again. "You plan on getting her with child so you can go back to your old ways when we get to France?"

Niall grinned. "I have my duty to think of."

Anne spent the day with Seana who, after examining her grandniece, asked no questions. They walked along the shores of the loch, a soft breeze blowing their skirts. Faithful Bard walked beside Anne, close enough so her fingers could touch his rough coat.

She looked down at him. "I am forgiven for keeping him from my room last night. I was afraid…"she blushed.

Seana said, "You were afraid he might attack MacGregor? "

"Aunt..." Anne hesitated.

Seana Drummond had had a happy marriage and had chosen to stay in Edinburgh after her husband died. Had she enjoyed the coupling part because she loved her husband, or just because it felt good? It certainly was more enjoyable with MacGregor, a man she didn't know, that it had been with the man she loved.

"What is the matter child? Did all go well last night? MacGregor didn't...?"

"No, he didn't hurt me. I just didn't know it would be like that, he wasn't like Hugh."

Seana stopped and looked at Anne. "I should think not. Hugh probably had little more knowledge about what he was doing than you did. I told you MacGregor would be different. Did you enjoy it?"

"Aunt!" Anne's face reddened, then she began crying in earnest. "Yes, I did. I shouldn't have!"

Seana wrapped her arms around Anne. "Oh, my sweet child, there is nothing wrong with enjoying a man. You are married to him, and if your love lies elsewhere it is wise to make a friend of your husband. MacGregor will be good to you, I am sure, and once you are with child, he'll be off and away, or less interested in taking you to bed. Best take this time to get to know him."

That evening, sitting in front of the fire in Anne's room, Niall said, "While we're away in Edinburgh, I want to have apartments for us built into the new wing. I have been drawing some plans."

"The rooms in the back?"

Niall nodded.

"But what about this room? It's mine."

"It always will be. I feel I'm only temporary here."

She turned halfway away from him, ducking her head and looking at him from the corners of her eyes, smiling. "I am relieved that you feel that way. Shall I invite you in when I feel like it, and shut the door on you at other times?"

He realized it was the first time she had smiled at him.

"Without doubt, in the future, but it would be unwise to keep me out just yet. After all, the heir of Caorann Castle is awaited impatiently."

He reached under her robe, stroking her breast, then leaned over and kissed her, feeling her response.

After, they lay curled together on the bed, neither wanting to move. Absently, he ran his hand up and down her spine.

"Niall MacGregor?"

"Mmm?"

"What were you saying to me, in French?"

"When?"

"Just now."

His soft laugh blew the tendrils of hair around her ear. "Don't you know French?"

"Of course. But I didn't understand those words."

He stretched and rolled away from her, standing up. "Ah, then. I'm not sure. I wasn't thinking of what I was saying. Probably something very indecent."

Anne grinned. Her knees felt a little weak as she rose, put on her robe, went to her table and picked up her comb. Niall pulled open the bed curtains, and she saw sleet hitting the windows, and for the first time, noticed the sound of wind howling around the castle turrets. She yawned, threw the comb down, and climbed into bed, dropping the robe and pulling up the quilts.

"Don't shut the curtains. I like to lie here, warm and comfortable, and hear and see the storm outside."

He pulled the quilts over them both. Sleep came suddenly and deeply, and dusk enshrouded them when Anne woke.

Niall slept beside her, his arm still around her, his face in her hair. By turning her head slightly, she could see his face. He wasn't handsome, she thought, with his long nose, flattened at the bridge, his sharp cheekbones, but with his dark lashes lying on his cheeks, the stern lines that usually bracketed his mouth smoothed by sleep, he looked younger. How strange that this could happen so suddenly. Not love, not like with Hugh. But an enjoyment of what Niall did with her. But it hadn't been like this with Hugh. She hadn't done those things.

Macgregor's Bargain

A heavy cloud began to settle over her again, as she thought of the years ahead, when Hugh would be no more than their clan chief. *But it won't have to be like that. We love each other, and our love will last.*

Her stomach growled, quite loudly. She was afraid to move, to try to get her hair from under Niall, and she found herself utterly ravenous. She sighed and frowned.

"What a noisy thing you are."

Anne started and looked at him. Niall's eyes were still shut, but there was a small smile on his lips.

"I was thinking how hungry I am, and how I was going to move you off my hair."

"I'm glad there was nothing insoluble causing that miserable sigh."

He raised his head, she gathered her hair into a knot, and got up, pulling her heavy woolen robe around her. Her breath left a trail of vapor as she walked to the fireplace. The fire was nearly dying, and she stopped to add more peat, shivering a little. Someone had slipped in while they were sleeping and set a tray of food on the table by the door.

"Shall I bring you something?"

"Nay. I don't want crumbs in my bed. The prickly creature I share it with is quite enough for me."

She pouted. "Prickly? I thought I was soft and warm, and quite rounded."

He laughed aloud as he rose from the bed and reached for his robe. "Only your body, Madam. Your mind is a veritable thorn bush."

Anne snorted. "You're probably used to silly creatures with small, soft minds who've never learned to think. You'll never be able to turn me into one of those. I am a Highland woman."

"This is a marriage we share, lass. I don't expect miracles." His laughter was loud, and Anne began to laugh too, as she tore the end off the loaf of bread.

Anne brought the tray to the rug in front of the fireplace, and they sat on the floor. Niall poured glasses of ale, and raised his own.

"To you, Anne Drummond."

Mockingly she raised her own. "To you, Niall MacGregor. And to the heir of the Drummonds, who may already be on its way."

"It's not for our lack of trying."

Niall sliced a hunk of cheese and studied Anne as he chewed. "What did you do here, Anne, so far from everything, after you returned from Edinburgh, and when you were a child?"

"I didn't mind, really. I had company of our clan, the Drummonds and the MacPhersons. Many of them are more loyal to me than to Grandfather. I played with Iain's children, and others, when I was small, till Jane came, from the Borders, you know. My grandfather would have let me grow up wild. She would have had me behave like a lady of the manor." Anne made a sour face.

Niall grinned. "She did well; you played the part well with our guests. But education? Did your grandfather and Jane teach you?"

"Jane found me a governess, a lady of advanced years who had strong views. She taught me French and Latin and mathematics and literature, and all sorts of odds and ends from her own store of knowledge. Mistress Ransome, she was, a confirmed Jacobite, and fierce. Her husband had died in the '15. She believed that women should be highly educated, and by the time my grandfather realized what she had taught me, it was too late. He believes, you see, that the less education women have, the better."

Anne finished her glass of wine and held it out for more."My grandmother, I've heard, was ideal for him, she brought him money and was a mousy wee thing; though he could never forgive her for giving him a sickly son and then dying."

"Why didn't he wed again?"

She shrugged. "I'm not sure. Though I've suspected for a long time that Jane may share his bed." She giggled. "Mayhap he tried to find a wife, but he does have a bad reputation. Probably no woman would have him."

She looked at him. One side of his face was in near darkness, the other highlighted by the fire.

"And you, MacGregor? What took you from Balquidder to France, and wherever else you've journeyed?"

Macgregor's Bargain

"There are only so many MacGregors who can be supported by cattle raids and stony ground. My father died in a raid, and my mother in childbirth before that. I went with some of my kin to find my fortune, and I might now be lying long dead on a battlefield," he stretched and grinned, "had it not been that I have extraordinary luck, and a love of my own skin."

Niall knelt to build the fire higher. "In Rome I met a man who was in King James Stuart's bodyguard. One of their number had been killed in a tavern brawl, and he introduced me to the King, who thought I would be a suitable companion to the Prince." He sat back and looked at Anne, an eyebrow raised. "And then I met a lady, a very kind older lady, of the Stuart court in Rome, who took it on herself to train me for all I needed to know."

"All?" murmured Anne.

He laughed. "She introduced me to the right people, and I became an assistant to an emissary of the Stuarts, raising money for the cause, and then I became an emissary myself, and traveled with them in France and Italy, and back to France. We taught Charles about Scotland, and how to fight."

"And you were rewarded?"

"Aye, very well. With a little money, though the Stuarts are not rich, and a great many introductions to people in power, who showed me how to use my little money to make a great deal more."

"All of which, of course, you gave to the Jacobite cause."

He looked at her through narrowed eyes. "Ah, the prickles again. Some of which I gave to the cause, most of which I kept for myself."

"And now you're back in Scotland, richer than all the MacGregors, and you have the Drummonds behind you, so you're no longer one of the People of the Mists."

"I'll always be of the MacGregors. They are my clan, though some be thieves..."

"Some?"

"Quiet, woman. Thieves they may be, but they were proscribed, disenfranchised. We can own nothing, we are not even supposed to marry nor christen our young, nor bury our dead in holy ground. We will survive, though. I simply chose an easier way to survive.

■ 60 ■

Remember, lass, your bairn will be half MacGregor, and whatever he's called, MacGregor or Drummond, he'll probably grow up to steal cattle. It'll be in his blood."

She threw a bread crust at him, and he roared with laughter.

Serious again, she looked into the fire. "Must we go to Edinburgh?"

"Of course. I have many people to meet there."

She chewed her lip.

"Don't tell me you're afraid of the Edinburgh *ton* cutting you? Well, the most upright of the Calvinists might well do that. But the scandal has had over a year to die down, and now they'll be curious. You'll meet friends of mine, who care little that you were caught tumbling like a tavern wench..."

He ducked the pillow she threw. "Madam, I've warned you. You must stop throwing things at me. I am larger than you, and stronger, and though I'm certainly not fiercer, I can do you damage.

"As I started to say, my friends will be a bit different, I think. They are more thinkers and doers than you met before. They will talk to you without flirting, and you will be able to discuss a book, or politics. You will be the mistress of my house, and you will be treated with courtesy."

She nodded, accepting what he said for now. She leaned against a chair and stared into the fire.

"Why so pensive?"

"I feel so strange, and I wonder what will happen to me."

The guilessness of her statement touched him. "Is that something your Sight does not tell you? We shall live long together and have many children, and raise Castle Caorann estates to be the best in the Highlands."

She said wistfully, "And shall we finally be content, together?"

"I don't believe in the romances. We are partners, and we must try to be kind to each other. If we expect no more than that, we shall not be disappointed."

She looked down, and he watched her lashes quiver on her fire-pinkened cheeks, and the firm set to her lips.

But she only said, "Of course."

Chapter Eight

"Anne?"

Anne opened her eyes, and moaned as she saw Fiona standing over her, a tentative smile on her lips. She squinted in the gray light and sat up to accept the cup of chocolate offered her.

"Is it late?"

"It's past nine. Your...MacGregor said to let you sleep. Jane's bringing your breakfast up."

Fiona looked down at Anne, and drew in her breath. Anne, too, looked down, and realized she was naked. She pulled up the quilt.

"Shall I get your sacque?"

"Please. It'll never do for Jane to see me thus."

Fiona giggled as she fetched the robe from the floor by the fireplace. She shook her head at the food spread around.

"Whatever happened..." she halted.

Anne scrubbed her face in the bowl of warm water Fiona had brought, and then sat at her dressing table while the girl unsnarled her hair.

Macgregor's Bargain

Fiona giggled again. "It looks as if mice have nested in your hair."

Jane pushed the door open and brought in Anne's breakfast tray.

"Will there be anything else?"

Anne shook her head, then thought of the morrow. "Yes. I'm sure you know we leave for Edinburgh tomorrow. Please pack my new clothes. I'll take Fiona with me if Iain will let her go."

Fiona's eyes widened at this.

"Also, send MacGregor's Hamish to me. And send Fergus too. I'll speak to him after I've talked to Hamish. Fiona, will you open the curtain so I can see the loch?"

Jane stood at the door, the picture of martyrdom. "Is that all, Mistress?"

"You'll stay here, of course, and manage things. We'll not be here for Christmas or Hogmanay, nor will my grandfather. Make sure everyone receives gifts."

The woman nodded, her black eyes showing nothing, her hands clasped tightly at her waist.

Anne grinned. *Old bitch. Wait till I return.*

"That's all, then, Jane. I'll kiss you goodbye ere I go."

Jane sniffed, and pulled the door shut behind her.

Anne looked out the window. "It's only misting today. I'll not get another chance to ride free for a long time, so today I shall. Will you get my old shirt, and my short skirt and heavy petticoat?"

Fiona clicked her tongue. "What'll your husband think of you riding off like a landless reiver's woman?"

"He'll probably not see me, nor mind if he does."

Anne devoured her oatmeal. Fiona answered the knock at the door.

"Hamish, come in. I know you will make sure all MacGregor's things are packed, but will you help Fiona and Jane in our packing and carrying, should they need it?"

Hamish MacGregor stood at attention, heavy black brows drawn together. "Indeed, ma'am, I'm much used to caring just for my cousin Niall. I'll find someone to help you ladies."

■ 64 ■

Anne's lips tightened. "I asked you to help us. I also want you to train Fiona's young brother Fergus, if Iain will let him go. He'll come as my man, and I'm sure he'll learn from you. I'd like to take my harp. It will have to be packed carefully."

Hamish glared at her. "I'm Niall's man, and his cousin, is all. Not a common laborer, not your servant. I'm a MacGregor, too."

Anne took another bannock, and sighed.

"Now, then, Hamish, I seem to be a sort of MacGregor myself now. Must we make your MacGregor unhappy? I simply wanted to make sure his needs are met, and his needs now include me. And I want the best teacher I can find for young Fergus, so who else but you? The temptations of Edinburgh would be too great for a young country lad without a mentor. And Fiona here could use help with the heavy parcels and trunks. Look you, if you could supervise the servants' work, t'would help me greatly."

Her lashes dropped, then she looked up and her chestnut eyes met Hamish's black ones..

"Well, then, perhaps I can be of help. The clarsach in the drawing room is to be packed?" He looked sideways at Fiona. "Perhaps Fiona will help me see to that."

The girl looked down demurely, and took a deep breath. Hamish's eyes dropped to the snowy scarf that covered her breast. Hamish was much traveled, he had been with Niall in Rome and Paris, and knew when he was being cozened. But the thought of traveling with Fiona was a pleasant one, and his new mistress had made amends for her abruptness.

He left as Fergus came in.

"Fergus, I'm going to ask your father if he will agree to your coming to Edinburgh with your sister and me. I need my own man, and MacGregor's man will train you. Would you like that?"

Fergus Drummond, just twelve, his red hair several shades brighter that his sister's, stood dumbstruck. Then he grinned, showing deep dimples. *Edinburgh!*

"Oh, yes, I'd like that."

"Then it's settled. I'll talk to your father, and if he agrees, we'll have you measured for the proper clothing when we get to

Macgregor's Bargain

Edinburgh. Now, go help your sister and Hamish prepare for our journey."

The boy ducked his head, and ran from the room. Seconds later, Anne and Fiona heard his loud crow of delight.

"Fiona, now that you'll be a lady's maid, we'll have new clothes made for you, too."

Fiona said, "MacGregor's man, he's passing bonny, isn't he? I fancy dark men. Odd these MacGregors are all cousins, yet he's the only black haired one. Yon Calum is bonny too, but..."

"Do watch what you're doing. You're plaiting my hair with my robe ribbons, ninny."

Dressed, Anne clattered down the stairs and out through the massive front doors into the windy day. Whitecaps moved across the gray-black loch. The great double gate in front of the courtyard stood open, but she went through a small door in the west wall and strode out to the stables.

The granite stable block was warm from the heat of animals, and smelled of horses and hay. Bard came bounding toward her, forgiving her again for exiling him from her bedroom these past two nights. He reared onto his hind legs and put his front paws on her shoulders, licking her face. She laughed and pulled his velvet ears, talking softly.

"Morning, lass." Iain, working on the hoof of one of the great draft horses, looked up at her.

Niall's stallion snorted and whinnied from his box stall.

"Iain, would you object if I take Fergus and Fiona to Edinburgh with me?"

"I'd welcome it, lass .'Twould give me comfort of mind to know you had the two to look out for you."

Calum MacGregor came into the stable and looked at Anne, taking in the skirt that swung around her ankles, the loose blouse made like a man's shirt. Anne once again thought how much Niall and Calum looked alike, yet were so different.

"Good morning, Anne. Do you look for Niall? He's walking with your grandfather."

She shook her head. "I only came to talk to Iain and to get my mare."

■ 66 ■

Iain called to his son Lachlan, and the young man led her mare out and saddled her.

"Where d'ye go, the glen?" Iain asked.

Anne nodded, stepped into Lachlan's cupped hands, tucked up skirts and petticoats, and threw her leg over Vixen.

Calum grinned. "D'ye want company?"

She laughed and shook her head. "I need no company. I like to be alone."

Anne nudged the little mare past the men, and out into the breezy sunlight as her grandfather and Niall walked toward her. Alasdair ignored her and Niall took in the plaid and the shabby skirt but merely looked at her. She made her way up the hill along a wide burn, Bard following, and then doubled back, to the place where the top of the glen widened and sloped down toward a mass of rock in the middle. She climbed off Vixen and left the little mare to graze as she paced through the tall wet grass, her plaid wrapped around her, the big gray dog at her side. She looked up at the interlaced branches of the trees, thinking of how homesick for this she had been in Edinburgh, times she had thought of this small glen, of bluebells and foxgloves, and the sweet smell of pine trees. She sighed as she thought of Niall. He demanded little, treated her pleasantly, had made enjoyable love too her, yet she sensed a distance, as though the life around him was merely amusing theater, and she an incidental actress. Not that she expected love. It would be easy to like him, and soon he would leave her alone. She had dreamed of a girl child last night.

Vixen snorted and pawed the ground. Bard, too, seemed to be responding to something. Suddenly wary, he looked around, growling deep in his throat. He came to stand by Anne. That same chill she had felt last time she had come here crept over her. The grass in front of her seemed to bend, as though something lay there. She reached for Vixen and mounted the nervous mare, prepared to run from the menace that brought the chill. As suddenly as it had come, the chill was gone, and with it the fear.

Anne's heart slowed and she patted the mare to soothe her. Then she heard the sound of a horse moving up the glen.

Macgregor's Bargain

Vixen turned her head toward the bottom of the glen and whinnied. Anne frowned as she saw Iolair and his rider coming toward her in the thinning mist. Bard stood, watchful.

Niall looked at her briefly, then at the mare.

"She'll make a good foal. I think we'll breed her in the spring."

She stared coolly back at him as the plaid slipped from her hair to her shoulders. "I think not."

The stallion sniffed at the mare's hindquarters, and Vixen sidestepped and kicked him.

Niall said, "Her manners remind me of yours."

"And his remind me of yours," Anne retorted. "And I don't want her to foal, yet. She's but three."

Niall's voice held a hint of amusement. "By spring, she may be more amenable; and so might you be. But then you have been *most* amenable."

She ignored him, and pressed her heels against Vixen's sides, calling over her shoulder, "How did you find me?"

"Iain told me."

Iain told him of her secret place. Would no one stand against this man?

Anne nudged the mare forward and started downhill. She looked over her shoulder at her husband, her cheeks pink, her hair limned with moisture.

Niall urged Iolair beside Vixen and looked down at her, his eyes belying his teasing smile.

"'Tis a shame it's so wet, Annie. I'd have you off that mare and on your back for that insolent look."

Her smile was every bit as offensive as her look had been. "No doubt you've gotten soft, living so long in dryer places. In Scotland, when a man wants a woman, or a woman a man, a bit of wet only adds to the fun. But then, as I don't want you, and you're much too effete," here her voice dropped and changing to lowland Scots from Gaelic, she added "wi' nae pintle in yer breeks, and na hair on yer chest, I'll be on ma way."

Before he could stop her, the fleet little mare was speeding down the mountainside, and he saw the plaid slide further down Anne's back, and her braid of brown hair bobbing before the mare disappeared in the trees, followed ghostlike by the great hound.

He kicked his horse and headed after Anne, but slowly, unsure of his path, unwilling to go at the breakneck pace his wife had taken. When he returned to the stables, Iain was unsaddling the mare, his ears red, his face grim. Niall dismounted and led Iolair into the stable. As he passed Iain, he gave him a sympathetic glance, and the older man rolled his eyes. Anne had not allowed her love for Iain to halt her angry words at what she had seen as a betrayal.

Iain put the mare in her stall.

"She'll go to Edinburgh tomorrow?"

"Yes, we'll ride there. I hope Anne wasn't too harsh."

Iain said, admiringly, "She has an unco' sharp tongue. Even when she was a wee thing, she did."

"I put you in the middle."

"Aye. I should not have told you the way to the glen." He grinned. "But I remembered that the grass was soft there, and when I was a lad, it was a good place to take a lass."

Niall thought of Anne's words. *Mayhap I have gone soft,* he thought.

When Niall entered the great hall, Anne stood in front of the fireplace, a glass of whisky in her hand, her drying hair beginning to curl loose from its plait. She cocked her head and watched him, her smile mocking. She had pulled off her boots, and her bare toes curled in the deerskin rug. Her plaid steamed on a chair near the fire, and her damp shirt clung to her.

He poured whisky for himself, and came so close to her that she had to tip her head back to look at him.

"So I have no pintle in my breeks?"

She shrugged, and her smile grew.

"Anne!"

Her grandfather's roar made her turned her head. He stood in the doorway, a scowl on his face, Seana directly behind him.

"Yes, Grandfather?"

"Jane tells me you're taking Fiona and Fergus with you."

Niall raised his brows, looking down at her.

"Aye."

"Ye did this without asking me? Who d'ye think is laird at Loch Laggan?"

"It had nothing to do with who is laird at this castle."

"Ye don't take people away without consulting me. Did ye know of this, MacGregor?"

Niall shook his head, amusement on his face as he watched grandfather and granddaughter face each other. Seana stepped around her brother and pretended to be fascinated by something in the minstrel gallery.

"I wanted some of my clan around me. I didn't want to be surrounded by MacGregors."

Mildly, Niall said, "But MacGregors are your kin too."

"Not my blood kin, nor ever will be. Fiona will be my maid, and Fergus my man. Their father agrees to it. It's done."

Alasdair Drummond stalked toward his granddaughter, his hand raised. He stopped when he saw Niall's face. The cold hazel eyes held his. Then he grunted, spun on his heel and strode out, shouting over his shoulder, "Ye better make sure dinner's ready on time, ye little bitch."

Seana turned and raised her brows at Niall.

Anne smirked, and sipped her whisky as she strolled to the door.

"I think we have a conversation to finish," Niall said.

"I think not, sir. If you come swaggering around, you can expect no courtesy from me. Now, sir, I will go and change my clothing, see to dinner, and go somewhere quiet, where I may read in peace."

Anne didn't see Niall for the rest of the afternoon. She heard the two men's voices as she passed her grandfather's study, but Niall chose, it seemed, to stay away from her.

So much the better, she thought, and pulled a book from the shelf. She wondered where her aunt was, and decided she must be staying in her room to avoid her brother. Anne thought of going to find Seana, but laziness and the book held her.

She didn't look up until Jane came in to light the lamps. Shortly afterward, Seana materialized, her lace cap askew, carrying a bit of needlework. Bard raised his head from the hearth, then lay back with a groan. Drummond's bitch Flur lay beside him, her belly heavy with the litter she carried.

"My dear, you should wear that color more often. It does become you."

Anne looked down at the blue-green frock with its lighter stomacher trimmed in lavender bows. She had forgone large hoops as too uncomfortable for sitting, and the full skirt billowed around her. The fire had flushed her face, and a small lace cap haloed it. Niall joined them, changed from his riding clothes to a dark gray satin coat and breeches, the coat fashionably long, his black vest trimmed in silver embroidery, his stock snowy.

"What do you read, Anne?"

"*Gulliver's Travels* again. It's long been a favorite of mine."

"What makes it so? "

"Why, because it's written exceedingly well, and it tells much about people. Have you read it?"

Niall nodded. "It has always seemed to me that most people would be very comfortable in Lilliput."

She gave him a genuinely agreeable smile. "Small minds are quite prevalent in any society, I suppose."

"I'm glad you like to read. I fear I'll be away a good deal in Edinburgh, but I have ordered an excellent library from Peter Williamson. You may contact him for any books you choose. You will be content to read the days away waiting for my return?"

Her smile faded. "I shall be more than content, sir, filling the time with my interests."

Their eyes held, for a moment, then Anne looked away.

"Auntie, come nearer to the fire. You mustn't sit so far away."

"My dear, I am not that old. I am quite comfortable. Sir, I do hope you will allow my grandniece to visit me often, and that you will accompany her."

Niall bowed to the older woman. "Would I deprive myself of your delightful company for long?"

Seana giggled and looked flustered. "My dear Niall, I am too old to be treated so by such a handsome rake."

"You can never be that old."

Macgregor's Bargain

They both laughed, and Anne stared at them over the top of her book.

When Alasdair Drummond stomped into the room, he destroyed the peace in it.

"Well, lass, is the meal ready?"

"Grandfather, it is not quite three by the clock."

"Ye may have learned dissolute ways in the city, but here we go the way we have for years. We eat early, we go to bed early, we work hard all the day."

Anne stared insolently at Alasdair's corpulent body and returned to her book.

"Well, my boy, shall we have a tot before dinner??

Niall poured glasses of canary for his wife and great aunt by marriage, and Alasdair, looking as if he wished the women in hell, poured whisky for himself and Niall…

"So, lad, you'll do great things in Edinburgh, I'm sure. There are men there, many men, who will rally to the cause. Mark me well, the next year will be a great one, for Drummonds and for Scotland, and for all Britain."

Seana snorted, and her brother glared at her.

He continued, "We'll not be ruled by the damned Germans for long, I'll wager. The Stuarts will return by the will of the people.

Anne muttered something.

"What, girl? What bit of nastiness was that?"

"I said it would be good if they could manage to keep their heads on their shoulders and their *bods* in their breeks."

Seana, horrified, looked at her niece, then at her brother's choleric face, and hastily asked, "Do tell me, Niall, is Prince Charles all they say. Is he so handsome?"

"Aye, Madame. He has the Stuart looks. He's tall. He has red hair and dark eyes."

Drummond laughed coarsely, and asked, "Is it true he has the unco' great Stuart *bod?*"

"Alasdair!" his shocked sister cried.

Niall noticed his wife looked interested for the first time, and when she saw him watching her, a small half smile curled her lips.

Macgregor's Bargain

For no reason he could discern, it irritated him, and it must have shown, for her smile widened, the small space between her two front teeth giving her an childlike innocence he was sure didn't echo her thoughts.

Drummond was still guffawing when Jane announced dinner.

His conversation did not improve as they ate. "Tell me, then. Is that Tearlach, that good prince, a man, or one like his forebear, that liked the lads?"

Seana fanned herself and looked heavenward. "Now, sir, tell me of where you have been. Rome, I think?"

"It's sadly decayed, and I find it hard to believe what it must have been. But the Romans are taking an interest in its antiquities now that more English are touring the continent."

"And Paris? It's been years since I was there."

"I like it very much. They lead the world, I swear, in pleasure. At court they think of little else. The style of building now is very ornate. In truth, I expect Edinburgh will soon follow. But one learns to clear one's throat before entering a room, to warn whomever might be doing whatever."

"La, sir, you are as bad as my brother."

"Though he phrases with a bit more nicety," murmured Anne.

"Why thank you, Madame. I do believe that's the first time I have received your praise. Or perhaps, there was a time, ..." His eyes glinted as he remembered the fulsome compliments she had heaped upon him, in a breathless voice, the night before.

Anne, knowing full well what he was thinking, forced herself to look serene, and sipped her claret.

"And have ye packed off half the goods in the castle to take with you?" Drummond growled.

"Very little, Sir. My husband informs me that he has especially ordered all we might need, as far as household goods go, so I leave the castle, and you, in Jane's hands."

Anne was rewarded with an uncomfortable scowl from her grandfather. She grinned. She had been correct in her belief that Jane had supplied him with more than clean linen.

"At any rate, I take my own things, and my clarsach."

Macgregor's Bargain

The evening seemed very long to Niall. He listened attentively to Drummond's monologue over port and joined Anne and Seana in the library as soon as possible. Anne, seemingly unaware of him, played her harp, her expression distant, and Bard lay by her, his head on her foot.

Gratefully, Niall heard the clock strike nine. "Come then, Anne, we must get an early start tomorrow."

"But I'm not through."

Seana gave them one uncomfortable look, and made for the door. "Oh, it is late. Anne, dear, there'll be many very late nights in Edinburgh. Now is the time to get your rest."

"Rest?" Anne raised an eyebrow.

Her aunt blushed violently and her grandfather guffawed as he led Seana from the room. "Little rest she gets with that young stallion, I'll wager. Do her good. Nothing like it to quiet a restive filly."

"Horrible old man." Anne rose and followed her husband up the stairs.

Fiona helped her undress, and Anne picked a heavy opaque satin nightdress. When Niall came in, he sent Fiona away.

"Twill be a pleasure to have our apartments done when we return. Why not take off that nightcap? It will come off soon, anyway."

He swept her up and dropped her on the bed, pulling off his clothes. "You look like a nun tonight. Are you trying to entice me with forbidden pleasures? I find it enchanting that the first time I took you, you lay as if you were being martyred, and by the fifth you were telling me some naughty things to do."

Laughing, he held her down on the bed, avoiding her thrashing legs. Bard, lying by the fire, raised his head and gave them an anxious look, then apparently decided it was just human play and went to sleep.

Next morning promised fair, the sun rising in a cloudless sky, the loch a flat mirror reflecting mountains and castle. Anne, dressed in her riding clothes, watched the preparations for their trip, then made her way to the shore of Loch Laggan, where a small boat was pulled up. She pushed it into the shallow water, climbed in and took the oars, heading for the small island in the middle of the loch.

As she approached it she looked over her shoulder at the ruins of a small chapel surrounded by gray stones. She nudged the boat against an ancient rock pier and climbed out, standing for a moment, looking back at the far shore and the great pile of castle with its one tower-her tower, the hills and mountains rising behind it, and horses being led out from the stables.

Then she turned and walked up the slope to the ruined chapel, there for hundreds of years, and around it generations of Drummonds and their kin slept under grass studded with the wild flowers of autumn. Two graves with one stone were newer than most, the storms of winter not yet having erased the lettering: Dughail Drummond and Catriona Grant, who had loved each other and the baby daughter they had left behind.

Anne laid her hand on the gray stone. As always, it seemed warm to her touch. She came here often to talk to her parents, and often felt as if her mother stood beside her: the mother who, according to Morag, had left her with The Sight.

There had been times in her life, especially in the past year, when she felt as if she could turn quickly enough, her mother Catriona would be standing there beside her. In early evening, a breeze often caught the petals of roses in her mother's garden, as if a skirt had brushed against them.

"Mother," Anne murmured, "why can I feel the fear, and not know what to look for? Mother, will you keep me safe in what is to come? Will you keep Loch Laggan safe while I am gone?"

Chapter Nine

Residents emptied chamber pots into the Edinburgh streets, sometimes on the heads of passersby, adding to the piles of rotting refuse in the gutters which ran down the narrow streets and wynds to feed the Nor'loch 's dark waters below the crowded city.

Anne, used to the clean expanse of Loch Laggan, the smell of thyme and heather, regularly gagged as she left their home, high wooden clogs on her shoes to keep them from the city's filth, carrying an orange stuck with cloves under her nose.

She had learned that wise pedestrians walked in the middle of the streets to avoid the dangers from above and those lurking in the wynds.

Over all lay a dense cloud of smoke. One could tell when dinner was being cooked by the increase in the cloud. Travelers saw the dark smoke long before they saw Edinburgh castle on its hill. Cramped, in tenements rising eight, ten, fourteen stories, the wealthiest and the poorest shared buildings. The rich lived on the lower floors, usually above shops, and the ascending stairs corresponded inversely with descending wealth.

Niall owned an entire house in the Canongate near Holyrood, and, practically unheard of Edinburgh, shared it with no one save his people. The ground level held the kitchen and storage rooms, the rooms of clansmen, the second and third the rooms where they entertained: two dining rooms, a drawing room, a library, a music room and a guest room. Many of their rooms had stoves in them, and Anne luxuriated in their warmth.

Anne's favorite was the small drawing room on the fourth floor, near her bedroom. The room seemed made for her, in soft shades of green and rose, with cream walls and wainscoting. It was intimate, and reserved for visits from Aunt Seana and Lucy, who was in the city staying with her father. Now Anne sat there alone.

Anne had met Niall's friends, and, true to his promise. they cared little for her past. They were, on the whole, of lesser social status than people she had met before, but better educated. Anne was still having trouble keeping their occupations straight, but she knew that Robert Crichton taught at the university, that Finlay Duncan had inherited great wealth from his father, who had been a merchant.

She poked a needle into her crewel work and frowned, looking over the frame at large snowflakes whirling past her window. She heard the bells of St Giles strike two, and wondered if Niall would return for the ball tonight.

The assembly was to be her first real venture into society since her return, and she was unsure whether she would be daring enough to go without him. He had been gone two weeks, on an errand about which he had told her little. She knew he had gone to the north, to Sutherland with his MacGregor troop, but nothing else.

Fiona came in, carrying a tea tray. "MacGregor's back." Anne could see a bloom on her cheeks.

"I suppose, then, Hamish is back too."

Fiona nodded. "Hamish says MacGregor will be with you shortly. They were both cold and wet."

"And you were helping Hamish get warm, and that's why your cap is awry?"

Fiona blushed and giggled.

"And Fiona, not one word about the babe."

"Aren't you going to tell him?"

"Not yet." Anne frowned, and looked down at her needlework. "You know missed courses can happen, and babes lost before they're fair started. I want to be sure. I'll tell him in another month or so. And not a word to your Hamish, if you know what's good for you."

"My Hamish!"

Anne said, "Best go and fetch some brandy in here, too, before MacGregor comes roaring in for it."

Would I be sitting here, if it were Hugh come home after two weeks away? She shook her head. She was curious about where MacGregor went, but she wouldn't ask. She didn't hear the door open.

"Ah, my sweet domestic wife, doing her needlework with her little cat smile on her face. Are you glad I'm home?"

Niall's mocking voice made her start.

"Indeed, I am. Remember the ball?"

"*Rach air mun!* I'd forgotten."

He brushed his hand through the curls at the back of her neck, then kissed her there, just below the frills on her lace cap. She sat very still, and he moved away from her, and stood across from her, watching her at her embroidery.

Fiona came in with his brandy.

He pinched Fiona's chin and said, "I saw Hamish heading for the back stairs with a leer on his face and something large in his breeks. Could it be a gift for you, lass?"

"Sir!" Fiona fled.

"MacGregor, you are too crude. Fiona's a virgin and her father'll kill me if she's not that on her wedding day!"

He laughed, and said, "Tell me again about the ball. I remember it's your first invitation to your old set."

She tipped her head to one side. "Well, I have spent a fortune of your money on a new gown in the latest French style, with a silver embroidered petticoat, and slippers..."

"And what am I to wear to complement your entrance? I am sure you have planned it."

79

Macgregor's Bargain

She made a face at him and poured herself more tea. "Black, I think, a shadow behind me."

"And?"

"Aunt Seana comes with us. And my wedding necklace."

"Tell me, are your hoops so wide that no man can come near you?"

"Do you wish that? I shall manage. I will dance, you know."

He dropped into a chair, laughing. "Come here, lass, and give me a proper kiss, or I'll not go."

"Nay. I know your kisses. We'd never get to the ball."

"If you want to go, you had better come here."

"D'ye promise you'll do no more than kiss me?"

"I promise I'll try to do no more."

Anne gave in. He pulled her down on his lap, and, as his mouth met hers, he slid his hand up her leg.

"You promised," she whispered.

"I promised to try. God, lass, it's been two weeks."

"Two weeks - without a woman?"

"I swear. The first ten days, I was so tired from your demands, I wanted only peace." Laughing, he dodged her fists. "And the last four, there were none about."

He winced as her sharp teeth bit his earlobe.

"And what did you do while I was gone?"

"Little, really. I ordered books by Aphra Behn and Jane Barker. Arabella Crichton and Margaret Duncan came to call one day. They suggested the books. I felt they came because of duty, but we had a good time. And I went riding, with Bard and Fergus to protect me. Like a lady," she added. "But I do miss riding astride."

He grinned as his hand slipped higher and he kissed her behind her ear. "Perhaps we can remedy that. If I unbutton my breeches, and you pull up your petticoat, this chair should do nicely."

"Beast," she said, but weakly, knowing she was lost.

As they walked into the assembly room, Seana examined her grand niece. Anne had a bloom to her, and it occurred to Seana that Anne might be breeding. She must ask when they had time alone. The low neckline of the gown Anne wore showed breasts that seemed fuller.

The crush of bodies, some of them not too well washed, made Anne wrinkle her nose as they pushed their way into the ballroom. A gentleman dressed in blue satin bowed as she threw back her cape, and he eyed her bosom.

"These routs are beginning to be excuses for the most immoral behavior," Seana grumbled as she avoided a waving wine glass.

Niall moved the women through the crush by the door. A woman blew him a kiss. Her breasts were almost totally uncovered, showing the tops of rouged nipples. Niall took two glasses of punch from a waiter's tray. Anne was whisked away by the blue satin suit. Seana accepted her goblet and a chair as she watched Anne go.

"Oh, my, this tastes as if it might do damage to me." She fanned herself and looked around. "There goes young Mistress Boyd, I'll wager."

"How do you know?" Niall eyed the buxom young woman in pink.

"How do you think I know? Not many are as endowed as Ellen Boyd. She was Ellen Fleming when Anne knew her. A nice little thing."

The music stopped and Niall bowed to Seana, then turned to find Anne.

"Go, dear, I shall seek my friends," and Seana headed for the card room.

Niall saw Anne standing between the blue suit and a handsome young man. She curtsied to the blue suit, took the young man's arm and walked with him to the open doors leading into a garden. He sauntered after them, wondering what Anne was up to.

Walking swiftly around a boxwood hedge, Niall nearly collided with Anne and her escort. They sat on a marble bench, Anne's skirts taking up most of it. They were laughing.

The young man said, "And do you remember when Charlotte.." and the saw Niall coming toward them.

Niall bowed, and Anne grinned up at him.

"This my friend Richard Burns. I met him at Aunt Seana's. My husband, Niall MacGregor."

The young man stood and bowed. "Servant, sir."

"Richard was just telling me I must go to Hope Park. Much has been done to improve it, and it is a lovely place to stroll, he says."

"So I have heard. Mayhap we will explore it on a fine day."

Something about MacGregor's stance told Burns he would be better off in the assembly rooms.

He bowed again. "'Twas good to see you, Anne. May I call on you?"

"Certainly," Niall said comfortably. "We shall look forward to seeing you soon. Mayhap you will join us in a stroll in Hope Park?"

"My honor, sir." Still bowing, Burns backed off, then turned and moved quickly back into the building.

Anne stood and sauntered toward the open doors above the terrace.

"Where are you going?"

"Why, to find a partner and dance, of course."

"I will be your partner."

Seriously, she said, "It isn't done, you know, going into the garden or dancing with one's spouse. Perhaps..."

"Don't tease me too much, woman. My patience is limited."

"Then I suppose I'll dance with you. But only once. I must rescue Aunt Seana from the faro table. She has no sense at all about gambling."

Niall enjoyed leading Anne out, watching her small flirtations with other men as she passed along. After the dance ended, they walked into the card room and watched Seana lose what seemed a great deal of money.

Anne caught his eye and shrugged. A tall blond man moved to stand beside her, and whispered in her ear. She giggled and turned her back on Niall while she spoke to him. He saw the man's hand slide around her waist, and moved quickly toward them.

As Niall walked up he heard her say, "Ah, but sir, you'll not know if a Highland woman always carries her knife unless you try her patience too far. And then it might be too late."

The man made an exaggerated face of fear and swaggered away.

Niall leaned down and whispered in her ear. "It appears to me I'll never have to protect you from unwanted advances.."

"Nor could you from the ones I want."

She took a glass of claret from a tray and drained it. The rest of the night went by swiftly. Niall gave up trying to keep an eye on Anne, convinced now she could take care of herself. He found himself at one point between two women, both offering their dance cards. Then Anne strolled by, on the arm of his friend Crichton, who seemed to be telling her an amusing story. She laughed, and catching Niall's eye, winked in a very bawdy manner. She disappeared again at supper, and he ate with Seana. Anne reappeared, looking even more flushed. She dropped into a chair beside her aunt.

"Niall, please, do be a dear and fetch me some food. I cannot walk another step."

Niall summoned a servant and gave him instructions.

"And how much walking have you done?"

"Well, around the card room several times, searching for Seana. Then up the staircase, where I saw one of your dance partners, against the wall, with the...."

"Anne, I do think you get more like your grandfather," Seana said.

"Nonsense, Aunt. I begin to resemble my husband." Anne grinned amiably at Niall.

"How much have you had to drink?" Niall asked

"A great deal, I believe. May I propose we leave soon? I think I shall soon be asleep."

Seana rose. "Oh, my dear, I should like to. I feel I have lost a great deal more money than I ought, and if I stay, I shall only lose more."

Niall said, "Have you tried winning?"

Seana slapped his arm with her fan and giggled.

After escorting Seana to her door, they elected to walk the few streets home, Anne wearing high patens borrowed from Seana, to protect her slippers.

"Well, did you do what you set out to do?"

"What do you mean?"

Macgregor's Bargain

"I think you were determined to enchant every man at the ball. Did you do it?"

A sidelong glance. "Did I enchant you?"

"You're flirting with me, Madam."

"It was pleasant. Before I was one of so many maids, and closely supervised."

"Obviously not closely enough."

"Must you always mention that."

"I was simply stating what must be truth."

"Well, at any rate, it was somewhat heady tonight. I saw you watching me. Were you protecting me or simply making sure I didn't kick over the traces?"

"Actually, I think highly of your honor. I believe that you'll not bed another man till we've a bairn or two."

"And then?"

"Then we shall see. I am a reasonable man. I do not expect too much in the way of fidelity."

"Shall we dismiss the discussion of fidelity until a later time? I find it tiring."

The torchbearer who had led them through the dark streets stopped at their house.

Inside the house, candlelight showed her face still flushed, her eyes sparkling. She climbed the stairs ahead of him, unpinning the brooch that held her cloak, swinging it off.

A glance over her shoulder, her eyes heavy lidded, and Niall climbed the stairs swiftly. He bent and kissed her neck, just under her ear, and she shivered.

"You continue to bewitch me."

They stopped often, that last flight of stairs, and Niall followed her into her bedroom.

"We must try my bedroom sometime." he murmured, as he stood behind her.

Fiona, yawning, stood at the door Anne's dressing room. Anne pushed Niall away.

"Oh, Fiona, I'm sorry we're so late. If you'll help me..."

Niall said, "My wife needs your help in freeing her from skirts and petticoats and stays, which I am unable to do, it seems."

Fiona blushed, and Anne followed her into the dressing room. Niall took off his coat and vest and sat in one of the fragile chairs at Anne's desk. "Where is Hamish, Fiona?" he called.

"Indeed, I don't know, sir. I expect he is in your rooms."

"When you leave, will you tell him I'll not need him tonight?"

Anne opened the dressing room door, dressed in a loose robe, and Fiona slipped past her. They heard her humming as she walked down the hall to Niall's room.

"Wasteful," murmured Anne.

"Mmm?"

"Maintaining two body servants and not using them."

"You still have to learn to shave me. I can't dispense with Hamish till then."

"Ah, but you profess not to trust me."

He slid the robe off her shoulders and she stood nude and simply looked at him.

"And so to bed, as the dear old Mr. Pepys said."

Anne moved to the opposite side of the bed from him, eyeing him as he stalked her.

Chapter Ten

Niall passed the port decanter to the six men who sat around the dining table. Adam Murray cleared his throat.

"King Louis still will not acknowledge Prince Charles, Niall. I know not what else to do. Cameron of Lochiel and John Drummond are doing all they can, and your men have been moving through Italy and France, and have promises from perhaps two hundred exiles who will come back to Scotland when the Prince is here. But the French - I can get no more promises from them. Have the guns been sent around the country?"

"Aye," Calum answered. "We've late been to Sutherland, and our men have delivered arms to the north. But," Calum paused, "but the northern clans are not so sure they have a cause to be with us."

Murray drew a deep breath, shaking his head. "There is other news. Prince Charles has announced he will be in Scotland by June."

"*By June?* But we can't raise enough men by then," Niall said, stunned. "If King Louis won't recognize the Prince, and we have no more sworn guarantees for French support, there is not a way we will be prepared."

■ 87 ■

Crichton sputtered. "I have not more than a handful of men from the Borders who will follow us now. They still fear the Catholic Church. And Hepburn? How does he in gathering Borderers?"

"He is in Peebles or thereabout, I believe. He may be back in France by now." Murray looked at Niall. "I fear, Niall, you must go back to France then too. There is much to be done. With some of the men in the Prince's favor, I fear he is getting bad advice."

Niall and Calum looked at each other. They knew whom Murray spoke of. Those men who were furthering their own causes, who would agree with the Prince on all things, and encourage his dissolute ways. Then there was the priest Father Kelly, whom no one but Charles trusted. Rumors persisted that some young men on the Grand Tour, who made it a point to visit Prince Charles in France and King James in Rome, were actually Hanover spies.

Murray continued, "I propose we send a letter to the Prince asking him to stay away unless he can bring men and money."

"Do you think he will listen? How many men?" Niall asked. "How much money? Alasdair Drummond and the Duke of Perth want him to come as soon as possible. We have a mighty conflict here."

"At least 6000 men, and arms for three times as many. And 30,000 louis d'or," Murray responded.

"I believe, though," added Crichton, "that with or without French money, arms, and troops, many of the clans will rise if the Prince lands."

Niall sighed. "Aye. They will rise, and we will fight. But I wish the odds were better."

Calum said, "But have we ever been careful gamblers, Niall?"

"And Jacobites in England?" Niall asked.

Murray said, "Manchester seems to be the only city that will bring many men to us."

Niall shook his head. "Who do we have in London? Do we have information on what the Hanovers are doing?"

"We have a few informers, but I fear the English spy system is far ahead of ours. We know who leads it. Newcastle has replaced Walpole," Murray answered. He hesitated before continuing. "Another problem is the Prince himself. He delights in masquerades

Macgregor's Bargain

and aliases, and part of the time we don't know where he is. But he has asked for you. Francis Hepburn has a steadying influence, but as I said, I am not sure where he is at the moment. But I think of everyone, except those damned Irishmen who are closest to him, you seem to be his favorite."

Niall took a deep breath, trying to keep his temper, and pushed his glass away. "We cannot solve the problems tonight. Shall we join the ladies? We will meet tomorrow and discuss this again. Duncan, you have said nothing. Tomorrow tell us what the Edinburgh merchants might do."

Duncan said, "What merchants always do: protect their interests."

"Anne, you must play for us."

Arabella Crichton fanned herself and sipped her coffee.

Anne pulled her clarsach to her and absently ran her fingers over the strings.

"What shall I play?"

"Something romantic."

Anne nodded, and played a love song she had known since childhood, *Adieu, Dundee.* There had been eleven at the table tonight, and now five women sat in the drawing room. As she played, Anne listened for the sound of her husband and his friends. Soon they would join the ladies, for Niall made it a practice not to sit too long over the port. In fact, they had been much longer than usual tonight. The women had discussed fashion, and books, and the latest concerts, and still the men lingered. Anne looked at Jeanne Murray. She had just met the Murrays tonight, they having come over recently from France.

Jeanne Murray wore more makeup than any women of Anne's acquaintance. Her face was whitened, her lips and cheeks carmined, her eyelids darkened. Her elaborate gown had rows of scarlet bows on her ivory stomacher. She looked at Anne now, her fan hiding her mouth, her eyes cool.

Anne looked away, concentrating on her music. Niall's eyes had strayed to Jeanne often during dinner. Niall had mentioned he had known Jeanne Duclos in Paris, and had been surprised to

Macgregor's Bargain

find she had married Adam Murray. Anne wondered how he had "known" her, but forbore to ask.

"Somehow, I can't imagine her with such a dry stick, and away from Paris." Niall had said.

Jeanne sighed, looking bored, and at her deep breath her breasts threatened to pop out of her bodice. At that moment a servant opened the door, and Niall escorted his guests into the room. Jeanne straightened up immediately. Anne stopped playing, looking at her husband's furious face, but Niall motioned her to continue. She grinned, and slipped from the soft air she had been playing, to one with a definite martial tone to it.

At the end, Arabella asked, "What was that?'"

"It is called 'The Glen is Mine.' It's a pibroch, a war song. It tells us no one can take our land. It rightly should be played on the pipes, it has much more of a swagger then." Anne looked at her husband. His face was tight and his eyes had that green flare she was beginning to recognize as pure temper.

He caught her stare and frowned at her before going to sit by Jeanne Murray.

Although nothing was said, Niall's mood cast a pall over the guests and they left early.

Still grim and silent, Niall escorted Anne upstairs. He followed her into her boudoir, and motioned to Fiona to help her mistress undress. Anne modestly stepped behind a screen, and Fiona unlaced her outer clothes and slipped them off. She unlaced Anne's corset and Anne sighed with relief as she stepped from her hoops. Dressed in a robe and night dress, she sat down at her dressing table, and Fiona stood behind her, pulling the pins from her hair. Anne, conscious of Niall's brooding stare, sent the girl away and began brushing her own hair.

"Well?"

"Well, what?"

"Your black mood drives our guests away, even pretty Mistress Murray, who seems to think she has some prior claim on you. You sit here with a scowl that'd intimidate anyone- except me, of course. Why are you sitting here, rather than skulking in your own room? D'ye want me to ask you something?"

"I don't want your saucy tongue tonight, Madam."

Sighing, she began to braid her hair.

"Something was said over the port, obviously."

He frowned and stretched out his legs. "D'ye want some brandy?"

She shook her head and waited.

"Well, my dear, our plans in France don't go well. I shall be busy until we go to Drummond Castle, then we'll be away to France. Prince Charles wants to see me. Murray says the French are still ignoring him. They plan another invasion of England, and Charles wants to make sure they give him support in Scotland. And this goes no further."

She made an impatient gesture.

Niall continued, "Others in Edinburgh say we should let the Stuarts stay in France, or Rome, or anywhere but Scotland. They say England will always win, and we'll be so depleted we'll not survive." He scowled at her. "I know, that's what you believe too. But I don't want to turn our country over to the Germans. Soon they'll bleed us dry. Look at Ireland."

"No, I think we'll not be the same as Ireland, although we fight among ourselves as they do. You forget one thing: Ireland is a hospitable land, gentle and green and good natured," Anne said.

"They won't have to conquer us by invasion. They will strangle us. And so many don't mind accepting the Sassenach among us. We see their soldiers here, and the lowlanders and the Campbells connive with them..."

The despair in his voice startled her. Never had he shown his feelings to her before, though she knew that all he had drunk tonight had lowered his guard. She watched him in her mirror for a moment, then a perverse thought made her mouth turn up at the corners. She leaned forward to examine herself in the mirror.

"MacGregor.."

"What?"

"D'you think I should take to using white lead? My skin is much too dark for fashion."

Now he really looked at her, his own face becoming darker.

Macgregor's Bargain

"Are you daft? I won't have your skin all scarred and pitted. And I've been told that's the cause."

"Is Mistress Murray's, without her makeup? You seemed uncommonly taken with her tonight. Is she all pitted? I noticed she only smiled behind her fan. Are her teeth bad also?"

Anne smiled then, showing clean, even teeth.

Amused in spite of himself, he asked, "And what makes you think I know Mistress Murray well enough to have seen her skin without her makeup?"

"You mentioned you knew her before her marriage. Did you know her in the biblical sense? Well, I'm sure she kept all her paint on, even when you were having at her."

"She always had a gentle way with words, she was sweet and thoughtful always."

"And did she sigh a great deal, so her enormous boobies popped out of her bodice? Are they as snow white underneath as they are on top?"

"What matters this to you?"

She shrugged, and glanced at him over her shoulder. "'Tis only that Adam Murray is uncommonly handsome, and has a most wonderful calf and thigh, and I wondered he didn't do better."

"So, Murray made you notice him. I shouldn't wonder. I saw him peering down your front in a most loathsome manner."

She laughed. "And how could you notice. You didn't just have one eye on Mistress Murray's décolletage."

Anne picked up her hand mirror, and using it was a fan, did a fair imitation of Jeanne Murray's manner.

"Ah, la, sir, you are too bold," she lisped, with a heavy French accent. "Pray, do not tempt me further, or I'll simply be forced to push dishes aside, lie on the table, lift my skirts, and let you have your way with me, in front of your wife and my husband."

Niall, eyes glinting, began to undress.

Still mocking, Anne said, "What, sirrah, another night in my boudoir without my permission? Have you no decency, sir? Have you no honor? What would the beau monde say if they knew my husband spent every night in my bed? My reputation would be ruined."

Macgregor's Bargain

Niall, down to breeches and stockings, advanced on her. "Not tonight, Madam, my bed has yet to be slept in. Without your knowing it, I have entrusted Hamish to put in various straps and chains and evil devices to torture you and destroy your mind with most evil pleasures."

She whirled and said, "Niall, you haven't."

His face grim, he advanced on her, backing her against the wall. Still not touching her, he placed one hand just over her shoulder, and reached down to remove one stocking, then the other. Then he braced the other hand, effectively bracketing her body. He leaned forward and she could smell the brandy fumes. His face looked very stern.

She said in a placating voice, "Now, MacGregor..."

"Now, Anne, " he mocked, and she realized he was more than a little drunk, a most uncommon occurrence.

"There are straps to hold you on my bed, to tie an arm or a leg to each bedpost, and I will stand and look at you, and then do things to you." His voice lowered to a hoarse growl, and his eyes never left hers.

Suddenly, just as she planned to duck and flee, he grabbed her robe and ripped it open and stripped her of her nightdress. He tossed her over his shoulder, so the breath was forced from her and strode from the room and down the hallway. He opened the door to his bedroom, kicked it shut behind him, and tossed her on the bed.

"Now, Madam," he said, "prepare yourself for all I have in store for you."

Anne raised one hand and ran her fingernails down the spine of the man next to her. Her eyes were still shut, the sweat on her body evaporating. Her skin glowed in the firelight. Niall turned his head to look at her, and grinned at the small smile on her lips.

"You lied to me, Niall MacGregor."

"Aye. I did."

"Where are the straps, the chains, the evil things?"

He laughed softly. "Ah, well. I thought they might entice you."

Her teeth nipped his shoulder.

"You are an evil man, MacGregor. I shall remember this, and pay you in kind."

"I can only hope, Anne Drummond, that you do."

Chapter Eleven

Niall threw down his cards. His luck wasn't with him tonight and he hated losing. He looked around the room for Murray and Crichton, and decided they had already left. The few men who were left in the card room were chance acquaintances. It had been a long day, meeting with other Jacobites, planning, discussing, arguing the best way to deal with the Prince. The three of them had gone to Will Forsyth's at midnight, knowing they would find card games to relax them for a few hours.

"Are you alone tonight, Niall?"

Kitty Seton pouted up at him.

"Ah, Kitty, where is Angus?"

"Why, asleep, of course. You did not answer my question."

"Yes. My companions seem to have deserted me."

"And your wife? I have it on very good authority that you are seldom seen without her."

"My wife is at home, far as I know. I went to dinner with Murray and Crichton, and they invited me to come to Forsyth's rout."

"Were you and your wife not invited?"

"Of course, but she chose to stay quietly at home."

Macgregor's Bargain

"I hear she is a hearty one. They do say that men find her irresistible. Do you find her so?"

He said, "And do tell me, Kitty, how are you and Angus?"

She pouted again. "Much you care. You have seen me at half a dozen dos, and have managed to be no more than civil to me. One would think you didn't know me."

"Kitty, married folk must be above reproach." he grinned, feeling a little lightheaded from the amount of rum punches he had drunk.

"La, no, sir. Single folk must be above reproach. Married folk need only be discreet."

Together they walked from the card room. They halted by a window to watch snow swirl onto the terrace. Kitty shivered.

Her black hair, unpowdered, was swept up in a cascade of curls, and she wore a royal blue gown, the same shade as her famous eyes. Niall looked down at her as she tipped her head up to him. He had forgotten how beautiful she was. He pulled her into the window embrasure and kissed her. Her mouth opened to him, her tongue slid along his, her leg sought entrance between his thighs.

"Ah, Niall, you haven't changed."

He bent and kissed her neck, sliding his hand into her low bodice, feeling her nipple harden.

Kitty moaned, and then pulled away from him. She took Niall's hand and led up the staircase.

When they found an empty bedroom, Niall reached for her again. She laughed, and moved from him.

"Ah, you haven't forgotten me after all. And all the ton are saying you're being led around by your wife."

"All the ton should be saying I must get a son on her, and I find it pleasant."

Again the practiced pout. "As pleasant as you have always found me?"

He unbuttoned his breeches. He did not need to answer her.

"It's good to see you're randy as ever, Niall. D'you not get enough of this at home?"

He laughed. "A man needs variety, Kitty, and you are still a lovely little package."

Later, she rearranged her skirts and led him to the door. "I do hope," she said, "That dear Angus is still asleep in the library."

Niall heard the bells of St. Giles chiming two when he handed his reins to his groom, and walked up the stairs to the second floor.

The lower floors were dark, except for wall sconces and the lamp Hamish held when Niall was admitted. As he climbed higher he was surprised to hear the sound of Anne's harp coming from her sitting room.

'Tis too late for Seana, he thought, the punch still making him feel a bit befuddled.

He heard Anne's clear alto, but he could not understand the words she sang. Then he heard a second voice, a baritone, and the words to the air were very clear. They sang in Gaelic, a very old, very bawdy tune. Both voices were full of laughter.

He opened the door and saw Anne, sitting at her harp, and behind her, leaning over her, his lips very close to her ear, stood his cousin Calum. Anne's head was tilted toward him, the long white column of her throat glowing in the candlelight.

Niall shut the door loudly and was gratified at their startled expressions.

Anne smiled brightly. "Niall, Calum brings word from Grandfather. He will be here within the week. We're to leave for Hugh's wedding as soon as he arrives, and will spend Hogmanay at Castle Drummond."

His cousin? Calum still stood, his hand on Anne's shoulder.

Niall walked to Anne, tipped her head back and kissed her. For a moment she responded. Then her teeth clamped together, narrowly missing his tongue, and she pushed him from her with such force that he staggered.

Her eyes hot, she said, "When did you start wearing a fragrance of musk and roses? I always associated it with Mistress Seton and other bawds who do not wash too well."

She stood up, regaining her composure.

"I'll bid you goodnight, cousin. Should you need anything, just call for Fergus."

"Anne!" roared Niall, and made for the door. It slammed before he reached it, and he turned, hearing Calum's chuckle.

Macgregor's Bargain

"What did you do with my wife?"

"Why coz, I sang with her. She has a most remarkable memory for naughty ballads." Calum grinned reminiscently.

"You do take liberties."

Calum, still grinning, sniffed as his cousin came near. "Anne's right, you know. You smell like a whore."

Niall thought of hitting him, but whirled and ran up the stairs to Anne's bedroom.

"Anne! Open this door to me, now!"

"Not likely, sir!"

"I'll kick it down, Anne!"

"Then I'll hit you with this poker. You're too weak to fight me now. Did you enjoy your doxy?"

"Woman, have a care. You will regret this."

"Not as much as you will, if you come through this door."

Niall leaned against the door and pondered, head down. He took a deep breath and raised the collar of his shirt and sniffed. He did smell most strongly of Kitty's perfume. Perhaps it had been unwise to go directly from Kitty to his wife.

"Very well, Madam," he said. "I give you the night alone to regret your hasty behavior. And I'll remind you that Calum is my cousin, and you seemed to show more than a cousinly interest in him. Do alter your behavior."

He heard a scream and something heavy struck the door.

Niall sauntered down the hall, realizing, with a small pang, that this would be the first night they had not slept together when he was at home. The nights were cold, and she seemed to generate a great deal of warmth as she slept. He sighed. The irrationality of women. She loved another. He loved no one. And yet she was most put out at the thought of sharing him. Kitty, on the other hand, was concerned that he enjoyed his wife's body. He grinned, then remembered the scene he had beheld in Anne's sitting room. Calum's lips had been so close to Anne's ear that he had seen small ringlets moving with his cousin's breath.

I'll speak to Calum. It isn't seemly to show such affection to a cousin by marriage, he thought.

"Hamish!"

Macgregor's Bargain

His serving man appeared from the small dressing room, and looked around.

"Where's mistress?" he asked.

"She sleeps alone tonight. As I do." Niall caught Hamish's frown, and said, "'Tis my business, man. Now help me get undressed, for I'm perishing, I'm so tired."

Hamish sniffed, and wrinkled his nose. "Shall I get some hot water for you?"

"Never mind. Just help me undress and be gone."

"I'll have hot water brought in for your bath in the morning."

"Why in hell is everyone so concerned about the way I smell?"

"Everyone? Is that why..."

"I think, Hamish, you overstep yourself." Niall pulled on his nightshirt and climbed into bed.

"Leave me now, and should you say another word about a bath, I'll send you back to Balquidder, and you'll long for the easy life you have here."

Hamish snorted as he left the room

Chapter Twelve

Dressmakers seemed to spend most daylight hours in Anne's bedroom. Niall walked in on her, several days later, as she and Arabella Crichton debated the qualities of several fabrics. Anne stood in front of the pier glass, clad in a lawn sacque, with a length of raspberry velvet draped over one shoulder. Over the other was a length of pale pink satin.

"Quite fetching, Anne. The colors suit you."

She made a mock curtsey to her husband.

"And where is Roderick, Arabella, that he can spare you for such frivolity?" Niall asked.

Arabella laughed. "In an interminable discussion with his friends, of course. When I left they were speaking of the needs of the poor, or perhaps 'twas the duties of the wealthy. It is ever so, and sometime, though I do agree with them, it is wonderful to escape to talk of not so serious a subject."

Niall made a face of mock horror. "In Edinburgh, that most righteous of all cities, you wish to talk of something ungodly? Indeed, Madam, I fear your husband toys with his immortal soul, according to the worthy leaders of the church, in thinking that

Macgregor's Bargain

the poor should be helped, and the wealthy help them, when it is obvious that God meant them to be so."

"Sir, you mock me. But you are right. The kirk has too strong a hold on Edinburgh. Even though we may go to the theater and hear secular music, still they rant from their pulpits that we're damned."

"But things are getting better," interjected Anne. "Niall and I are going to see a performance of "Taming of the Shrew". Not exactly new, but still enjoyable."

"I thought it appropriate for Anne to see it, " Niall said, ignoring Anne's icy stare.

Arabella pulled the fabrics from Anne's shoulders. "I shall ignore that bit of marital discord. Anne, what do you think of the russet wool, for a day gown?"

"I like it, " said Niall. "Russet suits her."

"Well, then, Arabella," Anne said, sarcasm heavy in her voice, "my lord says it suits me. Therefore, I must have it."

Arabella motioned to the seamstress, hovering in the background.

"That's four decided on. That should surely suffice for, what, a week?"

"More like two. So I must have more, and a special gown for Hogmanay."

"Madam, you beggar me with your extravagance."

"Surely, sir, you have something more worthwhile to do than observe women."

Niall leaned back on Anne's blue satin chaise longue, and grinned.

"In truth, I can think of nothing better than watching women."

Anne studied him for a moment, then reached for a length of green velvet. "Perhaps you'd like to pick my perfume too. Something in rose and musk?"

Arabella's bright black eyes shifted from one to the other as their duel continued.

"I think, Anne, that you are not the sort. That perfume is for women of the drawing rooms.."

"And brothels.."

Macgregor's Bargain

"...but for you, I think of heather, or mown hay, or something earthy, pine, perhaps? Do they make such stuff?"

Anne made an unladylike sound and turned back to the mirror. "What do you think, Arabella, for a riding habit?"

"It doesn't wear well. Your seat would be shiny in two wearings."

"For the jacket, then. And something sturdier, for the skirt, in a darker shade."

Arabella laughed. "My dear, are you out to bewitch all the men at your cousin's wedding?"

"Only one, I think," murmured Niall, "or I miss my wager."

Arabella stood hastily, seeing the look on Anne's face, and gathered her cloak. "La, hear the clock, I must be off. You're coming to the recital at the Grants' tonight?"

Anne nodded, still examining her face against the dark green velvet.

"We shall be there, never fear. Anne's determined to master the harpsichord, and she insists on watching the best people play."

"Ah, but sir, it's important to be to become excellent at everything I do, to make myself a more perfect wife for you."

Forgetting Arabella, Niall said, "Indeed, Ann, you do make it a point of practicing your interests to the exhaustion of yourself and some around you."

His meaning was clear enough for Arabella, who blushed like a schoolgirl, and with a great flurry of skirts, hustled out of the room, bidding them good day.

The seamstress, seemingly blind and deaf to all around her, stood up, to drape the raspberry velvet and pink satin around Anne.

"I think, mistress, this would be most suitable for a ball gown. Perhaps with embroidered stomacher and petticoat, in dark red flowers on the pink satin. And for your other, the silver and blue brocade."

Anne nodded. "Can they be ready in ten days' time?"

The seamstress lifted her eyes heavenward and sighed. "Yes, if it's necessary. Of course, I'll have to hire more people and.."

"Yes, I know, the cost will be greater."

Macgregor's Bargain

"The ball gowns, with the new hoops, will be seven yards around."

"I shall never get close to you, Madam, if you hold me off with yards of fabric and hoops."

"How convenient. Then, the green velvet made into a coat much like the latest style for men, but shorter, with wide cuffs and flaring skirt, and I think, silver buttons. A lawn shirt, a matching tricorne, and oh! I know, a plaid skirt. 'Twill be most unusual. Green and dark blue, perhaps with a white - no, a red stripe through it?"

The seamstress, enraptured with the picture of Anne clad in her new creations, rounded up her helpers and piles of fabric, and left them.

Fiona materialized and followed Anne behind her dressing screen.

"MacGregor, have you nothing better to do than loll about my boudoir?"

"As a matter of fact, I do. But I wanted to speak to you with a minimum of people around. Your grandfather comes in two days. We shall return to Edinburgh after the wedding and leave for France from Leith. We shall be gone for a month or more, so, in all this frenzy of ordering clothes, you may want to save some of my money to purchase court clothes in France."

Anne stepped from behind the screen, in corset and shift, blue silk stockings gartered at the knee, and high heeled red shoes. Niall was tempted to dismiss Fiona.

"The French court. Why would we go there?"

Patiently he explained. "Because Prince Charles is in France. And though King Louis does not acknowledge him, I am accepted in court. I must find out what is going on. The French are becoming fractious, since their invasion of England failed so badly. It's hoped I can help poor Cameron, who's had to endure them for so long. John Drummond is so firm in his talk to the Prince about coming as soon as possible that a more moderate voice is needed."

"You know what I think."

"It matters not what you think. The Prince would never listen to a woman anyway. But you do represent a powerful clan."

"Even so, I am simply a woman, your wife. Why doesn't the Laird go, or Hugh, or even my grandfather to join John Drummond?"

"Because they have other tasks to do. Your grandfather and the Duke of Perth must raise men here, and your Hughie must try to get an heir on his new bride. You go as my wife, and though I admit that women are not called upon enter in discussions of war, you still carry a great name, and Charles is not immune to a pretty face, though he mistrusts the sex and prefers bawds."

Anne, who had retreated behind the screen, stepped out again, dressed, to Niall's regret, in a demure mauve day dress, a fichu modestly covering her bosom.

She sat at the dressing table so Fiona could brush her hair. "So you throw me at Prince Charles, to bring him here?"

He grinned wickedly. "Wouldn't you like to discover if the rumor your grandfather mentioned is true?"

"You mean, the size of his..." she caught Fiona's eye and they both blushed.

Niall stood, laughing. "Mayhap Jeanne Murray can tell you about fashion in France. They'll be at the recital tonight."

"I wonder if Mistress Murray will be generous with her advice as she is with her..ah..charms. Perhaps you had better ask her. And ask if I can buy white lead here, or should I wait till I get to France."

"Madam, you have heard me on this point. Your face may be unfashionably colored, but I will not tolerate your using it. D'ye understand me?"

Anne made a mocking face at him in the mirror.

He realized as he left the room, that she had not agreed with him, nor did she seem particularly pleased to be going to France.

Chapter Thirteen

The trip to Drummond Castle took three days. The first night had been spent with kin in a large comfortable house near Falkirk. Rain the next day had shortened their time in the saddle, ending at an inn near Stirling.

The landlord, a large blustering man, seemed overwhelmed by the number of guests. Alasdair Drummond, Anne and Niall, Calum, Hamish, Fiona and Fergus added to a number of other travelers who had also sought shelter. wind, knife-edged, seemed to blow straight through her fur cloak and the plaid wrapped around her. But though it stung her cheeks, the wind was fresh, and smelled of pine.

Early dusk settled around them as they approached Castle Drummond, and their outriders hallooed the castle. The great doors opened and Niall led the way into the bailey. Anne was aware of light, and Niall's hands helping her down from her mare.

"You're stubborn, lass. You should have ridden in the coach."

"And be bumped and shaken for miles?" She stood for a moment, looking around.

The original keep towered over them, but added wings stretched along the hill around it. Anne had heard about the

Macgregor's Bargain

castle's beautiful gardens, but the winter showed nothing of them except for the geometric lines of shrubs and trees.

Alasdair Drummond greeted his laird with a deference Anne seldom saw in him. "You remember, of course, my granddaughter Anne, and her husband, Niall MacGregor?"

Anne curtseyed, her lashes demurely lowered. She dared not look around yet for Hugh. The Duke of Perth took her hand, pulled her to her feet, and kissed her cheek. All was forgiven.

"You bloom, lass. Has that husband got ye with child yet?"

Anne hoped her flare of anger would be mistaken for a modest blush.

"Indeed, sir, we've been married but three months."

"Well, then, surely he's done his work. Though I hear," he turned to Niall, "that you do leave her, to speak to others of our cause. 'Tis good for our king over the water, but no way to get a bairn."

Niall said, "There are times, sir, when I must choose between working for the good of Scotland, or working to get a bairn."

The men laughed uproariously, and Anne, her back very straight, turned to look for Fiona, and saw Hugh standing by the door.

The laughter didn't seem to matter then. He was so beautiful. Those golden brown eyes, the symmetrical features, the full mouth that curved like her own at the corners. He walked to her, hand outstretched, and she saw a look in his eyes she recognized.

"Anne."

"Good day, Hugh."

He took her hand, kissed it gently, and led her to the young woman who had been standing at his side.

"This is my bride to be, Alice Fraser. Lady Anne Drummond is my cousin, married to Niall MacGregor."

Alice, blue eyes clear and childlike, nodded, and her golden curls bobbed. "I'm most delighted to meet you. Hugh has told me of his cousins to the north, and of your husband's work to bring our Prince home."

Anne, her voice carefully controlled, said, "Welcome to the Drummond clan, cousin." She leaned forward and bestowed a kiss on Alice's cheek as Lady Drummond, the Duke's mother, bustled in.

"My dear, such a long ride. I am sure you must be exhausted. And this is your famous husband, who travels over all Scotland for his king."

Niall stepped forward and kissed her hand with the grace of a courtier, then took Alice's. "Best wishes on your wedding, cousin. And, thank you, Lady Drummond, though I fear you overestimate my worth." He put his hand on Anne's waist, and he and Hugh bowed to each other. "Yes, my wife is most tired, and I'm sure you will forgive us if we ask to be served in our room, so we may retire early. I look forward to seeing you tomorrow. Anne?"

He offered his arm with a look that brooked no discussion, and she laid her hand on his and allowed herself to be led away. She stole a glance over her shoulder. Alice Fraser was looking up at her betrothed, and he was looking at Anne. She turned away.

As they mounted the stairs, led by a maid to their room, Niall said, "I am beginning to recognize that smile. You are pleased with yourself. Wee Hughie is still besotted, I take it?"

"Do stop calling him that. Just because he's not huge. I find him very handsome, and he's certainly tall enough for me - or any woman, " she added hastily.

The servant halted at a door on the third floor, and opened it for them. It was a large room, with a fire that was burning brightly, but it was still chilly. Though the walls were covered with tapestries they could hear the wind buffeting the small windows. Fiona, who had been led up earlier, bustled around hanging Anne's gowns, putting things in chests. Anne pulled off her plaid and tossed it over a chair as she walked to the fire and held out her hands. She shivered.

A servant appeared carrying a steaming jug and two goblets.

"Sir James thought you would like a het pint, sir."

"Could you see to getting a tub and some hot water to us, and a warming pan for the bed?"

The man's brows rose.

"I'll see to it, sir. Meg will be up shortly with a meal for you."

Macgregor's Bargain

He left and Niall chuckled as he poured the steaming brew. "I could read his thoughts. Mad people, bathing in the cold."

Anne watched Hamish and Fiona straighten the room, exchanging glances. She would have to watch Fiona more closely.

"It's passing strange, isn't it, that we share a room. There's just a wee dressing room over there."

"Not so odd. We are married, and I'm sure the castle will be filled to bursting. And besides, I'll wager Sir James wants me to watch you carefully. No slipping away in the night to find your true love."

Anne's eyes blazed and her hold on the goblet tightened. Fiona and Hamish exchanged a another look. But at that moment there was a timid knock on the door.

A small, pretty girl carrying a large tray came in. Niall thanked her as he took the tray. She blushed and retreated.

Fiona asked, "Will that be all, mistress? May Hamish and I find where we're to sleep?"

Anne nodded. "Go ahead. But come back and help me bathe."

Niall interrupted. "Nay. I can help your mistress. You're asleep on your feet, girl. Go away and find some food and your bed. And Hamish, make sure that your bed is not Fiona's"

"Sir!" Niall laughed at Fiona's outraged voice.

After they had gone Anne said, "I would have liked to have Fiona bathe me. It isn't seemly that you should, and the servants will talk."

Niall tore off the leg of a grouse and bit into it. "Ah, but it's one of my joys. Here." He handed the other leg to her.

She took it from him and collapsed on the sheepskin rug in front of the fire. He sat beside her.

"You are very tired tonight, Anne. I'm not used to seeing you succumb to weariness."

"You're not used to seeing me travel so many miles in such harsh weather," she said tartly and rose to get more food.

He grasped her ankle to halt her, and looked up at her.

"Could our cousin be right? Are you breeding?"

She frowned and pulled her ankle free. "Of course not."

110

Niall surprised her when he helped her bathe. He asked no more questions, nor did he try to excite her. He washed her as gently as Fiona might, and helped her into a warm bed gown then set her in a chair and brushed her hair until it was dry, and poured some more of the hot drink for her. She leaned back in the chair and slept. Vaguely, she felt herself being carried, and then the warm bed, and then Niall's arms enclosing her. She snuggled against him, and knew nothing else.

Fiona opened the bed curtains and brought Anne her morning chocolate. Still half asleep, Anne struggled to raise herself on the pillows.

"'Tis snowing very hard, Mistress. I doubt many guests will find their way today. I do hope it doesn't ruin the wedding."

Anne yawned. "I doubt that. Anyway, the wedding's still five days away. Where's MacGregor?"

"He's with the men, below. Lady Drummond sends her compliments, and asks you to come to her rooms this morning. She and Mistress Alice and her mother and some others are sewing."

Anne sighed. "Very well. I suppose I must, but I'd rather sleep the day away. Let's see the russet gown, I think. It's matronly enough. Is that food by the fireplace? I'm famished."

Fiona grinned at her. "How long d'ye think you can keep this from him? He's not blind, and he's very smart. You want to sleep or eat all the time. And your temper's not that good."

Anne scowled back at her and yawned again as she raised an oatcake to her mouth. "I'll tell him when I'm ready. That great ass James Drummond. Did you hear what he said to me? I care not if he is our laird. I could have strangled him."

She finished her breakfast and Fiona helped her with her hair and her dress. She covered Anne's upswept curls with a lace cap and stepped back.

"You look beautiful. There's not a woman here can come close."

Anne said, her temper soothed by her breakfast, "Have you seen Alice Fraser? She has the face of an angel, and Hugh's sisters are supposed to be very pretty."

Fiona sniffed. "Mayhap. But who will men be looking at?"

Anne laughed. "Come, flatterer, let us find our way to the lady's chambers."

Soon Anne sat, needle diligently working, eyes demurely downcast, as Lady Margaret talked to her future good daughter about being chatelaine of Drummond Castle.

"Now, then Cousin Anne," she said, "I am sure that you also can help our Alice. For you have had the running of your own home for many years."

"Aye, Madam, I have, for most of my life, and though we have a housekeeper, I am the one who must make many of the decisions."

The older woman gave her a piercing look, and said, "Then you are happy to give up the charms of Edinburgh for Loch Laggan?"

Of course, Anne thought, *she knows*.

"Do you go often to Edinburgh, Madam?" Anne asked

"Never." Lady Margaret shook her gray curls. "I have gone, but not for years. That life does not appeal to me, and I cannot abide the filth of it. And my dear son humors me in this. I stay here, and I teach our people that they must rally to the Prince. I fear the Hanovers will take our religion away from us."

Anne looked at Alice's mother Janet and saw, by the woman's baleful stare, that she knew too, and found Anne totally repugnant. Anne lowered her eyes to her needlework and hoped that the innocence of Hugh's bride and the tolerance of his mother would continue, for she liked both of them.

Alice said, "But, then, Anne, you were raised with no mother? Your father died just after? Your grandfather must have been bereft. How fortunate he still had you"

Anne opened her mouth to make a tart reply, then saw the distress on Alice's face.

"My grandfather seldom speaks of them. "

"He must be very happy, for you to be wed to such a brave and handsome man, and look forward to being surrounded by you and your husband and all your children..." She halted, blushing.

"I know not what he thinks."

With some asperity, Mistress Fraser said, "Alice, I do think you are too unworldly. Now, then, Lady Margaret, what do you think of this pink floss with the dark blue?"

Macgregor's Bargain

The talk went in to weddings and births, and Anne's mind wandered. The men would be talking of the Stuarts, without a doubt, or trading hunting stories. Which was more boring? Anne sighed as her needle stabbed the silken fabric that was to be Alice's dressing gown.

Finally, Lady Margaret put her needlework away and said, "My son likes his dinner at two, so we must prepare. Tonight, if the snow allows, we shall have the ball, so I'm sure we shall want time after dinner to rest." Vaguely, she nodded at Anne, who stood, bobbed a small curtsey and left, followed by Fiona.

"God's breath, Fiona! I thought I would fall asleep over my needle. Hurry, let's find a way out of this maze, and I shall walk a bit before dinner and then dress."

Anne discovered that by climbing up instead of down, she had the advantage of not meeting anyone, and she had the battlements to herself. With her plaidie over her hair, clasped tightly under her chin, she peered through the lessening snow, It was high enough, she was sure, to see very far on a clear day. On a day like this though, the snow hid even the lower part of the keep from her.

"Anne."

Suddenly, Hugh appeared out of the whiteness. She gasped, then stood very still as he walked up to her.

"I expected no one to be here."

"I come often, for that reason." He spoke softly to her, his eyes almost on a level with hers, and his closeness made her heart beat faster.

"I, uh, I have been sewing with your mother and Alice, and..."

"And my esteemed mother by marriage?"

"She knows."

He nodded. "She and her husband spoke to me quite firmly about my, ah, past."

She turned from him, a little, and he watched her clear profile against the dark of her plaid.

"And am I that, Hugh, your past?"

"My dear, I still love you, if that is what you wish to know."

"Oh, then why, Hugh, didn't you come for me?"

"I am to be laird of the Drummonds. My brother pointed out..."

■ 113 ■

Macgregor's Bargain

"That it wouldn't do to marry a lass found with you in a dirty tavern in Leith?"

He sighed. "I had to accept that, like it or no. I had to do the best for the clan, and he had already arranged the match with the Frasers. James is not well, Anne, and it looks as if he has the coughing sickness. He must depend on me. D'ye like Alice?"

Anne nodded. "More's the pity. I shan't be cruel to her, if that's what worries you."

"It concerns me that my brother was so cruel to you, that he insisted you come - with MacGregor. Is he good to you?"

She nodded again. "He gives me almost anything I want. He doesn't beat me. He talks to me as if I had sense. I can ask no more, can I?"

"He knows of us?"

"Of course. My grandfather and your brother told him all. Then he was promised that our child would inherit Loch Laggan. That was tempting enough for MacGregor."

"Anne, my dearest, do you regret what we did?"

She looked at him, clear eyed. "No. I regret the way it turned out, but you were my love, and you are."

He put his hand on her shoulder, and she swayed to him. His lips were gentle, as they ever were, and his kiss was sweet, as it ever was. Her plaid slipped down, and he gently lifted it again, to cover her hair.

They stared at each other, and she ran down the stairs, leaving him to watch after her.

Fiona, fussing, hurriedly stripped her and helped her into a yellow silk gown.

"I'll wager no one else has as many gowns as you. Mistress Frasers's maid told me she had but three."

Anne adjusted her lace cap. "Has MacGregor been up yet?"

Fiona shook her head. "I've seen no one. I feared you'd be too long. Wasn't it cold?"

Anne turned so she could look out the window.

"I didn't notice," she said.

Niall waited for her at the door of the great hall and led her into dinner.

Macgregor's Bargain

"Your cheeks have a hectic flush. Are you well?"

She nodded, a little breathless. Damn. They were to sit together. She didn't want his eyes on her now.

"Did you have a good morning?"

"I sewed, sir. Sewing is not something I do for entertainment."

He laughed and helped himself to salmon. "Why, then, you should have been with us. We went to the stables, and looked over Sir James's fine horses. He has the fastest ones in Scotland I hear, and of course racing seems to be his main interest. He has a fine Barb I'd like very much."

Her interest caught, she asked him. "Did you offer for him?"

"Her. She would be a fine match for my Iolair. Yes, and he is mulling over my offer. I also discovered there's a music room here. Shall we try some instruments after dinner? Good God, Madam, you eat as if you're starving."

She looked up from her venison. "I had little for breakfast this morning. It's after noon. Of course I'm starving."

"You'll be a female Falstaff ere long."

She gulped some claret and looked around. To her left sat Hugh's young cousin Ian who was busily stuffing himself. Across from her, Alice Frasers' mother watched Niall and herself as if she expected them to sprout horns.

"Who's yon besom?"

"Poor Alice's mother."

"And what makes her 'poor Alice'?"

"She's truly a sweet girl, and her mother's an old besom."

"Ah, then, she knows." Niall directed his most charming smile across the table, and Mistress Fraser sniffed and looked away.

"And wee Hughie? Have you managed to find him alone yet?"

She took some partridge from a footman.

"Ah, then, you have met. And protested undying love? Ah, star-crossed lovers. And a snowstorm, so you can't escape from the castle...."

His voice was light and teasing, and, when she looked at him, his face told her nothing. She took another sip of wine and yawned.

"Are you going to fall asleep at the table?"

■ 115 ■

Macgregor's Bargain

She felt herself drooping, but shook her head. "Indeed, no. But 'tis a bit warm in here." She fanned herself and smiled at Alice, who smiled back.

By the time dinner was over, and Anne could escape, she was nearly asleep on her feet. Fiona unlaced her and tucked her in bed, and she slept immediately. When she woke, the bed curtains were closed tightly. She heard the crackling of the fire.

Niall, dressed for the ball, opened the bed curtains.

"Come now, Fiona waits with the spectacular red dress that will no doubt cause duels."

She made a face at him and stretched. He eyed her as she slipped from the covers.

"If we hurry, we can dismiss Fiona.."

She flounced out of the bed. "Do you think of naught else?"

"It's hard to think, with your nipples peeking from the top of your shift, and your face all soft with sleep. It gets much the same look to it ..."

She pushed him aside and went to the basin of warm water Fiona had brought for her. "If you wish to stay and watch me dress, then do so quietly."

He laughed and sat in a chair by the fire. She looked at him several times as she dressed, and saw nothing but his usual amusement at her behavior.

Finally, hair pulled smoothly to a crown of ringlets, the raspberry satin gown with its pink satin underskirt and stomacher in place, she admired herself in a mirror.

"If that bodice were any lower, even so understanding a husband as I would wonder about your plans for the evening."

"Mistress, will you not want a shawl?" Fiona asked.

Anne shook her head. "I can do without it. It will be warm in the great hall." She picked up her fan and looked at her husband.

He wore a coat of the new cut, shorter, with wide cuffs. It was of a dark green satin that went well with her gown. His vest was of gold brocade, his breeches the same green as his coat. He wore his usual simple wig, and the white of it and his lace stock contrasted nicely with his tanned face.

"Well, Madam?"

"Well?"

"Do I look a suitable escort?"

She tilted her head to one side. "I suppose, sir, that you will have to do." She swung her arms wide and turned in a swirl of red and pink. "There are no others, you see." She grinned at him.

She led him from the room, casting one more look over her shoulder at the mirror.

"Never fear, Anne. You will have every man at the ball envying me."

Alice looked at Anne admiringly as they entered. Hugh stared at her, then turned away as he caught Niall's look.

Anne danced until her feet, in their pink satin high-heeled shoes, hurt unbearably. Finally, sitting beside Alice, she fanned herself, watching Hugh approach with cups of punch for them. Niall stood nearby, talking to a woman she vaguely remembered seeing in Edinburgh. The woman was very pretty, and she leaned against Niall in a familiar way.

"Shall we make them all stare?" Niall had left the woman to bend over Anne and whisper in her ear. He sat and leaned past Anne to compliment Alice on her gown. She blushed and looked at him shyly from under her lashes.

"Winsome little thing, isn't she? And does that make it harder for you?"

"Bastard."

Anyone watching the exchange would have thought it was simply the soft words of love between newly weds.

She made to rise, and tottered.

"Anne, are you well?"

"Of course. These shoes have higher heels than I usually wear."

He said nothing, simply cocked his eyebrow at her and led her around the room, to speak to those they knew, to nod at others.

In spite of all her plans, Anne's heart wasn't in the evening. She thought longingly of bed, and escaped as soon as she could after supper.

Much later, she felt his bulk settle on the bed, and heard him whisper her name. But it was too much trouble to answer him.

Chapter Fourteen

By morning the snow had stopped, and the younger people planned to ride out. Anne, dressed in her new velvet jacket and plaid skirt, walked beside Niall to the bailey. Vixen snorted and sidestepped as a groom helped Anne mount. The horses danced in the clear cold air. Anne looked over her shoulder at Hugh as he pulled at his brown gelding. Niall strove to guide restless Iolair through the gate. The riders rode through the foot deep snow, bare branches of trees casting blue shadows, hounds baying in front of them.

"The deer may be out, down the glen," shouted Rab Lindsay, as his wife Morag cantered after him, her habit the same dark blue as the shadows.

Anne urged Vixen forward, to walk beside Hugh. "Where is Alice this morning?"

"She is staying with my mother and hers, readying herself for the morrow."

Anne said sympathetically. "'Twouldn't do, would it, to come down with chilblains or a broken leg on the eve of the wedding."

Niall rode up between them, exasperation showing on his face. "You two have little sense. D'ye think your kin and Alice's will not

Macgregor's Bargain

notice the time you speak together? Come then, Annie, ride by your husband and be a devoted wife."

He moved the stallion between them and sent Hugh's horse ahead with discreet snap of his whip.

"Twas innocent, I swear," Anne's face did look mild and sweet under the cocky tricorne. "I just questioned him on the whereabouts of his betrothed."

She urged her mare forward as the hounds began baying. " A stag. Hurry, Niall"

The great beast broke through the broom at the bottom of the hill and leaped up the next slope, the dogs in close pursuit. Vixen snorted and surged forward. Niall held his own mount back, to follow Anne.

They reached the rest of the riders just as the hounds brought the stag down, and Anne, reining in, saw bright blood spattering the snow. Hugh and Calum MacGregor jumped from their horses, driving the dogs away from their prey. Anne halted, feeling she was watching the scene from far away, but feeling the final pain of the deer. She, who had always enjoyed the hunt, swayed and bent her head. Before she could fall or regain herself, Niall jumped from Iolair and ran to her side, pulling her from Vixen's back.

He held her, looking down at her white face, at the blue shadows under her eyes.

"Will you faint?"

She grinned weakly and opened her eyes. "I never faint. I just had a fancy, for a moment, that I was the prey, and 'twas my blood spilling on the snow."

She pushed away from him, her legs still unsteady, and walked toward the hunters, and then decided she definitely did not want to see more. She turned and nearly ran into Niall.   "Must you follow me so?" she asked pettishly, thinking her stays were too tight.

"Calum," Niall called, and Anne watched their cousin detach himself from the men around the stag and saunter toward them, his hands bloody. Anne turned her head away.

"Will you lead Anne's mare back. I think she's not well enough to ride. I'll take her back with me."

Macgregor's Bargain

Calum asked, "You'd trust that devil horse with such precious cargo? You're daft, man."

Niall swung into his saddle, and Calum boosted Anne to sit in front of him.

"Anne."

She turned to look past Niall as Hugh walked through the snow toward them.

"Anne, what is the matter?"

Niall said, "My wife is a bit sickly."

"I'm not." said Anne, and sat up straighter.

Niall made an impatient sound and reined his horse around. Iolair danced, feeling the unusual weight on him, then settled into long strides, leaving Hugh standing staring after them.

"You'll have to ask wee Hughie to be more discreet, Anne. He acts as if you're his bride."

Anne said, " What use are all my lovely gowns if I just fall asleep or faint?"

She felt the chuckle rumble through his chest. "Ah, poor thing. It's not pleasant to watch one's plans fail."

"You always manage to make me feel like a child."

"Indeed, I didn't mean to. You have only to see the way men look at you, to know you're a woman. You may think like the craftiest general, but you most definitely look like a woman."

She shifted a bit, and Iolair snorted. She watched the great gray pile of the castle as it loomed over them.

"'Tis quite a fortress, Castle Drummond."

"Aye. At one time, it would have been nigh invulnerable, but gunpowder has made it of little use."

"They'll come, you know, Niall. The English will come, if you continue this madness, and they will flatten Castle Drummond, and Caorann Castle, and every croft, and all of Scotland. They don't want a Stuart."

His arms tightened around her.

"Does your mind never stay on women's things for long? Better for you to regret the clothing no one has a chance to see, than to tell me to abandon the Stuarts."

■ 121 ■

Macgregor's Bargain

He guided the horse through the gates, and a groom helped them dismount and led the horse away.

"Now, then, Anne, you and I will take ourselves to our room, and order a het pint, and talk a bit."

She backed away from him. "I should seek out Alice, and see if she needs my help."

"Madam, you will come with me."

He took her arm in a way that brooked no resistance, and led her up the stairs. By the time a servant had brought their drinks, Anne was seated in a chair facing the fire and Niall stood before her, booted feet placed far apart, his face in shadow.

"Now, then, Anne, do you wish to speak of these, ah, indispositions?"

She looked beyond him and said nothing.

"Then shall I tell you? You're bairning. You sleep at every opportunity. You get dizzy. Have you been ill of a morning?"

She shook her head, still not looking at him.

"And then, yesterday, when I woke you, I noticed those lovely pink nipples had gotten darker and a little swollen.   Do you think I don't know your body by now? How long have you known?" He waited. "Answer me!" he roared.

Finally she looked up at him. "For over a month."

"And why didn't you tell me?"

Anne stood up and went to the window. Clouds were obscuring the sun. "I didn't want you to know. I didn't want you to boast about getting me with child on our wedding night. I didn't want to miss Hugh's wedding."

She turned around, and her voice was fierce. "Well, then, Niall MacGregor, you've done what you set out to do. You can go after Morag Lindsay and Jeanne Murray, and all the whores of the French court, and I can go home to Loch Laggan with a big belly."

"Is that what you want, lass? D'ye want me to stay away from you now?"

In spite of herself she could not lie to him. She turned back to the window, and felt his arms go around her.

"For all your nasty tongue, Anne Drummond, I still want you. It would take many armed men to keep me from your bed."

He bent and kissed her on the neck, the place that he knew. She shivered and leaned back against him. He spoke as he nuzzled her shoulder.

"You did look most fetching today. 'Tis a lovely costume. But you'll not wear it again for a while."

She turned in his arms to look up at him. "Why not?"

"I'll take you to France, to keep an eye on you, to make sure you don't ride again till you've had the babe."

He was unprepared for her fury, as she pulled away from him.

"So you're at it already! Scarce three months gone, and you're telling me to stop riding" Shall I then not take walks, nor dance, nor do anything I like?"

He grinned as he backed her into the bed. "I understand there's no harm in walking, nor dancing nor – anything else you like, save riding. I think there's something we can do for a long while yet, that you like very much, if I can keep you awake long enough..."

"But they say you must not-it will harm the babe! MacGregor, you must stay away from me now."

"An old wives' tale. You may trust me on this." Niall reached out and stroked her.

"Lecher!" she blazed at him, and ducked under his arms. She stalked to the door, calling for Fiona, and her kinswoman, who had obviously been just on the other side of the door, appeared more promptly than Niall would have hoped.

"Fiona, I must nap now, before dinner. Please help me with my clothes."

Fiona gave MacGregor a measuring glance as he strode from the room.

"Did ye tell him?" she asked

"Aye."

"Was he pleased?"

Anne frowned. "Seems he knew already."

"I shouldn't wonder. Belike, he knows something about bairning."

"I shouldn't wonder. Perhaps, though, he's never stayed around long enough to learn too much."

She stared out the window as Fiona unlaced her.

Macgregor's Bargain

Alice Fraser looked like an angel as she stood beside Hugh in the ancient chapel. The flickering candles brought out golden lights in her hair, and her voice was so soft that Anne, sitting five rows back, heard very little of her vows. This was the first time Anne had the opportunity to watch Hugh without worrying about others noticing her. She cast a sidelong look at her husband. Yes, without a doubt, Hugh was more handsome. His profile was classic. The dark red satin of his coat went well with the white of his wig and his coloring.

As they turned to leave the chapel, Niall whispered, "You sighed a great deal, Anne, are you well?"

"You know I am," she muttered, glaring at his grin.

Anne thought the festivities that followed were much better than at her own wedding. She enjoyed herself more, without the dread she had felt. She watched the bride and groom whispering to each other, and Alice's quick, happy glances at Hugh.

Niall seemed to be watching her closely this evening. Now he came toward her, his face, as usual, showing nothing of his thoughts.

"You've no need to stare at me, you know. I'll not faint, nor go daft, nor cry."

"Indeed, Madam, you do not look like you'll do any of those. You simply look mildly irritated, as though your stays were too tight. You must strive to look happy. This is a joyous occasion. Aren't you happy for Alice? Or do you think she deserves better?"

"There's no better man than Hugh Drummond, certainly none here."

Before she could turn away, he grasped her hand and pulled her into a reel, and she found she was enjoying herself very much.

She flirted with Calum and handsome Roderick Fraser, Alice's older brother, and some of her distant Drummond kin. Roderick proved to be a magnificent dance partner, and made sure he led her out often. Niall seemed to be taking all this with his usual good humor, and Anne noticed that he was often with beautiful Morag Lindsay. She saw Alice's mother looking at both of them with disdain, which made her enjoy herself more.

Macgregor's Bargain

There was a roar as Alice, blushing, stood up and left her husband's side.

"What a horrid custom," said Anne to Roderick, but he was whooping with the rest, and didn't heed her.

Alice's mother looked at her daughter with horror as Alice beckoned Anne to join the handful of women making their way through the crowd. The older woman and Anne both tried to go through the door at the same time, and their hoops caught. Anne stepped back, smiling her sweetest smile, and Janet Fraser swept through in front of her.

In the bridal room, Alice grasped Anne's hand, her own cold.

"I did want you here," she whispered. "You're little more than a bride yourself, and you understand."

Anne said, "I do indeed, cousin. I too had one of my own age to help me."

Together, Anne and the others prepared Alice for bed, dressing her in a gown of palest blue silk. Finally, golden hair brushed, quilts pulled up, she sat in bed, waiting for her bridegroom.

They could hear the men roaring up the stairs, and the door flew open, revealing Hugh, clad in a nightshirt, held by his kinsmen. Anne, standing in the shadows, watched him smile at his bride as he walked to her. He climbed in beside her, and his mother handed them a goblet of wine to share, and led the others from the room.

Later, when the noise of the dancers had reached an alarming height, Niall realized that Anne was nowhere in sight. He wandered through rooms of people until he heard the faint sound of a harp. He made his way to the music room. Anne sat near the fire, her face absorbed, a clarsach in front of her. She was so intent on her music she did not raise her head as he picked up a lute and came to sit opposite her.

"Portpatrick," he said, "I never heard it played better."

Her eyes still holding a faraway look, she said, "Did you think you'd lost me, sir?"

He shook his head. "But I wondered..."

125

Macgregor's Bargain

"You know Hugh and I wouldn't be together. In fact, I doubt Hugh thinks of me tonight. Men, I've learned, can separate the one from the other."

"Are you grieving?"

"An odd question for a man to ask his wife, even in such a marriage as ours. My heart still beats." She placed her palm over it. "Therefore, it could not be broken."

His keen look made her uncomfortable, and she looked down at her hands on the harp strings.

"Perhaps," he said, "you plan the future."

Her smile turned into the secret smirk that enticed him and irritated him all at once.

"Perhaps. D'ye know The Paungs of a Desperate Lover?"

He nodded and bent his head to the lute. Together, in the quiet room, they played until she yawned and pushed the harp to one side.

"I'm most terribly sleepy, MacGregor."

"D'ye plan to sleep the winter away, like a bear? If you do, I shall have to leave you behind."

She looked at him in mock surprise. " In fact, as I think of it, I'm hungrier than I am sleepy."

He laughed. "Then let us fill you up, and send you off to bed. Whatever lecherous thoughts I had are being dispelled. But, Annie, I do hope you wake soon."

Chapter Fifteen

Anne looked down at the dirty street below her. In truth, Paris was much cleaner than Edinburgh, but she missed Scotland, and, more, she missed her home and the clean air of Loch Laggan. Anne still had Fiona and Fergus with her, Fergus by now well trained by Hamish.

In the two weeks they had been in France, she had met no one, and her hopes of attending salons and concerts and operas seemed doomed.

Niall was much away and had forbidden her to go out without an escort. In fact, aside from an occasional absent-minded kiss, he seemed unaware of her presence. He came home uncommunicative late at night, and often left before she woke. He had taken to sleeping in his own room.

Bored, she turned away and looked around her sitting room, done in the rococo style that was all the rage. They had a suite of ten rooms, done in the latest fashion, with paintings hung from the ceiling to mid wall, and ornate mirrors in odd places. She felt she kept bumping into herself. The apartment belonged, Niall said, to some sort of ambassador to Italy. Niall was rather vague about his connection to the man. He had found a spinet for her to

Macgregor's Bargain

play, but now it didn't hold her interest, nor did the books she had bought here to perfect her French.

"Anne," Fiona slipped through the door. " Niall is at home, and desires you to come downstairs. He has brought guests with him."

Anne's annoyance showed on her face. "He brought home guests without warning me?"

"Aye, and they will stay to dinner."

"Well, they'll just have to see me as I am. "

Actually, as she saw herself in a mirror, she looked quite good. Her yellow gown was in the latest style, full in the back with pleats at the shoulders, open in the front to show an embroidered ivory satin stomacher and petticoat. She allowed Fiona to straighten her lace cap, and then swept down the stairs and into the drawing room, where Niall and Calum stood with two men.

She recognized John Cameron from an earlier meeting. The other man, taking a glass of brandy from Hamish, turned to her and bowed. Her first thought was that he was quite the handsomest man she had ever seen. Her second was that she was very glad she was wearing her new gown.

"My wife, Lady Anne Drummond, Sir Francis Hepburn."

His gray eyes held her for a moment, then he bowed, and dark lashes covered them. He wore a fashionable bagwig, three curls above the ears on either side, a queue tied with a black ribbon. His simple gray coat and breeches were set off by a dark blue waistcoat.

"Sir Francis is helping me keep track of His Highness," said Cameron. "'Tis not always an easy job."

Niall interrupted. "Anne, Thursday next week we go to a court ball. "

"Next Thursday? That's hardly time to..."

"It's a masque. It's most important. Now then, would you like some wine before dinner? I've sent Hamish off to have cook prepare a simple meal for us."

Anne turned to Calum and raised her brows. He looked back at her, noncommittal.

"Of course. Gentlemen, do be seated."

For the next hour, Anne enjoyed the conversation as the men spoke of court gossip, music, books. They did not, she noticed, speak of Prince Charles. Francis Hepburn seemed intent on amusing her, and discovering her love of music, offered to take them to the opera. Anne's eyes shone, and she became more animated on learning he too had read a book she was reading, David Hume's *Treatise on Human Nature.*

"And now, tell me, Sir Francis, what is it like in Paris circles? Shall I be a barbarian?"

"You, my lady, could never be a barbarian in any circles in the world." He stood to lead her into the dining room.

"I do speak French, of course, but I hear that the way it is spoken is very important. I fear I'll make a faux pas if left on my own."

"You have my word that at the ball you will not be alone."

Niall raised an eyebrow. "I have found that so at balls in Edinburgh. She does not seem to lack for company. At this ball, however, we must try to be inconspicuous."

"Why...."Anne began

"I shall explain later." He looked at Hepburn. "My wife is a veritable Pandora. She has an insatiable curiosity."

"Which is why, I am sure, she is so very clever."

Hepburn looked down the table at her, and Anne experienced a small flutter. He *was* a most attractive man. His mouth curved in such a way that made her think he would kiss very well. She saw Niall looking at her in a measuring way, and hastily picked up her fork.

Despite the short notice, the cook had managed to do a creditable job. In winter there were seldom many fresh vegetables, but he had pureed carrots, and served them with a leg of veal with a coulis sauce, preceded by fish pastries and a stuffed partridge.

Anne, as the only woman, chose to withdraw, but she was surprised to be followed shortly by Hepburn and Calum.

"Your husband and Cameron had something to discuss, something about money, for which we have no skill at all. Calum tells me you play most beautifully, and have a fair voice, and I would much prefer your company to theirs."

"He exaggerates. I'm only passable, except with the clarsach."

"And have you brought your harp with you?"

Macgregor's Bargain

She nodded. "But I know no fashionable tunes. Mostly airs from my home."

"Just the ones I'm most fond of."

Cameron and Niall had withdrawn into his study to discuss, not finances, but the Prince's cronies.

"There is one, Niall, who worries me a great deal. He is a Borderer, which alone does not make him suspect. But I do not trust the man. He always is there during the Prince's most outrageous behavior, always there with more to drink, more whores. And he sits, all ears, when the plans for the purchase of ships, and arms, and the sailings, are made. Also there are rumors that a Highlander has been seen in London, in suspect company."

Niall froze, his glass halfway to his mouth, his eyes cold.

"He is also a spy?"

Cameron frowned. "I do not know, but, yes, I fear he may be."

"See what you can discover. And is this Borderer particularly friendly with anyone?"

"Well, you know the Borderers are inclined to stick together, so Comyns is seen with Hepburn, and with Fraser and Burns, but not one more so than the others, and I do not see that they encourage the Prince's debauchery. Certainly Hepburn is above reproach. As for the other, the Highlander, I have nothing to be sure of. I have my suspicions, and I have a man I can send to London."

"Perhaps in the meantime it would be wise for us to watch all the Borderers near the Prince."

Cameron nodded. "Another thing. I have heard from Scotland that some of the clan chiefs are often telling too much when they've taken the drink."

Niall shook his head. "I know. Alasdair Drummond was shouting all over Edinburgh that King James will be on the throne before Hogmanay. But I cannot stop them; they will not listen."

Calum looked from Anne to Hepburn, as she played the clarsach and he sat beside her, listenig intently. The spark of attraction was obvious, and he wished heartily that Niall would finish his business and appear to watch his wife.

Macgregor's Bargain

As if he had heard, Niall stood in the doorway of the salon, Cameron behind him.

"I did not realize how long I had kept John. I thank both of you for entertaining my wife. She looks quite delighted with your company."

Calum heard the slight edge to Niall's compliment, and said, "'Tis Anne who's entertained us. We three share a liking for music."

Hepburn said, "Indeed, sir, if you would, I should like to take you and Lady Anne to see an opera being performed here. She has told me that she has not had the opportunity to go to many events here, and I am sure that such a state must sorely try her."

Anne nodded. "And I do accept, for myself and my dear husband. He has had much on his mind lately, and it will do him much good to sit and enjoy good music."

"Then I shall arrange it. A new programme will be starting this week, and I look forward to escorting both of you, and of course, Calum, you're most welcome. I will exclude Cameron, as I know his most favorite music can only be played on a bagpipe."

They laughed, and the guests rose to leave. Hepburn bowed over Anne's hand, then looked up at her, his eyes intent, his mouth unsmiling.

"Until we meet again, Lady Anne. It has been a most...exciting evening."

Niall caught Anne's eye over Hepburn's bowed head, and raised his brows.

She smiled prettily at Hepburn and curtseyed as she withdrew her hand, and said, "Sir, I look forward to hearing the opera. I thank you for your invitation."

When the men left, Niall turned to see Anne heading for the stairs.

"Anne."

She turned, her gaze abstracted. "I must make sure that my gown is ready in time for the opera. And what did you plan for us to wear to the masque?"

He caught up with her and walked with her up the stairs. "The Prince says we go to the masque as King Arthur, Guinevere, and the Knights of the Round Table. You see, Anne, Prince Charles

■ 131 ■

plans on going to the masque although he was not invited. And we will make sure that he is with friends."

She halted at the landing and stared up at him, her jaw dropping. "But I thought the King Louis did not welcome him."

Niall shrugged. "He doesn't. This is the Prince's wee joke. He likes to think he is making a fool of the king, who probably will not know he is there. Or, if he does, can safely ignore him in masque."

"And does our being with the Stuart prince mean we shall become personae non grata in court?"

"I daresay it will make little difference. But even if it did, we must go along with the Prince's desires. Else he will find someone who will, and who might make even more mischief. I do not think Sheridan and O'Sullivan can keep him in check."

"How many of us shall there be?"

"Well, the Irishmen, probably. Cameron. You and me. And your devoted servant, Hepburn."

Thoughtfully, Anne continued up the stairs.

"And tell me, my dear, shall I play the cuckolded king to Hepburn's Lancelot?"

She gave him a sideways smile. "And who shall be Galahad, the fine young Prince?"

"The fine young Prince can play Elaine, for all I care."

He stopped her as she stood on the stair above him, and pulled her face to his. His lips against hers, he murmured, "It has been a great long while, hasn't it, Annie, or does it seem so to you?"

She pulled back slightly. "Or could it simply be that you find me more attractive now Hepburn pays court to me?"

He kissed the white tops of her breasts above the yellow satin, and ran his tongue between them. She drew in a deep breath.

"MacGregor, the stair is no place to be amorous."

"Then, lady, let's go at once to your boudoir."

She walked up the stair, Niall just behind her.

"I wonder, MacGregor, what brought on this surge of passion."

"Anne, you do question too much."

"Is it Hepburn's attention, or possibly Meghan Sevigny, whom I hear has some claim on you, that has raised your lust to such heights after so long a drought?"

Macgregor's Bargain

"Do you regret my lack of time with you?"

As he opened the door to her rooms, he leaned to kiss her shoulder. Fiona, just inside, responded to his gesture and fled the room.

Anne pulled away and eyed him. "Not at all. I might have enjoyed more activity. However, Sir Francis seems to be willing to fill those needs."

"Don't flirt with me, Anne. And don't try to play me against Hepburn. We play a much larger game."

"And the prize is Scotland. I damn all of you to hell." Her voice was very low, and the look she gave him was devoid of emotion.

"Shall we not talk politics in your bedroom? I should think you would be quite touched that, after these months of marriage, I still lust for you."

"Would it make any difference if I said I don't want you?"

"Only if I believed you. There was a certain flush, as I kissed you on the stair."

She walked away from him, to give herself a distance from him, and turned, her face showing a cool interest, her mouth slightly tipped at the corners as she looked him over.

She undid her necklace and dropped it on a table, unhooked her earrings, pulled the combs from her hair, so it fell softly past her shoulders. Leaning against a chair, she reached down to pull off her slippers, still watching him as he dropped his coat to the floor, and his vest, walking over the gleaming satin to hold her shoulders under his hands.

"I hear, sir, that it is most important to appear wise in the ways of love - or lust- at this Court. Mayhap you'll be my teacher, that I not disgrace you, by having your friends think I'm a simple Scots country lass."

"Anne, you are a shameless besom. I've half a mind to turn you loose on the French court, and devil take the hindmost." His voice dropped to a murmur as he began to unlace her gown. "But not yet, I think. How do you unlace this bodice? You wear too many clothes. I prefer you in nothing."

And she wore nothing, very soon, and set about undressing him, pausing now and then to stroke him, or kiss him, or, once, to

■ 133 ■

Macgregor's Bargain

bite his neck hard enough to make him wince, and pick her up, and toss her onto the bed.

"Annie, it's a good thing you are not a lady of the court. I think you could topple thrones. And now, I think, I shall prove that I can still teach you a few things."

Later, he looked down at her rosy body, her sweat dampened hair, and grinned.

"And you see, I am still ready to serve you. 'Tis a wonder what a capable man can do, with a little imagination."

He pulled her to the side of the bed, and watched her face as he slowly moved into her.

"'Tis a fine feeling, is it not?"

"I find it.. stirring."

"Stirring? I thought that's what you did with a spoon, like this." She gasped.

He continued. "But, of course, the stirring is most effective when we have a small container, such as we have here. It enables the spoon to get all the way to the bottom....Ah, don't scream, don't move like that, you disturb the chef. If you don't take care, you scrape the bottom out of the pan, or worse yet, bend the spoon... Ahh, Annie, you have me."

She watched him as he slept, her eyes calculating, reviewing the evening, the unspoken words between the men, the holding back. There was much to find out about Francis Hepburn. Still sorting out impressions, she curled up and slept.

Chapter Sixteen

Fiona knocked gently, then opened the door. Hamish followed her with a tray. Sunlight caught bright satins strewn on the floor, and, in the curtained bed, a glimpse of the two sleeping there, Anne's hair spread across Niall's chest, her fine profile etched against the darker skin of his arm.

Hamish set the tray near the fire, stirred the coals, added wood as Fiona closed the curtains.

As they went out, he grinned at her. "I daresay there's little for us to do this morning. They look fair exhausted."

Fiona blushed and pushed past him.

Struggling from sleep, Anne brushed away the bothersome tickle on her nose. It came again, and she sighed and opened her eyes.

"Good morning, bonnie Annie."

Niall grinned down at her, a lock of her hair twisted round his finger, the ends very near her nose.

"I smell chocolate. Aren't you hungry? "

She sat up. "Famished."

Macgregor's Bargain

He had not expected such a precipitous departure from their bed. Before he could reach for her, she was off, tearing at the loaf of bread, pouring chocolate.

"Damn. The chocolate's cold." Reaching for the bell pull, she looked down at herself, and turned to him, grinning. "I suppose I'd better dress myself."

"Not for my sake. You're one of the few women I know who do not benefit from a bit of covering."

"One of the few? But then, I forget your great experience. And you see, I have no idea if other men look better without clothing. Hepburn, perhaps. He has a fine leg and a broad chest."

She found a robe and slipped into it, and rang the bell.

"I'm surprised, MacGregor, that you're not already away, doing whatever it is you do, the day long."

"As a matter of fact, today I need meet no one." He pulled himself up in bed as Fiona entered with a fresh pot of chocolate. "I intend to loll about, perhaps take you out to see some of the sights of Paris."

"I'd like that." Her eyes looking at him over the rim of her cup were serious and level. "I'd also like to know what you spend so much time doing here. Are you collecting money? Arms? Promises? Or are you following the Prince around, hoping to make plans? Even I have learned that he does not take kindly to advice from any except his closest people. Who are not, I hear, all that reliable."

He frowned. "Well, I suspect there'll be no dalliance this morning. You must have been very busy, picking up bitty fragments to prove your dislike of the Stuarts."

"I don't dislike the Stuarts. I simply dislike them in Scotland."

He swung his legs out of bed and strode toward her, and, in spite of herself, she backed up. Gently, he took the cup from her. Gently, he took her shoulders in his hands, but his face was fierce.

"Madam, if you, by any way, let your feelings be known, if you in any way jeopardize this cause, I, personally, will make sure you feel the wrath of us all."

She forced herself to stare into his blazing eyes, forced herself to face him, her expression cool.

Macgregor's Bargain

"MacGregor, you would make a much more intimidating presence if you were not bare naked."

She pulled away, picked up her cup and saucer, and turned her back on him, saying over her shoulder, "You do misjudge me, if you think I would, if I could, do anything that would stop this foolish plan. But mark me, Niall, I fear it will make Scots think, those that will still live, that they are already in Hell."

By unspoken agreement, they dropped the subject as Fiona and Hamish came in with their breakfasts, and nothing more was said as they prepared to go out.

Anne had replaced her plaid with a scarlet wool cape, the hood lined in brown fur almost the same chestnut as her hair. As they drove through the streets in their carriage, feet kept warm by heated bricks, her eyes sparkled with excitement; her nose and cheeks were tinted pink with the cold. Niall glanced at her admiringly. Her features were too cool, too sculpted for the kind of beauty he admired, but she was a fetching piece.

"That's the Palais Royal. It was built during the reign of Louis XIV."

She made a small face. "It's impressive. But then, after Edinburgh, most Paris buildings are impressive."

"Wait until next Thursday. We will go to Versailles for the masque. I warn you, you will stop and gape like a country lass."

She looked at him over the top of her muff. "Thank you for warning me. I shall try not to disgrace you."

The cold drove them back sooner than Anne wished. They entered their apartments and went into the library. Idly, Niall looked through a pile of books on a side table.

"I hadn't realized you brought so many with you."

"Fortunately I did. I have had the opportunity to read more than a few," she said dryly. "Then I have ordered these from a local bookseller." Anne motioned to books on another table.

He ignored the goad. "Ah, *Joseph Andrews*. Did you enjoy it?"

"Very much. I found it more entertaining than *Pamela*."

He laughed. "I should think so. *Pamela* was meant to instruct girls of the lower orders.."

▪ 137 ▪

"In how to avoid losing their maidenheads. I know. 'Twould have done me no good though. I was intent on losing mine."

"You speak quite frankly to the man who's not responsible for taking it."

"I'm but being honest."

"Sometimes, Annie, your honesty rankles."

She raised her brows. "Jealousy, MacGregor?"

He snorted. "Never jealousy, dear girl. Simply irritation at your indiscretion."

She shrugged. "This conversation tires me. Tell me what is happening. You've spent much time away. I've picked up things now and then. And I know all is not well, and you say the Prince is still not welcome at court."

At that moment Calum knocked at the door and opened it.

"Ah, sweet coz. Why such a serious face? Has Niall been cruel again? Shall I rescue you?"

She shook her head impatiently. "I'm trying to find out about the Prince, about his going to Scotland."

Suddenly serious, Calum looked at Niall. "She can be trusted, you know."

Niall scowled at him, and motioned for them both to sit. "All right, Anne. The Prince's plans are in jeopardy, for several reasons. The English, of course, want him safe in Rome, knowing that the French would use him to their own ends. The French had promised Charles help - ships, men, guns." He walked to a table set with glasses and bottles, and poured brandy for the three of them. "Year before last, as you know, they lost most of their fleet in a storm, when they were trying to invade England. The Prince came from Italy into France without permission, and King Louis will not recognize his presence. The Prince can be rash. He has been in several drunken scrapes, and the men around him are not reliable. He loves to slip about the country in strange garb, under other names. And the news I brought him is also bad."

Calum continued. "Too many of the Highland lairds remember all they lost in the '15, when Charles' father came. I could get little but vague offers of support, and several asked Niall to tell him not to come. Oh, the Drummonds and the Camerons will fight, and

Macgregor's Bargain

the MacDonalds, a few more. But Scotland is divided by religion, as you know, and most of the Border lords have no wish to see a Catholic king."

Niall leaned back in his chair. "I still believe we may pull Scotland together. I believe that the Stuarts are rightful rulers of Scotland, and the Hanovers should take their German asses back to their own country," he said grimly to Anne. "And I must do my best to keep His Highness under control, and keep those bloody Irishmen from giving him bad advice. And I must try to talk to the French, to get what we can in men and arms from them, for a Prince they do not acknowledge, for a cause that could well help them defeat England. What a web we have here, and I see no way out."

"It seems, husband, that you are on the horns of a dilemma." Anne rose, and went to the door. "I have little sympathy, but I will hold my tongue on the matter, as best as I can. You alone will hear my opinion."

She said her goodnight to Calum, and left the room.

Calum grinned. "Yes, I believe that you will hear her opinion on the matter. I must say, Niall, I am surprised that you show such patience to her. She's not an easy lass."

Niall shook his head, and stood to pour brandy for both of them. "That is true, but she's an honest one."

"Do ye think you made a good marriage?"

His cousin shrugged. "What is a good marriage? She fills my bed nicely; she doesn't demand much; and she got with child quickly. Other than her contrariness, she makes a fair companion, in such time as I am home."

"I think you don't do her justice. She's a fine, fair lass. I wish I could find such a one."

"Fond of her, are you?"

"She has the way with her. She may not be much to your taste, but some men seem to find her fetching."

"Besides you? Who? Hepburn?"

"Ah, there, I'd watch those two. There was a bit of a spark between them." Calum's eyes glinted. "With him taking you to the opera, and being with you at the masque, and I heard him ask

Macgregor's Bargain

Anne if she wanted to go to a salon, to hear some poet or other, and a musician."

Niall said, "Well, let them go. We'll be gone soon, and she is carrying. Naught'll come of it." But he frowned at the fire, and missed Calum's sly smile.

Their conversation moved to other matters, to Niall's men, who were getting restive.

"Let them know we'll go back to Scotland in a fortnight's time. We sail to Inverness. Perth is bringing some lairds to Inverness to talk to me. Mayhap I can convince at least some of them to wait on the Prince when he lands."

"He will come?"

"Aye, he'll come. The man will let nothing stop him. And in the meantime, Calum, would you pay a bit of attention to the Borderers - one James Comyns in particular. Tell no one, not even our men. I want nothing to get out, but I have been warned."

"A spy? What about the others - and Hepburn?"

"That is for you to look into. I was only told of Comyns. And perhaps there is another-a Highlander."

Chapter Seventeen

Francis Hepburn and Niall waited for Anne in the salon, making small talk.

She swept in wearing one of her new gowns, of dark green brocade with a paler green stomacher and petticoat. Her hair was powdered, pulled back from her face, with a knot of curls in the back, and a small wreath of flowers surrounding them. Her gown was quite dangerously low, and a lace choker called attention to breasts swelling with her pregnancy. She moved into the room, managing her enormous skirts with practiced ease. She fluttered her fan and smiled, first at Hepburn, then at her husband.

"I am ready, gentlemen."

"Lady Anne, I fear that no one will be watching the singers tonight. Poor Scarlatti might well have written nothing at all, for all the attention he will receive. "

Indeed, in spite of his promise, people did listen to the music, but at intermission several young men found their way to Sir Francis, to bow and be introduced to Anne, and, with less interest, to Niall.

"I thought perhaps you might join me at the Sevignys' for supper after the opera. You know them, I believe," Hepburn said.

Macgregor's Bargain

Niall nodded, his face showing nothing. "Yes, I met them on my last visit."

"Madame Sevigny has a most popular salon. I had hoped you might allow me to accompany Lady Anne there, while you are about your other duties."

Niall nodded again. "It is most kind. I am sure she would be appreciative. But can you spare the time from the Prince?"

"I help the Prince by finding out the mood of our hosts. Tonight, when she found whom I was escorting to the opera, Madame Sevigny insisted I bring you along to supper. See, she smiles at us."

Hepburn gestured to the other side of the opera house towards a woman in the box opposite them. Her fair hair was curled at the top of her head, cascading down her neck. A wreath of flowers held it in place. Her pink dress was even lower than Anne's, and she seemed to be looking directly at Niall.

Anne turned to her husband. "She does seem to remember you."

Niall, smiling back at the rosy vision, said nothing.

Anne, standing in the foyer of the Sevigny house, managed to look cool and unimpressed. She swept her surroundings with one look as they were led into the salon. Her face didn't lose its composure, but inwardly she was awestricken.

Dia! she thought. *These people have gone mad.*

Although she had seen the newer style of decoration in some Edinburgh homes, nothing compared to this: a room of shells and arabesques, of mirrors and nymphs being pursued by shepherds. Gilded chairs upholstered in velvets and brocades were set beside tables covered with objets d'artes.

Meghan Sevigny came to greet them, her skirt fully twenty yards in circumference, her lips and cheeks carmined.

Niall and Hepburn bowed to their hostess.

"Niall, my dear! What joy! And I have wonderful news for you. Jeanne Murray is here with her husband." Meghan slid a look toward Anne. "So you'll have a number of dear old friends to keep you company tonight. And this, I believe is the new bride whom everyone wishes to meet?" Her tone of voice indicated she lied.

142

Macgregor's Bargain

Anne curtseyed, then saw Adam Murray making for them, his handsome face alight with pleasure. Jeanne Murray followed her husband, her eyes on Niall MacGregor.

"Captain MacGregor and the lovely Lady Anne! How good to see you." Murray bowed over Anne's hand. "The finest flower of the Highlands."

"Ah, but then," purred Meghan Sevigny, "is not most of the country barren and plain?"

Anne's eyes widened, then she said, "Indeed, ah, Lady, the flowers of Scotland must of needs be sturdy. They then need no special artifice to keep them beautiful."

Jeanne Murray looked even more beautiful than Anne remembered. Her dark blue dress matched her eyes, and swept in a great oval around her. The tops of her nipples were rouged to match her cheeks and lips. Her look at Niall was one Anne was beginning to recognize.

"How good to see you, Murray. When did you arrive?" Niall asked.

Jeanne murmured, "A week ago. I was fading fast in that grim gray town. They seemed to have a law against everything I like to do."

Anne opened her mouth, and Niall's fingers dug into her arm. She closed her lips and smiled at Murray. He was a most handsome man.

Hepburn, at her side, led her away. "Lady Anne, I have others who want to meet you, ere we sit down to supper."

Murray bowed and moved away.

"Now, then, cher Niall. Why didn't you answer my note? Surely your man gave it to you. Or did your clever wife find it?" Jeanne tapped his arm with her fan.

Niall looked blandly down at her. "In truth, Madam, I've been hellishly busy. And, too, your being a recent bride of a friend of mine makes me think that perhaps we should be circumspect."

She pouted. "Surely, some of the morals of that dreadful country must be infecting you. When has fidelity been important in a marriage? Or perhaps the lovely Meghan is suing for your attentions." Her eyes narrowed as she glanced around.

"I think, Madam, it would be to my taste if jealousy did not enter into our companionship. It really isn't appropriate."

She muttered through her smile, "Perhaps it's that your wife has unmanned you, and you are no longer able to keep a woman happy."

As Meghan Sevigny came to join them Jeanne Murray swept away.

"My dear, what did you say to the Madame Jeanne? She is acting like a peasant, which I am sure she is."

"Sevigny must be treating you kindly. You are lovelier than ever."

"And what makes you think it is Sevigny who is kind to me? Perhaps I got tired of waiting for you, who are always disappearing, and found another. And my salon is becoming very popular, you know. Attention is always a necessity for beauty."

"Ah, yes, and rightly so. You are an object for poets and painters to worship. My wife has been invited to your salon, I believe, to hear the latest musicians."

"Indeed, Hepburn has mentioned it. He is a great, great favorite with the ladies, as it seems he is with your wife. In spite of his devotion to your Prince, he still finds time to delight us."

Across the room, Anne was laughing as the two men, Murray and Hepburn, seemed to be vying for her attention.

"And now, regretfully, I must usher my guests into supper. Perhaps, after they are replete, I may show you my new gallery. I have a collection of art that might interest you."

Only fourteen people sat down to Sevignys' "modest supper," as Meghan described it. Priding herself in being in the forefront of fashion, she planned her meals around many courses and few guests. Tonight, she had chosen white foods as her theme, and her guests were suitably impressed. Over the breast of chicken in white sauce, Anne chatted with Hepburn about Scotland.

"I've never been to the Borders, Sir Francis. I hear they are beautiful, but dangerous. Have you still many reivers?"

He laughed. "Alas, yes. As in your Highlands, a man's mettle is shown by his ability to steal cattle."

Macgregor's Bargain

"And the Hepburns? Does the family reputation linger? Are there still witches and warlocks?" Her eyes danced.

"Ah, the accusation against Bothwell. Our family always denied it, of course. But I have heard strange stories about a certain uncle who took to wearing odd clothes at certain phases of the moon. And I, too, my Lady, find that I..." he hesitated and smiled at her.

"...That you?" she prompted.

"That I believe in witchcraft, now, after my first seeing you."

She laughed. "Are you accusing me of being of the sith, the fairy folk? Sir, I think you toy with me."

"You say you do not believe in enchantment? But Madam, you have enchanted me."

Casually, he covered her hand with his. Anne took a deep breath as his smile disappeared. The look he gave her had no place at the supper table. Their hands were hidden from view, but a casual observer would have made much of his look and the sudden pink in her cheeks. She dropped her eyes, and then looked up, across the table, to find Niall oblivious to her, engaged in a deep conversation with Meghan Sevigny.

Anne withdrew her hand and spoke across the table to Murray.

"And how did you leave Scotland, sir? Are things well there?"

"Aye, although I fear Niall will not welcome the news I bring; but this is not the time to talk of such matters. Have you seen much of Paris? Is it not a lovely city? I look forward to seeing some of the new plays and Opera Comique."

"I am beginning to enjoy my stay here. Sir Francis has been most kind, in taking us to the Opera tonight, and in inviting me to a musicale at Madam Sevigny's salon."

As her women guests rose to withdraw, Meghan held Niall's hand. She said, "And later, Captain MacGregor, you must come see my newest acquisition. I am sure my husband will be able to entertain our guests while you judge whether I paid a good price for my art."

I'll wager she pays a very good price for her art, thought Anne. *And that my husband is to be her newest acquisition.*

145

Macgregor's Bargain

Murray waited until servants shut the dining room door after the ladies, and brandy was poured for the men, then he spoke softly to Niall.

"I am afraid that the clans in the north show little enthusiasm for joining our effort any time soon. What says our Prince?"

"I have spoken to him once, and his enthusiasm has not faltered. He still insists that this is the year the French will come forward. He says he has been promised arms and men by mid year," Niall answered.

Murray shook his head. "My own kinsman, Lord George Murray, who has more experience in warfare than any of us is adamant we cannot win without twice the numbers the French will send us."

Niall looked around, noticed Hepburn sitting quietly near them. Was he listening to them, or was his attention being paid to Count Sevigny? No matter, Hepburn had heard it all. He had been near the Prince for the last six months, while Niall and his men had been in Scotland.

"I think, gentlemen," Niall said, "that we Scots must look at a much wider world than our own country. So many of our own people are moving to the New World. My lord, do you see a rise in French emigration?"

The candles burned down as the men's conversation moved from topic to topic.

After an hour or so, Sevigny stood. "Shall we join the ladies?"

Anne sat next to Sophie MacGillivray, wife and daughter of Scottish émigrés. The young woman, who had been born in France as had her husband, seemed delighted to speak to another Scot.

"Do tell me, Madame, about the way of Scotland now. I hope soon to see it for myself, for my father yearns to return to his homeland. Are you familiar with the Black Isle? With Inverness?"

Anne nodded. "I know Inverness, for my family has a house there, though I have not been there for several years. My own land is to the west," she said to Sophie, who seemed hardly old enough to be a wife-perhaps 15 or 16, Anne thought.

"When we have driven the Hanovers away, we will return and claim our land. My father and my husband's father both left as

Macgregor's Bargain

very young men after the '15, when they would have been killed if they stayed."

Anne pitied the girl. What happened thirty years ago was all too likely to happen again. People would be killed, disenfranchised, put to the horn, sent across the Atlantic to die in the cane fields of the West Indies, or at best escape to France, to wait for another Stuart to follow.

She looked up with relief as the door was opened and the men came in to join the ladies at their coffee.

Meghan Sevigny stood and made her way to Anne. "Madame, I wish to show your husband a new piece of art I am thinking about purchasing. I do trust his judgment on such things."

"Indeed, I understand, Madame Sevigny. I am sure he would enjoy that. I shall not join you, do forgive me."

"Oh, such a shame! But of course I do." *How very sincere!* Anne thought.

The ladies bowed to each other, Anne without bothering to rise from her chair. She looked beyond Countess Sevigny and smiled sweetly at Niall.

"Was that wise, Meghan?"

"But, my dear, wise or no, let them think what they will. Your wife seems resigned, and Jeanne Murray's pouting is none of our concern. Come, now, and see what I have."

She led him up a broad curving marble staircase.

In a small gallery, hung from ceiling to wainscoting with paintings, a statue took pride of place. It was old, Roman, without doubt. It depicted Leda and the swan, and was so graphic that there was little doubt that Leda was enjoying herself a great deal. It was harder to tell the swan's feelings, though its long neck arched, its body tensed between her legs. There was a passing resemblance to Meghan in Leda's features.

Some time later, Anne, still flirting with Hepburn, looked around for her husband. Her corsets were becoming uncomfortable, and she longed for bed. Jeanne Murray joined them.

"If you look for your husband, Madam...but of course, no woman looks for her husband, when she is talking to such a handsome gallant."

Her smug smile made Anne realize how long it had been since she had seen Niall. In fact, she had not seen him return to the salon. At that moment, he reappeared and strolled to her side.

"The three of you look as if you have been talking about me."

Jeanne eyed him coldly. "We were actually wondering where you had hidden our hostess."

Hepburn looked uncomfortable. "I fear I must take my guests home."

"Indeed, Lady Anne does look rather tired," Jeanne Murray said. "Such skin shows late nights."

Anne, too tired to enjoy the fencing, said, "That's because my skin is not covered with layers of cosmetics, mistress. And now, since our lovely hostess seems to have disappeared, shall we say good night to our host?"

In the days that followed they spent very little time together and Anne said nothing about Niall's disappearance. Hepburn called daily, often bringing friends, and at times Niall, passing by their salon, heard conversation, music and laughter.

Chapter Eighteen

The night of the masque, Fiona helped Anne dress.

"Lucky for you this waistline is so high. The bairn is beginning to make herself seen. If you weren't so tall and long waisted, you would never be able to hide it."

"She moves constantly." Anne said, and laid Fiona's hand over the small mound of her belly. Fiona grinned as she felt the fluttering movements.

"Will we be back at Loch Laggan for her birth?"

There was no doubt in either of their minds that Anne carried a girl. Anne knew, and Fiona believed her.

Anne nodded. "MacGregor says that we should not plan on it, with the weather being so in doubt in the spring, but I have promised this bairn she will be born at Loch Laggan. And she will be."

Anne's russet gown, an adaptation of one seen in a tapestry, was gathered under the breast and hung full to the floor, with a sleeveless overdress in dark green. She wore no corset under it, and no hoops, and relished the freedom. A sheer veil fell from her gold crown, covering her unbound hair. Fiona clasped the ancient gold necklace, Niall's bride gift, around Anne's throat. In the flickering lamplight the Cairngorm stone glowed, and the magical beasts and vines surrounding it seemed to move.

Niall entered, looking large and impressive in robes of royal purple, a false beard and moustache, and a heavy gold crown.

"You were right, Anne. Charles chooses to play Galahad. And I was right, Hepburn will be Lancelot. However, if I were you, I would not let him embrace you. He might discover that you are not quite as barren as Guinevere."

Anne examined him coolly. "Won't it be hard getting out of those clothes, should the lovely Meghan want to show you her art again? Or do you just lift your skirts?"

Fiona fled, to warn Hamish that MacGregor and his wife were still not exactly warm toward each other.

The other Knights of the Round Table arrived. Sir Francis Hepburn, looking every inch a fine Lancelot, bowed over Anne's hand.

"Indeed, it is an honor to serve such a lovely queen."

Niall snorted, and Hepburn raised his head to give MacGregor a cool smile.

"And our illustrious King Arthur. His Highness wishes me to tell you that he will be here with O'Sullivan. He believes that there is less chance of his being recognized if he arrives at the masque with all of us. We have three carriages."

Niall nodded, and led his guests into the salon. Anne tried to ignore the tension running between herself and Hepburn.

What have I become? she thought. Hugh Drummond seemed far away and, if the truth be told, uninteresting. In a few months, she had managed to relegate the love of her life to the far corners of her memory. Niall had brought her body to full consciousness, but she had carefully kept her mind from becoming embroiled in their passion. And now, another man captivated her.

Fickle Anne. You have become untrue.

Hamish, his voice reverent, announced, "His Majesty, Prince Charles Edward Stuart."

The men bowed low and Anne curtseyed as the Prince entered the room, followed by the faithful O'Sullivan and Sheridan. The Prince's clothes showed him off beautifully. He wore light mail, silver gleaming, and his hair was covered in a blonde wig. His dark eyes swept the room and stopped at Anne, who curtseyed even lower.

He took her hand as she rose, and touched it with his lips. "Madam, we thank you for accompanying us tonight." His words were mere formality, as was his practiced charm. But Anne had to admit he had a winning smile. He added, "I could not serve a finer queen."

Versailles was as extravagant as Niall had said, walls and ceilings laden in gold arabesques and cupids. The masque was held in honor of the marriage of the Dauphin to the Spanish Infanta, and King Louis XIV came as a yew tree. People in outrageous costumes filled its rooms. Candles glittered in enormous chandeliers, and reflected in tall windows and mirrors. Shepherdesses swept past in improbable hoops, carrying gilded crooks, skirts high enough to show pretty ankles. Satyrs and eastern potentates chatted with goddesses and sibyls. Although Anne had felt her group's costumes were far from simple, here they were unpretentious compared to most.

The Prince led Anne out in a minuet. He danced well, and when they met in the pattern of the dance he asked about her grandfather and cousins. He bowed and thanked her at the end of the dance, and then left her.

Calum took her hand to lead her out again."Well, Your Highness, and what do you think of our royalty?"

"I think he is a man most practiced in the art of being a Prince."

Calum laughed as they parted, and swung her toward him again. "I am not surprised, coz. He can be an engaging sort, when he chooses to be, even with his cronies and whores.."

"He smells strongly of drink."

"Say that softly, my dear. I agree with you in all things, but let us be discreet. He will be our Monarch some day."

Anne looked skeptical. Then, in the rush of dances and flirtings she pushed aside her irritation and enjoyed herself.

Hepburn led Anne in another minuet. "I am not certain which yew tree is His Majesty," commented Hepburn. "But I have it on good authority that he is in the forest over there."

Anne laughed, and allowed him to lead her to a quiet corner at the end of the dance.

"MacGregor says you leave in a week. I shall miss you, Anne."

"And I you. Our conversations have meant a great deal to me. Will you be coming to Scotland?"

Hepburn nodded. "I do not know yet when I will come. Perhaps with the Prince, perhaps before. We must wait for him to announce his plans. I am sure that O'Sullivan and Sheridan know something, but for once the Prince says nothing. I fear he has made your husband short tempered. And, by the way, I have not seen our King Arthur for some time."

"I believe that Meghan Sevigny came as an odalisque," Anne said.

"Madam, you are patient with him."

"Why sir, I have been told many times that such behavior is common here."

"It is, but you are a Scot, and I thought you would not take kindly to it."

Anne frowned. "Let us not discuss my husband and his paramours, I find it boring. "

"Then let us discuss when I may see you next."

"Why, when you wish, sir. But I feel I must tell you something. I am with child."

Hepburn's handsome face showed no surprise. "You are most beautifully with child. That does not make your lips less enticing, nor my feelings for you less strong."

He pulled her into a window embrasure and into his arms. His hand moved up to cradle her head, and he opened her mouth with his tongue. His kiss was as exciting as Anne had thought it would be.

When Anne drew back, they were both breathing heavily. The baby lurched, and she put her hand on her belly.

"I think, Francis, we might go and watch the card players for a while."

He bowed, and they walked into the card room. The Prince was there, and it was obvious from the concerned faces of some of his followers that he was losing. He was also very drunk. Niall suddenly appeared behind them, smelling, Anne noted, of

Meghan Sevigny's perfume. Anne drew away looking at neither her husband nor the woman..

"We must get him out of here, Hepburn, before the King is made aware of him," Niall said

"How do you propose we do it? Sheridan and O'Sullivan do naught but encourage him, and they are drunk too. And Comyns seems to have disappeared."

"Then we must draw them away, and find some lure..."

Jeanne Murray, dressed rather inaptly as St. Jeanne, armor made of yards of gilded cloth, played whist at the next table. The two men looked at each other.

A woman dressed as a saint, particularly with armor and a halo, would surely tempt the Prince. They spoke to her, and she rose , threw down her cards, and walked to the other whist table to lean over the Prince's shoulder. He turned around and gave her an admiring smile. She whispered in his ear, and he stood and followed her from the room.

Anne, standing between Niall and Hepburn, grinned. "'Tis a lovely sight to see someone so devoted to the Cause."

On the way home, the knights having gone to look for their own diversions, Hepburn diplomatically found it urgent to stay behind and watch out for the Prince, and Anne and Niall were alone in their carriage.

Niall laughed. "I fear the Prince will not have too many memories of this night. He did not behave as Galahad should."

Anne said, "Poor Murray. He is a good man, who deserves better than your former paramour. I fear, MacGregor, that you don't always show good taste. At least Madame Sevigny is intelligent. And probably inventive. Your tunic is awry."

Niall's laughter stopped. "And did you enjoy yourself? I thought I saw a Guinevere being pulled behind a curtain."

They said nothing else to each other that night.

Anne saw little of Niall that last week in Paris. She saw a great deal of Francis Hepburn, as they spent their time in conversation at salons, or at concerts. He did not try to kiss her again, but there was a certain tension between them when their eyes met, when he bent to kiss her hand, that gave her a small *frisson*.

Macgregor's Bargain

After one meeting with their Prince, Niall and his cousins rode away together. A damp, chilly wind whistled around corners, and Niall's horse shied as a piece of rubbish blew across the street.

"Does he say, yet, when he'll come?" Rab asked.

"He has received a letter from Edinburgh telling him not to come unless he can field 6,000 French troops, three times as many arms, and 30,000 louis d'or," Calum told his cousins.

Niall said, "Prince Charles says he will land in Scotland in June, but he waits on the French. Always and always, it's the damned French we wait on. They expend so much on the war with England in the Lowlands, that the Prince's plans are not getting attention. Our people in Edinburgh are afraid, as well they should be. I fear the Prince may be as good as his word, to come alone if he has to."

Calum frowned. "Then what will he have us do? If we can't tell the lairds when to raise the clans, what is there for us?"

Niall sighed. "He wants us to go to the clans now, especially in the West, and prepare them for his coming. So I must be away as soon as we get back to Scotland. We have found out Duncan Forbes is busily convincing those in the West the unwisdom of fighting for Charles. The damned Irish friends of his are the ones who fill his head with dreams of all Scotland and most of England rising to welcome him. Of all the old men, Father George Kelly, who is the worst. And his cause is religion."

Niall reined in his horse in front of his house. "Before we go, I must try to learn who among our people is telling the English of our plans."

"And what will our bonnie Anne think of your disappearing again?"

Niall's jaw tightened. He was sure Anne would take this news coolly, as she had responded to everything he said since the ball.

Rab hooted. "She'll be glad to see his back, I'll wager. I heard a strange tale about her husband disappearing at the ball, and not alone."

"In God's name, where did you hear that?" Niall asked.

"'Tis common talk, it's drifted down to such lowly folk as Davey and me."

Macgregor's Bargain

Davey added, "And 'tis said Anne wasna' lonely in your absence, that Sir Francis kept her amused."

"Shut your mouths, ye girning old maids," snarled Niall. "This has nothing to do with you."

"Only, cousin, it does." Calum's bland voice made Niall want to strike him. "We must live with you when your lady wife puts you out of temper. And besides, I have grown most fond of our coz. I mislike having her unhappy."

"Unhappy? She seems most happy to me, the little I see of her," Niall said bitterly.

His cousins exchanged looks, and rode on in silence. They bade Niall goodnight and watched as he strode up the stairs and slammed the door behind him.

"I never thought him a lackwit before," observed Davey.

Calum said, "A woman never bested him before."

The laughter Rab had been holding in burst from him.

Niall stalked up the stairs and paused in front of Anne's door. No light showed.

In his own room, Hamish helped him out of his coat and into a dressing gown.

"I have papers to look at, Hamish. Bring me some whisky to the library and then go to bed. 'Tis late."

He forbore to ask if Anne had gone to bed.

Long after that he heard the front door open and Anne's laughter. Niall walked to the landing and looked down. Anne stood in the foyer with Fiona behind her. Hepburn was taking her cloak, his hands on her shoulders.

Anne looked up and said, "See, Francis, my husband awaits my coming. Would you like to stay and have a dram with him?"

Hepburn bowed toward Niall, and shook his head. "I thank you for the gracious invitation, but I must decline. And I thank you, Anne, for a delightful evening."

Fiona ushered him out.

Anne, ascending the stairs, said, "Why, husband, I did not expect you back so early. We were at a musicale at Madame Sevigny's, and of course she asked me to be remembered to you. I assured her you would be delighted to know you were missed."

Fiona, watching Niall's face, slipped up the stairs and into Anne's rooms. As Anne started to pass him, Niall caught her arm.

"A moment of your time, Madam, if you will."

Her brows, more finely plucked than they had been in Scotland, rose in two questioning arcs. He noticed she had put a black beauty spot beside her mouth.

"Indeed, sir, 'Tis late, and a bairning woman needs her sleep."

"A bairning woman,"he grated, "needs to watch her health most carefully, and insure that she does not fall victim to violence."

He bowed low and stepped back, gesturing. Anne, with one swift glance at him from under half closed lids, swept past him. She wore, he noticed, another new gown.

Before he had shut the door, she turned on him.

"Before you talk to me, sir, I hope you remember the foundation on which our marriage is based."

"And I hope, Madam, that you remember also."

"I remember everything. I went to a musicale with Francis Hepburn, one of your sainted Prince's entourage, accompanied by Fiona. Do you think that Hepburn would dishonor your wife? As you have dishonored your friend Murray?"

Unknowing, he raised his hand, and she thrust out her jaw, staring furiously at him, unflinching.

"By God, woman, for the first time, I have sympathy for your grandfather."

He turned from her, and poured more whisky in his glass, willing himself to be calm. When he turned back, she had sat down, hands carefully folded in her lap. Her face was wary.

"I'll not hit you, though God knows I nearly did." He sat opposite her, and stared into her eyes. "Anne, I mislike explaining myself. But this I owe you, for I know without doubt that you are an honorable woman. I did not make love to Meghan Sevigny. I, too, have my honor. I would not have insulted you, either at her supper, or at the masque, by having her when you were nearby. We agree that this is no love match, and we have agreed that we owe each other little, but I swear that I did not make love to her."

She leaned back, her head tilted, her eyes half closed, firelight shining on one side of her face. He was reminded, as he often was, seeing her still face, of a renaissance painting.

"I think I know that, MacGregor. But others don't. And though I usually care little what others say, I did not want to be pitied, and I feared that Hepburn pitied me." She sighed and stood. "He knows of the child, but not of our agreement." Her lip curled. "Mayhap he shall come calling, after I have produced an heir. I think he would make a good lover. He is most thoughtful."

As she walked by him he took her hand. "Not yet," he said. "Stay. I have missed your body these last nights."

"Then, sir, you will miss my body these next nights. Another time, perhaps..." Gently, she pulled her hand loose and left the room.

Niall sat, long after she had left, staring at the fire. There was one more thing to do, before his affairs in Paris were settled.

"So you think it is Comyns?"

" I am sure of it. He takes information to someone else, someone who reports to London. He seems to be one of those creatures who does his best work for money. I am not sure that he has much loyalty to any cause." Calum took a drink of his wine and made a face. "Why is it impossible to meet in a better tavern?"

Niall ignored the question. He looked around at his cousins. Davey and Rab sat silent, watching, waiting for his decision.

"You know what taverns he goes to?"

"Aye,"Hamish , said, his black brows drawn together.

"Find him and bring him here," Niall said. "I have a room here for the next few days." He looked around at the other people in the noisy inn. No one would notice them, or remember them. He thought about Anne. He had told her that he and his men would be gone from Paris for a week.

She had shrugged and turned away, saying only, "How long will we stay in Paris?"

Macgregor's Bargain

"We will leave shortly after I return.."

"Then I will make arrangements," and she had turned away.

Now, Niall watched as his men left the smoky torchlight of the tavern and disappeared into the wet night.

"Cher, you look so lonely. You need a kind lady to care for you?"

He looked up at the baud who had come to stand by him. Her life showed under the white lead covering her face, the tired marks around her eyes and mouth.

He took coins from the table and gave them to her. "You are beautiful and if I had not urgent business, I would spend time with you. Here, take this, and find shelter for the night."

She curtseyed and smiled, showing blackened teeth. "You are a gentleman, cher."

Two nights later, the rain had stopped. Niall stood in a doorway a few streets south of the Seine. Stars shone, but it was the dark of the moon. The light from scattered torches at taverns beckoned late revelers. As one man passed into the wavering light, Niall tensed.

Comyns.

Niall drew back, pulling his dirk. As Comyns walked past the doorway, Niall reached out, wrapping his arm around the man's neck.

Comyns gasped. "Please, take my money pouch. Don't hurt me!"

Niall pulled the shaking man to him. "I don't want your money. Who pays you?" He smelled the stink of fear that came from the man.

"I…I don't know…"

Holding Comyns tightly, he let the man feel the edge of the dirk against his throat.

'Please! I don't…"

"Who!"

"I don't know!" Comyns squealed. "He wears a mask. I tell him what I hear and see and he pays me! He has the accent of a Borderer. Please! I've told you the little I know!"

The dirk slid across Comyn's throat. There was a gasp, and Niall stepped back, avoiding the gout of blood that spewed on the filthy cobbles.

Chapter Nineteen

I t was snowing again, after yesterday's sleet and the previous day's rain. Anne stood at a second story window of her grandfather's house, and stared down at the River Ness flowing past. The child lurched, and she pressed her hand to her back. The snow would lie heavy still in the sheltered places around Loch Laggan, and she longed to see its whiteness. Here, all around her, including her own mood, seemed to be only varying shades of gray. She waited for a clear day that would promise open roads to Loch Laggan.

If I don't go soon, she thought, *they'll try and stop me, tell me my child will not survive the journey.*

But Niall had been adamant. Though increasingly indulgent toward her, he would not let her go. "We will wait. When the weather calms, you will be free to go back to your dear Loch Laggan. But not until. Accept this, Madam. I will not be moved."

Aunt Seana had come to join her. They saw little of Niall, who seemed to be spending most of his time urging the good men of the Inverness environs to come to the Stuart cause. The powerful Lord Lovat, who had defected during the '15 to save his lands, would not commit himself.

Macgregor's Bargain

"Which is as well," said Niall. "He may veer to the other side again. Besides, he's an evil old sod. I would not trust him."

That evening, contrary to custom, the very pregnant Anne served as hostess to a dinner party. Although most of the people were men whom Niall had invited, Lucy and Alan MacPherson, who had wintered in town with their newborn baby boy, and Aunt Seana completed the party.

When the conversation came round to Prince Charles, as it invariably did, Niall watched, increasingly angry, as Anne argued with Ewan Grieg.

"And should he come, and should the French do as they promised, for the very first time, shall we be able to overcome the might of the Hanovers and all their Teutonic relatives, and all the English, who will fight to the end to keep a Catholic monarch from taking the throne?"

Grieg hooted with laughter. "The French have the weapons, and we have the strongest men in the world, who stop at nothing. Do not fret, Lady Anne, we shall overcome the might of the Hanovers."

Niall stared at Anne over his wine glass. "How can you question, when we have such bravery on our side?"

"I questioned, sir, because it is my nature to question. Because women, not being engaged in preparing for war, have more time to think of the outcome of war."

Young Donal MacGillivray said to her, "Then 'tis the wrong thing for such as you to worry yourself about, Madam. For, after all, haven't you and Mistress MacPherson the next generation of Scotland's soldiers to raise?"

His benign smile froze as he saw the fury on her face.

"I do not bear sons to have them die in some useless fray. I will bear children to take Scotland out of the Middle Ages, to set it beside the rest of Europe as a place of knowledge and civilization. Let your generation fight battles if they must, but do not promise future generations to the god of war!"

As the men sat stunned, Seana and Lucy stood hastily. None of them, not even Niall, had been prepared for such rage. She glared

Macgregor's Bargain

around the table, then swept from the room, followed by Seana and Lucy.

Alasdair Drummond said, "'Tis a pity. I thought you had that little bitch tamed. No good can come of this fancy French idea of women discussing such things with men. Ye've failed, MacGregor."

"Ah, well, then, she's breeding and they get passing strange," Grieg offered to red-faced MacGillivray.

Niall poured brandy for them. "No doubt you're both right. My wife has been on edge lately. She pines for Loch Laggan."

"And you, sir, where do you go next?"

"Caithness, I suppose, and then to the West. Some of he northern clans are less interested in joining us. The French promise the Prince he will have his ships and guns this spring, so all must be ready for him."

Calum, frowning, turning his glass to the light, asked, " Do you think you can convince the clans, Cousin? They all remember the '15."

"God damn it, man," Grieg, face flushed with drink and patriotism, glared at him. "Lady Anne may fear what will happen, she's a woman, and breeding. But you - what right do you have to think that Highlanders will not follow their rightful Prince?"

Calum said, taking no offense at the young man's challenge, "Perhaps because I know the French better, and I have seen them give the Prince short shrift, and treat those who went over after the '15 with scorn because they have no titles. I do not trust them, man. Their enemy is England, and only incidentally is their friend Scotland."

Gavin Cameron's face showed his anger. "Niall, I think you must tell your own people not to be doubters. 'Tis not the best of time to have so many questions about what will happen. The Prince will land, and he will have the French with him, and we will sweep the Hanovers into the sea, that they may swim back to their evil land. As for having a Catholic monarch, there are many of us, good Protestants, who will welcome him. I think you had best reassure your wife - and your cousin."

Niall's smile was unperturbed. "We have the right to disagree, I think. Calum will always be with us, he simply likes to play Devil's

Macgregor's Bargain

advocate. As for Anne, well, a breeding woman's liable to take offense at almost anything. She will soon be back at Loch Laggan, happy among her own folk."

"The sooner the better, the shrew," muttered Alasdair Drummond.

It was not until the first of May that the drovers' road along the Great Glen and into Glen Spean became passable. The ones at higher elevation, though shorter, might not be clear for another two weeks. And so Anne, with Fiona and Seana, Fergus and a baggage wagon, made the three-day trip in misty cold weather.

The last day, as they approached Loch Laggan, the heavy overcast broke, and patches sunlight shown brilliantly on the new green of the hills. The first wildflowers, bluebells and squill, star of Bethlehem and bugle, bloomed along the roadway and up the hills.

Somewhere, Anne heard the song of a lark as it soared high above them. Sitting in the cramped, uncomfortable litter swinging between two horses, she laughed, her heart soaring too, as she smelled the wind off the loch. Then they were turning onto the narrow neck of land that led to the castle.

She stuck her head out and yelled up at Fergus. "Stop. I'll walk from here."

He jumped down to help her, and, heavy and ungainly, she stood again on her own land. She ignored Seana fussing beside her, and motioned for them to continue.

As they neared the castle, a gray form appeared around the wall, and paused. Then, in great leaping strides, Bard ran to her. She felt the breeze chill the tears on her cheeks. Then, as the great dog neared her, still racing, she braced herself. He ran past her, gave one more joyous bound, and circled back to stand in front of her. He rose, putting gentle paws on her shoulders, his long tongue scrubbing her face.

"Get down, you silly cuif. You'll knock me over. I'm not that steady, just now."

He bounced down and away, and then back, glee in every movement. Then, as she began to walk to the castle, he fell in beside her, brushing her, letting her lay her hand on his back. Together, slowly, they walked to Caorann Castle.

Macgregor's Bargain

Anne hardly had time to enjoy her return. On an afternoon in late May, walking along the loch with faithful Bard, the first pain hit her at the small of her back. She stopped. It was gone.

I've been doing too much house cleaning, she thought.

For, indeed, she had felt an extraordinary energy that morning. Her grandfather and Niall were due home in a week, and she had known there would be guests in plenty after that, so she had supervised the turning out of all the rooms, the cleaning and scrubbing.

Morag, Iain's wife, had come up from their cottage to help.

"Do not overdo, child. Your time is near, and you must save all that energy to push the bairn into the world."

"Oh, it's not due for a while, yet. And the cleaning must be done, for you know once all those men get here, there's not a hope of getting anything done but the fixing of their meals," Anne had laughed.

Now she took a few tentative steps. Nothing. She whistled to Bard and turned back toward the castle. She saw Morag and Fiona by the stables, and waved to them, and felt the lash of pain across her back. She stiffened, and put her hand on Bard to keep her balance. Something in her movement must have alerted the two women. She saw Morag say something to Fiona that sent the girl racing toward the castle, and Anne heard Morag's voice, calling out for Iain.

She had to halt again. She felt her belly grow tight, and she leaned more heavily on Bard as she hesitantly made her way toward the now hurrying figures.

Morag reached her first. "Hold still, lass. Iain's on his way with Rob." She gestured to her husband and son.

Anne gasped. "'Tis early, Morag. Will it be all right?"

"Shush, now, sweeting. I've had six bairns, and they were all, except for sweet obliging Fiona, either early or late. Now, here's Iain and Rob. They'll carry you to your room. I've sent Fiona off to prepare Jane. All's well, dearie...."

The pain was gone, and Anne was embarrassed to have the men carry her, with anxious Bard trotting alongside Morag. Upstairs, Iain and his son beat a hasty retreat and the women stripped her and pulled a nightgown over her head.

Macgregor's Bargain

"I'm fine, really. The pain is gone."

"Here, lassie, here's a hot posset. 'Twill do you good. Now, just walk a bit."

The hours passed, and the pains grew closer together. Poor Bard lay on the rug in front of the fire whining and watching her passage around the room. Anne had insisted that he stay, against Jane's protests. Anne grabbed the bedpost as she walked past, her knuckles turning white. "Don't fight the pain, Anne. Just breathe and let it come. If you fight it, the pain will be worse."

"Worse!" Ann screamed. "God's blood, how could it be worse??

The pain went away and Anne began walking again. Bard rose and walked beside her, and whined softly when her fingers pulled at his fur.

There was a time, long after dark, when Anne, allowed finally to sit, felt a gush of water.

She turned her embarrassed face to Morag. The woman spoke softly. "No matter, we can clean it up. Now, let me feel your belly. I think you may want to lie down a while."

The next pain was so severe that Anne, in spite of herself, screamed again. She was glad that MacGregor was not there to hear her. She sat in the birthing chair now, her tangled hair pulled back, Morag wiping her sweating face and offering sips of water.

And then, there was the overwhelming urge to bear down. She gritted her teeth.

"Ah, that's it, my love," crooned Morag. "Push. That's it. Ah, look, Jane, its head is showing. No, now, rest a moment, Annie. Now, then, a bit more, ah, look at the lovely wee thing. Anne, it's a girl, a prettier one I've never seen" "

Anne, hair matted, lips bruised from biting them, looked at the small wailing creature lying in her lap. It moved. A small star of a hand stretched out, a leg kicked, and Morag cut the cord and handed the red babe to Jane.

"Now, then, bear up, girl, I'll press your poor sore belly, and we'll get rid of the afterbirth, and clean you up, while Jane's tending the bairn."

In all that followed, Anne's eyes never left the small form being cared for by Jane. Finally she held her daughter, unwrapping her

Macgregor's Bargain

blankets to see perfect wee fingers and toes, each with a wisp of nail, and gray blue eyes staring into her own. Bard sniffed the bundle, tail wagging.The baby had cried, briefly, but now she lay, eyes wide, small face serious, a fluff of reddish hair standing up on her head. She made small sucking movements with her lips.

"'Tis too soon for your milk to come down, but let her suck. That'll bring it. She'll be a special one, being born in the wee hours. They're always the smart ones, and ofttimes have the Sight."

Morag smiled fondly down at them, at Anne, combed and clean, with a look of peace on her face Morag had seldom seen.

"She is a beautiful bairn, Anne."

Bard, sensing all was safe, rested his head on the bed and sniffed. Anne held the babe toward him and Jane looked disgusted.

Morag said, "Ah, I nearly forgot. Iain sent Fergus to Inverness with a couple of men, as soon as he brought you up here. With a night on the road, if they ride fast, they will be there by tonight. He'll have the word passed to Niall, wherever he is."

"Has it been that long?"

"Well, it's nigh noon. For a first birth, 'twas fairly easy."

Anne groaned as she tried to move. "I think I'd not like to have a hard one. But MacGregor, you know, might not even be there, he was going again to Caithness and Sutherland, mayhap to Orkney. And my grandfather certainly won't stir himself just for the birth of a great granddaughter."

She bent again to look into the face of the sleeping baby. "How small she is, her head no bigger than my two fists. Look, Morag, look, she has eyelashes!"

Jane, bent on cleaning the room, muttered something that sounded like, "Ninny." But she too walked to the bed to smile down at the baby.

"Let me take her now, Anne, and put her in her cradle. She'll sleep the while; being born is hard work. And you'll need your sleep too for she'll not allow you much for a while."

■ 165 ■

Chapter Twenty

"They're in the garden," Fiona said as Niall walked into the great hall. She glanced over her shoulder at Hamish, carrying in bags, and he followed her up the stairs.

When Niall opened the gate he saw his wife sitting on a bench, a cradle at her feet, and their daughter in her arms. Faithful Bard lay beside the bench and raised his head, tail thumping. Although Anne must have heard them arrive, she gave no sign.

He heard her soft humming, and an image flashed through his mind, not of the portrait he so often thought of when he looked at her, but another, a Madonna. Her lips curved in a small smile, and her entire being was focused on the wrapped form in her arms. Then he shuffled the gravel under his feet and she looked up, and the tender smile changed to the usual ironic grin she displayed for him.

"Well, then, MacGregor. Your plans have gone agley. My grandfather, I hear, is none to happy with me."

He walked forward and she rose, and proffered the small bundle.

"Would you like to hold your daughter?"

Macgregor's Bargain

He looked down at the small sleeping face. "Should she be so tiny?"

Anne said, "I'm very glad she was no larger. But she has grown in her two weeks."

"I was in France."

Anne squinted up at him, the sunlight bright on her face. "Couldn't leave Jeanne Murray alone? Or is it Meghan Sevigny now?"

"The Prince is in Navarre. He has obtained two ships. He's getting arms to fill them with. The French are still fighting the English but have promised two more ships and weapons."

Nial thought about the English spies. There was one man less to mistrust, now. It was easy to follow a man intent on meeting representatives of the English, easy to pull him into a black alley, shining in the heavy rain. Comyns met his death swiftly, and his masters, hearing of his body being found, throat cut, purse gone, blamed thieves. They had others who would do their work.

The infant opened her eyes, and her fathomless gray blue gaze held his.

"She has blue eyes."

"All bairns have blue eyes when they're born. Haven't you ever noticed puppies or kittens?"

One pink hand found its way out of the blankets. Solemnly, Niall examined it as it closed over his finger. The tiny scraps of nails were perfect. Then her face contorted, turned red, and she wailed.

"She has the Drummond temper."

"She's hungry, is all." A young woman, who had been sitting in the shadows, came forward and took the child. She nodded shyly at Niall and retreated, turning her back to them as she nursed the infant.

"Have you christened her?" Niall asked.

" No, of course not. I waited for you. I thought perhaps Lucy and Alan could be godparents."

"What have you called her?"

"Catriona. My mother's name."

"Your mother's name. I didn't know it. "

"My grandfather would never have mentioned it. Though I hope our Catriona leads a happier life than her grandmother."

The baby slept and the girl handed her back to Anne. A bead of milk still trembled on her lips. Niall reached out to touch it.

"Well, Annie, it seems you must remain faithful to me for a while longer, until we get a son. By the by, Francis Hepburn is on his way here."

It was said idly, as if the one sentence had nothing to do with the other. He sat beside her and ran a finger over the reddish fuzz on the babe's head. The small light brows drew together in a frown, and in sleep she made sucking motions.

Niall continued. "And Hamish tells me he's going to ask for Fiona's hand. No doubt inspired by our domesticity."

Anne said, "No doubt."

"She is a bonny thing, this little lass."

He stood, and bent to kiss his daughter's head. "I have brought some men with me. No doubt you heard us ride in, and chose to ignore us. Calum discreetly waits to greet you, just behind the garden door."

At the door, hand on the latch, he looked back at her, at the sun striking lights in her hair, at her face looking back at him, telling him nothing. "Oh, and Hepburn. He arrives tomorrow. And in a week, your grandfather returns with some others."

"Our rooms are ready. I have moved your things to the new apartments."

He shrugged and opened the gate, and Calum, grinning, strode toward her, arms out, and she rose to meet him. Niall's last glimpse of them was of Anne proffering the babe to his cousin, and Calum's wide grin as he looked down at Catriona. He heard Anne's laughter.

The newly remodeled suite for the two of them was in the rear of the castle, and there was a room next to it for small Catriona and her nurse, Bride Drummond, a young relative who had recently lost her own child.

"So we share a bed again, Annie."

Anne examined herself in the new full mirror. It was the first in the castle. She wore one of her less daring Paris gowns, and was pleased to see it fit well.

"It depends on what you mean by sharing a bed, MacGregor. I'm told you may not have me for two more weeks. I'm still recovering. Besides, I've become used again to sleeping alone. Your own bed is a good one, in the next room; the mattress is new made from feathers of our own geese. And sometimes I get up with Catriona."

She turned back to look at him in a measuring way. "So, then, the Prince is on his way, and I hear there are not too many who will welcome him."

He frowned at her. "Are you still offering your opinion to all who will listen? Or have you learned to control your tongue?"

"You always encouraged me to speak my mind to you."

"Perhaps I had forgotten how very opinionated you are."

She stared at him again. There was something new to him, an edge that hadn't been there before. It would bear investigating. In the meanwhile there were safe everyday things to tell him, for in her grandfather's absence she had taken over the overseeing of the castle.

"You saw the barley, I'm sure, as you rode in. It doesn't do well; the weather was dry. Bard sired a litter of pups on Grandfather's bitch Mil. I'm choosing one for Catriona. Now, in addition to Francis Hepburn, how many others can I expect? You had better take some men out and bring down a few deer. We have little meat just now; the lambs are not yet big enough to kill."

"I brought my men from Paris with me. So ten, and Hepburn will come with just a few of the Paris Scots. They come by way of the Western Isles, to escape detection. Tis the way, I'm sure, that His Majesty will come, too, with all his Irishmen."

Her brows went up, but seeing the expression on his face, she decided to wait for a time when she might get more information. Now, he was liable to turn his anger on her.

"Anne, while we were in Paris, did Hepburn ask ought of you, about my work, or about what you knew?"

"An odd question, MacGregor. Are you asking if Francis was spying on you? He was near enough to the Prince to know

Macgregor's Bargain

everything you do, wasn't he? Do you think his attentions to me were a ruse?"

She was much too quick.

Niall said, "No. I only wondered if he might have spoken of the Prince."

Anne shrugged. "Only on occasion. We spoke more of our mutual interests, and I think the Prince interested him very little."

"An odd thing, for a man of his stature in the scheme of things."

Tired of the conversation, she frowned. "Hamish should have your things put away in your room. I must see to the preparation of the meals, and find out when Fiona and Hamish plan to wed. The chapel must be cleaned out, and proper food made. Perhaps..."

"What?"

"I only thought they might choose to settle here now, to work here rather than wait on us. It was only a fancy."

He said, "Hamish is not only my man, he is a fighting man, and I trust him at my side, or at my back. No, he'll bide here a while, but he goes with me, and I go when I hear the Prince has landed."

He stared at her for a moment, daring her to say more, then turned on his heel and strode through the door to his room.

Chapter Twenty One

Fergus had been visiting a friend on the Drummonds' holding in Glen Spean and ran home to tell the news.

"MacDonald of Keppoch's men captured redcoats at Spean Bridge! I heard the noise, the gunfire!" Dancing with excitement, he ran to where his father and Anne stood at the stable door.

"Oh, it was bonny, they say! The lobster backs just gave up! And now MacDonald is taking them as prisoners to Prince Charlie!"

Anne shuddered. A few miles away, a battle had occurred. The first, she knew of many.

"Hush, Fergus. Your brothers are with our men in the west and your mother's that worried." She and Iain exchanged a glance. It had started.

On August 19, Prince Charles waited with a handful of men at Glenfinnan. He had landed on July 16th, after having one of his ships so badly damaged by a British warship it had gone back to France. He had been begged by some to return to France, told that there weren't enough to fight.

Macgregor's Bargain

Then, pipes skirling, the MacDonalds of Keppoch came over the hill, and when the Stuart standard was raised, Niall MacGregor, Alasdair Drummond and his men, and 1200 others knelt to pay homage to the Prince. Wind blew cold off Loch Shiel, and the steep mountains surrounding them dwarfed the small bands of men who had made their way to join the Prince's army.

Word had reached Alasdair Drummond and his men that the Duke of Perth had barely escaped capture at Drummond Castle and was on his way to join the Jacobites.

During the days of waiting for other clans, the Prince's men made an attempt to form the Highlanders into companies.

Calum and Niall watched. "Do they not know that these men fight as clans?" Calum asked.

Niall shook his head. "There are too many men who know nothing of Scotland who have the Prince's ear."

Slowly, in clans and twos and threes, men came to the standard, then the growing army marched toward Fort William and on over the mountains to Lochgarry Castle, to avoid the fort's guns. Prince Charles rode among his men, talking to them, praising them for following him. He seemed unbothered by the steep terrain or by the biting midges.

"Yon O'Sullivan is a dolt," Calum said.

"Aye."

"Did you hear what he did?"

"You mean burying cannon and all rather than carry it across the mountains? Aye. Everyone knows what the lackwit did." Niall, sharpening his dirk, looked up at his cousin.

"Well, there's more. The redcoats at Fort William found our supplies! All of them!"

"Christ," muttered Niall. "That man was a problem in France. I had hoped someone would push him overboard."

As they neared Loch Garry, Prince Charles rode back along the lines of men and pulled up his horse by Niall and Calum. "And, MacGregors, you are not far from your own home here?"

"Not far, Your Highness. To the south and a bit west."

"And your wife? Where is the Drummond land?"

174

"Across Loch Lochy. In fact quite near where MacDonald of Keppoch captured the redcoats."

"Ah, yes, I released them on their word they would not fight against me. Well, should you see your wife ere I do, give her my compliments. I remember her as a lovely Queen Guinevere."

Niall bowed and the Prince rode away.

Calum made a disgusted sound. "Does he think those soldiers will be so taken by his charm they will throw down their arms and not try to shoot him?"

Niall shrugged and they rode on.

The summer had not been a good one for crops. The winter had been the worst in memory, leaving people with few supplies. There had not been enough rain early on, and later rains ruined some of the oats and barley. Few women took animals up to the shielings, because there were not men enough to care for the land.At last, in August, the weather turned benign, and grain ripened.

Now it was early September, the leaves already turning, the weather still warm. Anne stood, out of sight of the castle, her bare feet in the loch, the chill water and hot sun a pleasant contrast. She looked over her shoulder. Up on the mossy bank Bard lay, head on paws, and Catriona slept on Niall's old plaid beside him. While he had not switched allegiance from the Anne to her babe, he had resigned himself to being occasional nursemaid.

Anne pulled off her shift and added it to her gown on the rocky shore, and waded into the water until she could swim.

Niall separated from Hepburn and the MacGregors at the castle gate when Fergus pointed the direction Anne had taken. He dismounted and threw his horse's reins to Fergus, and strode down the loch shores. First he saw the pile of clothes, then Bard's raised head. The dog examined him carefully then laid his head again, his nose pointing toward the sleeping child.

Niall turned toward the loch then, and saw Anne's sleek dark head and one arm, then the other, rising to lower again, as she swam toward shore. She did not see him until she rose and began walking and then he stood before her, naked too, and picked her up and carried her to the bank, soft with moss.

▪ 175 ▪

Macgregor's Bargain

She didn't speak, nor did he, but the fierceness of her startled him.

While he still lay on her, he chuckled into the softness of her hair and shoulder.

"I have heard of selkies all my life, and their enchantment, but I did not know I was married to one. And yet you must be, for you swim without a ripple, and you hold me in your spell. But a Selkie is supposed to love her human mate...."

She pushed him off, and stretched. "You forget what you know about me, MacGregor. As yet, I've produced no male child, so I must endure long periods of abstinence that you, obviously do not."

"Speaking of such matters, your most fervent admirer has ridden into the castle, and no doubt seeks you."

She sat up. "Hepburn is here?"

"You knew immediately whom I spoke of. Slut." He grinned, got up, and walked into the water. "Best take the back door into the castle, lest he see you too soon. You have the look of a woman well fucked."

She ignored him and began dressing, then picked up Catriona and plaid and began to walk toward the castle, followed by Bard, who looked back at him. She didn't.

Anne managed to avoid both her husband and Hepburn, until dinner. She did corner Calum, though, and extracted news from him.

"We are on our way to Perth, gathering supplies. We'll be off again in two days. Some of our men had set up an ambush on Corrieyairack Pass, to catch old Johnny Cope but he found out about us, and fled to Ruthven Barracks." He started laughing "MacPherson of Cluny, who had promised his men would join Cope and the redcoats, switched sides and joined us. Then Cope decided Ruthven couldn't be held and left for Inverness."

Calum, grinning, said, "Anne, there are so few of us right now, and we have done so well, that I promise you I will dance with you in Edinburgh in a month."

Anne shook her head. "I'm not leaving Loch Laggan, Calum. Catriona and I will stay here while the rest of you go haring off after your wonderful Prince."

"I know you cared little for him in Paris, Anne, but he has the ability to make men follow him, and when Murray and the Duke of Perth join him, he'll have advisors who are not only skilled in warfare, but whom he'll listen to."

"I thought one of his problems is that he listens to too many people."

"Ah, Anne, argue as you will, the Prince is raising men as he goes, and he makes them think they can win, and that is the secret of a leader."

"I should think the secret of a leader is to know what he's doing, and the Prince does not."

They glared at each other, the closest they had ever come to anger with each other, then Calum laughed. "All right. Pax. If I don't give in, I shall have poor rations these two days we're here."

Anne, too laughed, but as she went about preparing for her guests, she was so abstracted that Jane had to ask her twice which rooms were to be aired and made up, and exactly how many there would be for dinner.

Conversation at table was on other things, although the men, including Niall, were in high spirits. They flattered her and teased her, and Francis Hepburn begged her to play her clarsach after dinner. Niall watched the interplay between the Anne and Hepburn over the top of his goblet, his eyes narrow. Motherhood had softened Anne, but there was still that turn of the head, that sideways glance, now directed at Hepburn. He had been surprised, finding her on the loch shore, just how much he had looked forward to seeing her again.

Anne, in her turn, watched her husband when she thought she was unobserved, and Calum, ever aware of her, saw the softening in her face before she turned to flirt with Hepburn.

Her playing was better than ever, because she had found time to spend at her harp as the child slept beside her. Niall, leaning against a far wall, watched the play of light on her hands and face, watched her laugh as Hepburn murmured in her ear. Bard moved closer to her, and laid his shaggy head on her foot.

"Jealous," she laughed, and bent to pat him, then raised her head and saw Niall watching her. Mockery replaced the softness in her face, and she launched into "The Glen is Mine."

"For all you, going to glory for Scotland and the Stuarts," she said.

Niall's own ironic grin matched hers. "Ah, Sweeting, you also will know glory, for the Prince has expressly asked for all the Drummonds to be part of his party in Edinburgh."

The harp strings made a harsh sound, and she stood. "Gentlemen, it is late, I must be off to bed early, to make ready for my grandfather's arrival tomorrow."

She curtsied and left the room.

Niall caught up with her halfway up the stairs. "I meant it, Anne. We are to bring Lucy and Alan, and as many as we can to show our solidarity with the Prince. In two days Calum and I and our men leave to meet him in Perth. We will gather there, prepare to move on when we are supplied. There is no doubt at all that Prince Charles will enter Edinburgh ere long. James Drummond has told your grandfather to go there, and so we will go."

"I can't leave now. The harvest is being brought in. It's a poor one, and I worry what will happen." She pulled away from him, and went into her tower room. "I seem to be the only one who thinks of Loch Laggan and the people here. What will happen to them? The women, the children. You and Grandfather want to take all the men, and leave them defenseless. I'm sure Grandfather has pledged most of our harvest, hasn't he?"

Bard had followed them, and now he stood between them, leaning against Anne's skirts. She brushed her hand against him, and comforted, he lay down.

"The women and children of Loch Laggan know, all of them, that some of their men will not be back, that they at home may face hunger for the first time in their lives, this winter. We Drummonds have a responsibility to the people of our clan, and I feel it strongly. And yet you are telling me I must leave, as their men leave, and they must make do with what little is left them."

He stared at her somberly. "Yes."

Macgregor's Bargain

"I won't do it. Please leave me." Her heavy lidded eyes stared back at him for a moment, and then she turned to the window, and looked out across the darkening loch.

Niall watched her for a breath, then shrugged and made his way to his own room.

Anne stood staring blindly as night closed around her. She didn't hear Fiona enter and light the candles.

"Is there anything you need?" she asked

Anne shook her head. A cold so intense she felt frozen to the spot enveloped her. In the glass of the window she saw Fiona leave. And yet, it seemed there was someone else in the room, and a sadness so strong it consumed her, even as the cold wrapped itself around her. A whisper of a sob, a sound inside her head. As she turned she saw Bard lift his head and stare at nothing. A wave of dizziness made her lean back against the windowsill. She shut her eyes tightly for a moment, breathing deeply, and when she opened them, her room was her own. She set her jaw and walked to the door, now full of anger at Niall.

Catriona's room was down the passageway, nearer the new apartment than her own room, and Anne went there as she did every evening. As she opened the door, she was startled to find Niall standing beside the baby's cradle, looking down at his daughter. He turned as the breath of air from the open door made his candle flicker. His face was unreadable in the dim light. Anne moved past him, and peered down at the sleeping child. Bride McPherson sat up in her cot, yawning.

"Is aught the matter, Mistress?"

"No, go back to sleep."

The two of them looked across their daughter's cradle at each other, and Niall was the first to look away and walk to the door. He looked back at them, once, before he opened it and left.

Catriona stirred, and Anne watched her as her mouth made nursing movements and a frown brought the two fine brows together. There, suddenly, on the tiny face was a reflection of Niall. Anne shook her head and made her way back to her room.

Macgregor's Bargain

In the dark hours when there were no sounds in the castle except for the soughing of the wind, Niall sat up from his sleep. His eyes sought light, for something that would give shape to the room around him. He turned his head and saw the lighter square of the window near the bed, with a star in its center. His heart was pounding, and a memory of a dream clung to the edges of his mind.

There had been Anne, in her room, and going up the stairs, and in the garden, and yet when he spoke to her she seemed not to see him, nor hear him, and it had come into his mind, in his dream, that he must be dead.

He took a deep breath and rubbed his face, feeling the sweat on it. Dawn still came early, this time of year, and he lay and watched the gray window become lighter, and the star fade.

Hamish came with warm water and towels and sharpened razor and was surprised to find Niall partially dressed.

"'Tis early yet."

"Is my wife up?"

Hamish nodded. "Have you spoken to her about Fiona and me?"

"Yes. When will you wed?"

"Before we go, God willing. Word is the priest is staying with someone in Spean Bridge. Anne approves?"Hamish asked

Niall said wryly. "She approves of the marriage. She does not approve of you going with me after. But she and Fiona will join us in Edinburgh, and so you'll have time with your wife."

"Before..."

"Why before we go with our Prince to drive out the Hanovers." There was an ironic note in Niall's voice. "Best get on with it man, you'll have to convince the priest we've no time to have the banns read three times."

When Niall went downstairs, Fiona informed him that Anne had gone riding with Francis and Calum. He went in search of Iain. The older man stared at him impassively and claimed ignorance as to where the trio had gone.

Macgregor's Bargain

"I think, though, it's not the glen up above. She doesn't go there anymore."

"I thought you said once that was her favorite place."

"Aye, I did, but my wife Morag says something besides the bairn has changed her, and not long ago Morag saw Anne come riding down the mountain as if the hounds of hell were after her, and great Bard came with her, tail between his legs."

"And did she not say what had happened?"

"She would not, Morag said, but told her to mind her own business, she did, which is passing strange, for Morag's like a mother to her."

Iain looked over Niall's shoulder toward the loch as he thought about this, than added, "Mind, ye didna hear it from me. Morag would have my hide."

Niall watched Hamish ride off toward Spean Bridge, and soon after, as he walked along the loch shore, he saw dust rising on the road and made out the bulky form of Alasdair Drummond in the lead. When Drummond led the way into the stable yard Niall counted some twenty men, Drummonds and Alan McPherson and his men, the castle filled to overflowing.

Alan stayed but long enough to speak to Anne as she came riding up, and then rode on to his own home, to Lucy.

Shortly after Alan and his men left, Anne, Calum and Hepburn rode into the stable yard from the eastern hills. Niall watched as Francis Hepburn sprang from his saddle and went to help Anne dismount. *As if*, he thought, *she needed help*. He caught her swift upward smile at Hepburn, as he lifted her from the saddle, and then as she saw Niall watching, her eyelids dropped and she pulled away.

Strumpet.

"Well, girl," Drummond bellowed, "have ye got sommat to eat for us, or have ye been wasting everyone's time riding your damned horse, and acting like a bitch in heat."

She eyed her grandfather. "There should be everything you want on the sideboard. I take it you haven't lacked for whisky, but that's there too."

Anne turned and pulled her mare toward the stables. Niall made to follow her, but Drummond called him back.

"Come, lad. We leave for Perth on the morrow, and ye must know what's afoot. I must make sure all our men are prepared-Iain, the women must make enough bannocks for several days' forced march, and have we enough oats to fill the men's sporrans? The Duke of Perth expects us Wednesday, and we'll no fail him."

"The harvest has been poor. We must leave enough for the bairns and the women, else our men will not go gladly," Iain said.

Drummond stared at him. "This is no time for women to be mollycoddled. We may not be back for a long time, and till we get to a place where we can live off the land, we must have enough for every man to eat."

Francis Hepburn spoke. "And does the Prince supply nothing?"

There was a murmur among the men at that.

Drummond rounded on him. "And are you for our Prince, man, or are you a traitor."

Hepburn said steadily, "I am no traitor, sir."

Something in his voice made Niall look at him, then he stepped between Drummond and Hepburn. "Let's get something to eat, and talk about our plans."

He cast a look back at Anne, nearing the stable. That particular battle would have to wait.

That evening, in the candlelit chapel where Anne and Niall had been married a year ago, Hamish and Fiona were married. It had to be a simple ceremony, but Fiona glowed with happiness and Hamish looked at her as if she were a princess.

What a difference , Anne thought, looking at the two, so in love, remembering her on elaborate wedding, and the fear of being alone with her bridegroom.

She managed to evade him until she had settled their guests for the night, and they were alone in their new rooms.

"I will not go with you, MacGregor. I will not leave the people of Loch Laggan wondering if they can make it though the winter."

"You will be in Edinburgh, if I have to tie you to the saddle."

Macgregor's Bargain

"If you do, everyone will know I come unwillingly, and that I hold no reverence for the Prince. This is what I will do. If you leave Iain here, if you convince my grandfather this is the thing to do, I will follow you to Edinburgh. I want Iain to care for Loch Laggan. His sons can go in his stead, they are good men, but they have not Iain's heart for the land. Iain's brother's son Cailean is a strapping lad, just turned seventeen."

Niall's face was shadowed in the candlelight, his expression hidden from her. "You choose who comes with us? Who may die?"

"Iain and all here may die, if the English come. And if Iain goes, all may die of starvation. I must make a choice, for will it or not, I must be laird of Loch Laggan, for all you men have given me the responsibility."

"Tonight, Anne, you are not the laird."

They all watched the men ride out, the next morning. Anne put her arm around Fiona's shoulders as the girl wiped her tears away with her apron. The MacGregors and Drummonds would stop for Alan McPherson and his men.

Niall carried a message to Lucy, that she and Anne could plan to ride to Edinburgh when they received word of Prince Charles's entry into the city.

"I should have gone."

"No, Iain, you should not. You and I must make sure that Loch Laggan's people are cared for. I could not do it alone."

Chapter Twenty Two

The news that General Cope and his army had retreated to Inverness meant the way to the Lowlands was open to the Highlanders with only two Royalist dragoon regiments stationed there.

Now the Jacobite leaders sat at a table in an inn in Perth: the Prince, his Irish cronies, Niall and Alasdair Drummond and other chieftains. James Drummond, Duke of Perth and Lord George Murray were the prince's two military advisors: one with no military experience, the other fifty three years old, a veteran with Alasdair of the '15, James Stuart's aborted attempt to take the throne.

Alasdair voice boomed out. "Do the Sassenachs still hold Drummond Castle? And is your mother still there?"

"Aye." The Duke answered Alasdair. "I will wager they are getting the worst of the deal. They offered to free her and she would not leave."

A servant brought in ale and bread and cheese. They ate, talking about the distance to Edinburgh, the best way to go.

Niall, versed in war, looked around him in dismay. There was Murray, a good tactician, hot headed, but the one man to be counted on. The Duke of Perth had little experience but his clan

■ 185 ■

stood strong behind him. Few of them would be able leaders in battle. As always, the Irishmen Sheridan and O'Sullivan concerned him. That Prince Charles would listen to two inexperienced men rather than Murray and Cameron, would allow them to lead men into battle, did not bode well for the future. All he could do was watch and hope.

Within days Niall's fears proved true when the first divisions showed themselves. Murray, arrogant and gifted, alienated the Prince. Niall heard from more than one source that Murray would seek to take the Highland army over to the English.

When Ogilvy, Maxwell and others joined Charles, they hesitated to tell him what they thought of the poor quality of leaders he had appointed, though they did voice their concerns to Niall.

Later in the evening some clansmen came to Niall's room. It was obvious they must have been in some tavern, for they reeked of whisky and it and their tempers showed in their red faces.

"Someone must tell him to rid himself of O'Sullivan!" Lord Ogilvy's face was indeed scarlet with rage. "The man's a stupid ass, and Sheridan is drunk again. I'd as soon have a Campbell leading this rabble as these men!"

"And the men, Niall," interjected Alan MacPherson. "They have not enough to eat. Hay has not got enough provisions for half the men."

Niall looked gloomily at the darkening streets, and wished that he was at Loch Laggan, where at that moment Anne was probably flirting with his cousin and a suspected spy.

"I do not know what you expect of me. I have not got the Prince's ear. Sheridan, O'Sullivan, Father Kelly, have always been closest to him, for years, so of course he listens to them." He looked around at the men. "The Drummonds' motto is Gang Warily, and I advise you to do just that. I will see what I can do, but do not get between the Prince and those closest to him. He will not believe you."

Calum came into the room. "Sheridan has had the Provost of Perth imprisoned for non-payment of taxes."

Macgregor's Bargain

"I'll go to Murray," Niall said, rising and heading for the door. "I think that silly old man must work for the Royalists." He threw on his cloak and left the other to simmer in their rage.

Lord George Murray and Niall spent their last day in the town soothing its leaders and assuring them that the Prince himself would never have done such a thing, that the perpetrator would most assuredly be punished. The Prince and his sycophants rode in triumph from the town.

"God help us all," muttered Alan, "if they act so in every town we stop at. We'll have all Scotland changing sides."

His usually sunny disposition was failing under the twin attacks of being close to his Prince and being separated from his Lucy.

The army passed by Stirling, its great looming castle too impregnable and not important enough to challenge. Niall rode beside the Prince as they passed, and a few shells were lobbed their way. He was glad to see that the Prince showed no fear, instead he was rather amused at the poor aim of the English garrison.

"We go now toward Bannockburn, Highness, where Robert the Bruce defeated Edward's army."

"Ah, yes. A great victory." Charles looked around the marsh that had doomed the English cavalry. "Tis fitting, is it not, that another conqueror of the English should come this way?"

"Most fitting, Highness." Niall inhaled deeply and looked away.

Two miles from Edinburgh, Prince Charles's army set up camp. As the Jacobite leaders made their way to the Prince's tent, Niall scanned the troops. The men of Loch Laggan, the Drummonds and MacGregors, looked well enough. But many others, suffering from the poor year for crops and the plague that had beset their black cows, looked weary and undernourished. Anne had been right, he thought, in insisting that some of her men be held at home to help with the crops.

Calum had just arrived with a cartload of food for their men, sent from Loch Laggan and intercepted by him outside of Perth. He told Niall Anne had gone on to Edinburgh with Lucy. His cousin walked beside him now, and frowned at some of the men gathered around their fires.

Macgregor's Bargain

"Does the Prince honestly expect them to follow him, them at the end of their strength?" Calum asked.

"The Prince expects a great deal from us all," Niall said cryptically.

"And does the esteemed Prince still depend on his Irishmen for battle tactics?"

"Thus far, as the battles have not been much to mention, they have fared well."

Calum glanced sideways. "And Murray? Does he keep patience with all this?"

Niall snorted. "When did Murray ever keep patience? Ah, Cal, I do wonder where all this will lead. I fear I don't have the faith I had a month ago."

"But we will go on?"

"Aye."

The message Prince Charles sent to Edinburgh's leaders demanded their surrender. A deputation was sent out twice to meet with him. They had just left the wicket gate the second time when Highlanders captured them.

On September 17, 1745, Prince Charles Edward Stuart, dressed in Highland finery, entered Edinburgh on a white horse, leading his triumphant men, to the shouts of delight from some residents, the dismay of others, and set up court at Holyrood Palace. Edinburgh Castle's occupants being loyal to King George, the Jacobites avoided the castle, entering by the south gate to the city.

Alasdair Drummond beamed, leading his men, with Niall at his side. Ahead, his clan chief the Duke of Perth rode just behind the Prince, whose white cockade on his blue velvet bonnet had become a Jacobite symbol.

At the gates to Holyrood, the Prince dismounted, and, to the roars of the crowd, moved among his subjects. In the palace, in his room, he waved to the crowds from his balcony, while his awestruck men trailed through rooms grander than most had ever seen. Niall, with Cal and Hamish, followed Alasdair Drummond as the old man peered around him.

"'Tis said," Niall spoke softly to him, "that Queen Mary's secretary Rizzio still screams for help as he lies dying."

▪ 188 ▪

Macgregor's Bargain

He grinned as Drummond jumped and glared at him. "Rot"

A footstep behind him made Niall turn as Francis Hepburn approached him.

"Niall. So good to see you again. Your wife has turned Calum and me into common laborers, but I'm sure he told you of our harvesting efforts. I hope the food was helpful."

"Indeed. My wife is well, I hope?"

"Very well. After we parted from Cal, we made our way with no difficulty into the city. Mistress MacPherson is in her father's home now, and Anne is in yours, and, I believe, already has plans to spend an afternoon with her grand aunt. The bairns were left at home, of course, but did Cal tell you Anne insisted on bringing that great gray rogue of a dog with her?"

"Anne?" murmured Niall.

Something kindled in Francis's Hepburn's gray eyes. "I forget myself. Forgive me if I presume too much." He bowed. "I must go and present myself to His Highness."

Calum watched Niall thoughtfully as his cousin stared just as thoughtfully after Hepburn. Niall turned to see Alasdair wandering out of the room.

"And tell me Cal, after laboring in the fields with him, is he just as he seems to be, or..."

Calum shrugged. "In truth, I do not know. He has become my friend, I suppose, and Anne's. Whether he is other than a supporter of the Cause, I have found nothing either way."

"Anne's...friend?"

"Just so. Jesu! you're not jealous, Niall."

Niall glared at him. "Not jealous. Just wondering how far Anne took him into her confidence. She does know certain things, that would be better left unknown by our enemy."

Cal bristled. "Anne is not lacking in brains. She may not like our cause but she'd never betray us."

He strode off, muttering, and Niall followed. "I think, Cal, I'll return to our house to greet my wife. Better yet, I'll stop by our aunt's and bring Anne home."

"I'll go too. I have no more patience with all these lackeys who seem to have formed out of nowhere."

■ 189 ■

Macgregor's Bargain

The cousins rode their horses through the crowds outside Holyrood and pulled up in front of Seana's. They heard music, then polite applause.

Seana greeted them as they came into the drawing room. "Ah, two of my favorite men. And where is dear Hepburn? He does love music so, I hate that he was unable to attend us."

"Dear Hepburn," Niall said sardonically, "is awaiting His Highness's commands. I am sure he'd rather be here."

"And I'm sure you'll want to see Anne. She's over there, talking to Arabella Crichton and Mungo Grant. They have looked forward to seeing you again."

At that moment Anne turned and saw him, and her eyes widened. Then she coolly nodded and walked toward him.

"Your Jeanne Murray is here, somewhere, rather the worse for wear, I fear. However, Arabella and Mungo have both been asking when they should see you."

Anne held up her cheek for Niall's kiss, then turned to draw Mungo and Arabella into their circle, and motioned for Calum to join them.

"I must take my wife home now. I look forward to your coming to our home soon, but now, we have not seen each other for some time, and we have much to discuss."

Mungo Grant grinned. "Aye, I'm sure you do."

Arabella tapped him with her fan. "Niall, you still are a rogue."

He bowed, and signaled for a servant to bring Anne's cloak.

"A sedan chair is waiting for you. I trust you'll want to be away before your grandfather comes to stay with his sister."

Her brows shot up. "Oh, poor dear Seana. Does she know?"

"She must not. Look, she is still laughing with her guests. Shall we warn her?"

"Indeed, we wouldn't want the old horror to spoil her party."

Seana being duly warned, Anne ensconced in her chair, Niall and Col mounted and rode slowly on either side of the laboring chairmen. It was but a short distance to their own home, not long enough for Anne. Her heart was thudding. Would he, shrewd as he was, see through her?

190

As they drew up in front of the house, she swallowed and stepped out into the lamplight. It had begun to rain and the mist settled softly on the fur framing her face. She shivered, and led the way into the house.

Upstairs in the small salon a fire was burning brightly, and Hamish, a satisfied smile on his face, served them brandy. Fiona bustled in to replace Anne's damp slippers, her cap slightly askew, her face rosy.

Niall grinned. "Marriage does become you, lass."

Hamish's smile broadened, and Fiona turned pinker and slapped her grinning brother as Fergus brought in more firewood. Bard nosed through the half open door, and trotted to Anne, tail waving.

Cal drained his glass and stood. "I must be off to bed. Niall will tell all the news, I'm sure, Anne. We must be at the Merket Cross tomorrow for His Highness to formally take over Edinburgh, and there is to be a grand ball tomorrow night."

Niall laughed. "Now Cal himself has told you the news, and I have nothing left to say."

"Why, sir, that would surprise me, indeed. " Anne's lids lowered as she idly picked up a book from the table beside her. She bade Cal goodnight and the door closed, leaving the two of them, the great hound lying at Anne's feet, his head on her knee.

Niall watched his wife over the top of his glass. She had changed, subtly, in the time they had been separated - or perhaps the change had begun earlier. The girlish roundness in her face was gone, and her cheekbones were more prominent. Her heavy lidded eyes under winged brows were wary now as she looked up at him.

What are you hiding, Anne?

She looked down again, and he began to make desultory conversation about the campaign, still watching her. The strong chin with its cleft was the same, the jaw firmer, her upper lip still curved at the corners as though she forever found life amusing. Her skin was darker, proof of the long hours of harvesting Cal had told him about.

"Anne."

Macgregor's Bargain

She looked up. "Yes?"

He stood up, and walked to her, and bent his head to touch her lips with his.

"Come, Anne. It has been too long."

There was a brief shadow on her face, then the old ironic grin. "Too long without me? Or without a woman?"

He laughed. "Both, but I daresay you will not believe that."

"Arabella and Mungo have invited me to sit with them at a friend's window to watch the ceremony in front of St. Giles tomorrow. I had assumed that you would be busy grooming His Highness."

He pulled her from her chair. "Indeed, he makes many demands on us. You'll probably not see much of your admirer Hepburn. Nor of me, but that might distress you less."

The ironic smile he found so irritating curved her lips, and he bent his head and kissed her until she leaned against him. As he drew back, he saw Bard staring at him.

"Shall we invite him to stay below tonight? I fear after all this time he'll think I'm murdering you, and tear my throat out."

She laughed, and motioned for Bard to lie in front of the fire. Groaning, he settled himself and stared after them.

It was not yet dawn when Hamish shook Niall awake and whispered to him. Anne lay on her stomach, her face buried in her hair. Niall rose as Hamish collected his scattered clothing. Hamish grinned at the bed, at the tumbled covers. He and Fiona weren't the only ones who had enjoyed the night.

Niall spoke softly, watching his sleeping wife. "I'd like you to stay and escort the ladies to the Grants'. It will be dangerous, with all the townspeople and the clans gathering in such a small place. I will meet Calum and Hepburn at the Palace. And Hamish. Have you heard aught about Francis Hepburn?"

"Only what you know, I'm sure. Cal told me he made himself very useful at Loch Laggan. Calum has a high opinion of him after that."

Niall sighed. " Aye, he seems passing perfect, doesn't he? But still, ever since France, there's something nagging..."

Macgregor's Bargain

"You mean, with the ..."

"Yes, the unfortunate victim of a cutpurse. They were seen together, and though we were sure of that one, Hepburn could have simply been with him in all innocence."

"Or not," Hamish said tersely. "Shall one of ours follow him this day?"

"It wouldn't go amiss. Even though he'll be busy most times... and tomorrow, too, I think. Now I'll go wash and dress in all my finery. If you haven't ill used your pretty wife, will you have her bring me chocolate and bread?"

They left Anne's bedroom and entered Niall's as they talked.

Hamish grinned, and gestured toward the clothes he had laid out: tartan trews, buckled shoes, elaborately slashed doublet, full sleeved shirt; lying by them, a silver hilted sword was sheathed in its scabbard. Hamish left to give the message to Fiona, and was back in time to shave Niall before he slipped into his lace-trimmed shirt. At last, wearing his bonnet with its white cockade, he surveyed himself in his mirror as Hamish straightened his plaid around his shoulders.

"Well, ye'll measure against any laird in attendance this day, and the ladies tonight at the ball will be fair swooning."

They turned as the door swung open. Anne, hair pulled to the top of her head in an unruly knot, decently clad in a long robe, though bare feet could be seen below it, stood grinning and eating an apple.

As they watched, she swept into a deep, graceful curtsy, the hand holding the apple outstretched to one side, her head tipped up, juice dripping from her lips.

"M'lud," she murmured around the mouthful of apple.

Behind her, Fiona's burst of giggles became infectious. Anne lost her balance and collapsed in the doorway, her head down on her knees.

When she finally drew breath, she grinned up at Niall. "Jesu, who are you out to stun with all your Highland dress. The ladies of Edinburgh will be overwhelmed with you."

"See that you match my grandeur when you come to the ball tonight, else I may look elsewhere for a partner."

▪ 193 ▪

Macgregor's Bargain

She cocked her head. "If all are half so grand as you, I shall be hard put to shine at all. And now the hour grows late while you're preening. I'm sure your Prince will be all dressed in his native clothing also- by the way, how do Polish gentry dress?"

Niall took her arm and pulled her, none too gently, to her feet. He held her face in his hand, and looked into her eyes. "Mind what you say, Madam. There are some who would be offended by you flippancy."

She jerked loose from him, and looked down to see the big dog nosing his way between them.

"Ah, your protector. I must be off now, Anne. Hamish will guide you and Fiona to the Grants. And I will see you at the ball. I will be occupied with the Prince till then."

Chapter Twenty Three

ater that morning, seated at a window overlooking the Market Square, facing St. Giles Cathedral, Anne chatted with Arabella Grant and her friend, Maria Hancock. Madame Hancock was a stately, solemn woman, unlike bubbling Arabella. Indeed, thought Anne, she gave the distinct impression that this occasion was not to her liking.

Anne, looking down at the massed people below, couldn't blame her. Townspeople, merchants, hawkers, cutpurses, doxies and drunkards, mixed with the Highlanders who had followed Charles, and Anne was hard put to see who made the poorer showing, for among the Highlanders there was every kind of weapon and dress. Clansmen clad in old plaids, barefoot, some of them, carrying pikes and scythes and rusty rapiers, matchlocks and firelocks; bagpipes skirling, then their own roars as the Prince, with his blue velvet bonnet and plaid rode his white horse into the square.

Riding behind him were his advisors, Sheridan, O'Sullivan, Strickland, Murray, Perth; then came Anne's own grandfather, looking, she thought, like a much finer man than he really was,

Macgregor's Bargain

with his great head of white hair and his big hooked nose, his florid face glowing above his red plaid.

Niall led his men behind Drummond, his bearing so regal that he looked rather like a prince, or so Arabella whispered to Anne. The horses thrust aside onlookers, and Niall's own great Iolair began curveting and rolling his eyes at the crush of people. Niall leaned forward and calmed the horse, and then all of them slid off their mounts and stood before their Prince as pipers played pibrochs. The only woman there was Mrs. Murray of Broughton, who was mounted on her own white horse, and kept an unsheathed sword in her hand.

Although Anne could hear little of what followed, first a herald read a declaration of King James' right to the throne of Britain, then another of Charles' commission as Prince Regent.

Maria Hancock sent a servant down to collect copies of the manifestos, then, as they were read, muttered about the offering of a pardon to those who had hitherto been loyal to King George. She caught Anne's eye and paled, as if Anne might turn her in as a traitor.

As the crowd dispersed, amid much ringing of bells and playing of bagpipes, Anne gathered her shawl about her and called for Fiona and Fergus.

"Did you enjoy watching the ceremony?"

"Aye," said Fergus, his freckled face shining. "Twas noble, don't you think? And our Loch Laggan people and the MacGregors put on a rare show."

"Where has Hamish gone? Isn't he going to see us home?"

Fiona shook her head. "He said he wanted to be out among his people, and I haven't seen him since we arrived."

"Well, then, we must simply depend on the Crichtons' men to see us home. I don't like the look of some of those who gathered. I daresay not a few people lost their purses in the crowd."

They thanked the Hancocks for their hospitality, and found their way home. Once Anne thought she saw Francis Hepburn in the crowd, talking to a townsman, but her party was swept away.

Calum appeared to bring her to the ball, and bowed low when he saw her. "I think you'll fair outshine your husband, dear coz."

Macgregor's Bargain

Indeed, Anne's gown had cost a small fortune, and looked it. Of emerald brocade, widely hooped, the low bodice and elbow length sleeves trimmed in fine gold lace, its mantua back floated behind her. Her hair was unpowdered, caught up tightly at the sides with two curls hanging at the nape of her neck. Green silk flowers were pinned in it, and more nestled between her breasts. She had powdered her face, but the golden flush from her hours in the sun shown through, making her darkly shadowed eyes brilliant. Her lips were reddened, and as she moved toward him, Calum inhaled sandalwood perfume.

Fiona brought her cloak, and Calum laid it gently over her shoulders.

"Well, I can see that I shall not spend the entire evening at your side."

"I would not impose on you so, dear coz," she mocked him.

Calum had found two sedan chairs, and they waited at the steps.

"Should your skirts be any wider, I vow you would have been forced to walk," he teased.

Holyrood Palace shown with lights. Most of the men were quartered in Duddington, outside the city, and some were within Edinburgh standing guard, and quartered where their stations allowed; only the highest ranks had comfortable quarters. On the Palace grounds Anne heard drunken voices raised in song, and as the great doors opened, heard more from within.

"And what does our bonny prince think of his loyal Highlanders now?" Anne looked around her as she entered.

Men in plaids and bonnets mingled with others decked out in satins and buckled shoes and brocaded waistcoats, and women in fashions of the past thirty years stood beside their men.

Upstairs, in a long reception room, Prince Charles stood with his court: all the Irish come over with him from France, a scattering of Frenchmen, Scottish nobles, and a bevy of Edinburgh ladies. Anne saw her kinsman the Duke of Perth, Murray, Stewart of Appin and others, and Niall, standing close to Perth, with her grandfather on his other side.

Francis Hepburn stood nearby, smiling and nodding with a short round gentleman done up in tartan trews. He raised his

Macgregor's Bargain

head as she came in and she was taken again by the beauty of the man. He had worked alongside her, with her people all the summer, to bring in crops, to make sure there would be food for the Jacobite army and her people. He had talked freely about his past: the death of his wife in childbirth, his two sons who lived with his sister on his estate. She found it hard to believe that Niall thought him a spy.

Niall was usually more discreet around her, she thought. This morning she had heard enough to convince her that Francis was in danger.

Now Anne curtsied so low to the Prince that Niall, watching, thought sure the Prince would not be able to take his eyes from her breasts.

Charles nodded, a slight frown on his face."Ah, yes, MacGregor's bride. Paris, wasn't it? Charmed, my lady."

Calum, bowing, led her into the adjoining chamber, where she saw Seana holding court with Alan and Lucy, who were laughing as she gestured, a look of dismay on her face.

Anne joined them, and they drew her in.

"You look so distressed, Aunt, you must have been talking about my esteemed grandfather."

The old woman nodded. "You know, my dear, I count myself fortunate that, until now, in our adult lives, I have seen so little of him. He was a horrible little boy, and he still is a horrible person. I shall be glad when the army moves on." She stopped, flustered. "Ah, Alan, I didn't mean...."

He laughed again. "Dear Seana, I take no offense. There is no bad thing without something good coming from it."

Anne snorted rather like her grandfather. "I fail to see how aught good will come of this."

Seana held her arm. "Quietly, my dear, if you please. There are stalwart supporters of the Prince. Indeed, with reservations, I am one. We must not be ruled by that German rabble."

Anne opened her mouth to retort as Calum took her hand, pulling her into a line of dancers.

"Shall we avoid bloodshed for now? I get so little chance to dance with you, and you know I am very, very good."

Macgregor's Bargain

And so he was, as were the next five gentlemen who asked for a dance.

"So, Anne, may I beg a dance?" Francis Hepburn bowed before her, and she flushed, looking behind her to see if Niall was in the room.

"I will, and gladly."

They joined the two lines of dancers. She curtseyed, he bowed, and they paced toward each other, joining hands, stepping forward. Her heart fluttered and she felt that she could not breathe properly. There was no help for it though.

He is my friend, and I must save him. "Francis, I must speak to you. After the dance, walk with me around the room. There are enough people I know here, that we may nod and bow, and I can smile and tell you..."

He looked at her, brows raised.

"Just do as I say," she hissed, smiling at him.

As the final notes of the dance were played, she rested her hand atop his and they began the circuit of the room.

"I overheard something this morning." She nodded at the Grants. "Niall suspects you of being a spy."

She felt his hand harden under hers; she glanced obliquely at his face. He still smiled, and only she could see the slight quiver around his mouth.

"And what has he said?"

"Only that you are to be watched, and something about another man, and a cutpurse."

Still smiling, he leaned toward her. "Did he say this something happened in France?"

She shook her head, noticed people standing near, and laughed. "I don't think so, I was half asleep, and truly I didn't really think of what was said until he and Hamish had left the room...."

"Ah.."

Anne blushed, realizing what he must have been picturing. They were nearly back to Seana and Alan and Lucy.

Seana took Anne's hand."My dear, I'm quite sure the entire room is now dazzled by you. I must go home now, but I wanted to stay to tell you good night. I have only to find someone to

Macgregor's Bargain

accompany me and I'll be on my way. I leave early, you see, and am in my rooms before your grandfather comes in. Therefore, I do not have to be around him." Seana looked around.

Anne elbowed Hepburn. "Dear Aunt, I have your savior just here. Francis Hepburn has said he must go to see to his men, and so he can escort you."

Hepburn made a graceful leg, said, "Honored, mum."

When Niall managed to break away from Charles's escort, he found Anne chatting with Alan, Lucy and the Grants.

"Have I missed your wonderful aunt?"

"I fear so. She must needs leave early to be in her rooms before my grandfather arrives."

Niall laughed. "I daresay he'll stay as long as he can. He quite relishes his role as a senior Drummond, whether he has power or no."

The Prince had released him for the evening, and he and Calum took turns dancing with Anne, whose gaiety, Niall noted, seemed rather strained. She laughed much more than usual. Anne and Calum had developed a deeper affection for each other. It would have been nice, Niall thought, to see her so unguarded toward him.

They left together, all three of them finally captured by the joy, the noise and brightness, the promise of great days ahead for Scotland. Even Anne allowed herself one brief flare of hope. And she also hoped, fervently, that Francis Hepburn would escape.

That night Niall led her, and she came most willingly, into his bed, and into a passion that tore them away from all reservations, and she betrayed herself. He might have heard, but might not have heard, in his own abandon, his own muttered words to her, her breathless words as her body fused with his.

When she woke in the tumbled bed, he was gone, and she slipped silently into her own room, and rang for Fiona.

"I'm going to Aunt Seana's this morning. Grandfather must be gone by now. I suspect he spends all his waking hours at the Palace. Aunt is planning a musicale this afternoon and I promised

Macgregor's Bargain

I'd help." Anne took a sip of chocolate and avoided Fiona's eyes. "Is…has my husband gone out?"

"No, I think something happened last night. I'm not sure what, but Calum and Hamish and a few others are in his study downstairs, and they're a grim looking lot. I heard him shouting at them."

Anne carefully lowered her cup to its saucer, and tried to stop the clattering of the two delicate dishes. She set them with great care on a side table, and clenched her hands together. She took a deep breath.

"Bring me water for washing. I'll wear the new blue brocade. I must hurry, before Aunt goes into a complete frenzy." She tried to keep her voice light.

Fiona said nothing but raised her brows. The blue brocade was hardly suitable for a morning call, and Seana had never gone into a frenzy about anything.

Anne could not seem to get dressed quickly enough. A stocking tore; a garter broke. Her petticoats would not lie right over their hoops. Her shoes seemed to trip her on her way down the stairs. Fergus followed her; Fiona stood at the top of the stairs and shook her head. Whatever was concerning her mistress, she was definitely going to find out.

Anne slipped past the study door, and heard Niall's loud, angry voice "… if that bastard has escaped, I want to know why and how…"

She fairly ran down the last flight of stairs, with Fergus at her heels.

"Quickly, Fergus, find a sedan chair." She took a deep breath, feeling her stays digging into her. "Aunt will be most disturbed."

Fergus obediently ran off, wondering.

Indeed, Seana did seem to be somewhat out of sorts, but that lay at the door of her brother, who had slept late, awakened feeling the effects of the tankards of brandy and ale he had drunk last night. He bellowed at the servants, vomited copiously, and roared off to the Palace to begin drinking again.

"I do wish, at times, my dear, that he detested me as much as I do him, then perhaps he would not avail himself of my home. You are, truly, the only good that has come from that man. Now, then,

• 201 •

Macgregor's Bargain

you look a bit harried. Shall we have chocolate and discuss the musicale? A much more pleasant subject."

"Aunt..." Anne smoothed the rich satin of her skirt, her head lowered so her aunt caught only a glimpse of her face below the fashionably tilted hat, "Aunt, last night-did Francis Hepburn escort you home, and did he say aught to you?"

Seana said, "Why, yes, my dear. He did. He spoke about you, and...now, that's odd.." She paused and gave her great-niece an odd look. "He said to give you his thanks for asking him to escort me home. At the time, I thought it most gallant, but it was a passing strange thing to say, wasn't it?"

Anne said, as the maid waited beside her, "Now, then, I think I'd like chocolate very much, and, Aunt, do you suppose I might have a bit of bread? I left home quickly and find I'm quite famished. Now, as you can see by my gown, I have every intention of staying with you and helping arrange the musicale, rather than returning home. Shall we start?"

Her aunt looked at her shrewdly. "Anne, you are no longer the naïf of a year ago. I did wonder why you chose to wear an afternoon dress to share a cup of chocolate with me, and I have been arranging musicales much too long to need help. Therefore you must either tell me what you have done, or I shall send you home and let your husband deal with whatever transgressions you have committed."

Anne tried to look offended. "I swear I know nothing I have done that could be called a transgression."

"And it could have nothing to do with the handsome Borderer who was my escort last night?"

Anne sniffed and examined her nails. Suddenly, a door below slammed open and they heard someone thundering up the stairs, and Seana's sitting room door was thrown open.

"Oh, dear," said Aunt Seana.

Niall scowled at Anne. "I sent to MacPherson to find if he had seen Hepburn last night. He said he saw the two of you dancing together, then you sent him off with Seana."

Anne studied her chocolate, willing her hand not to shake. She shrugged.

Macgregor's Bargain

"I could hardly have my dear aunt go home unescorted except for a footman, when Francis was there to be her protector. Jesu. One would think you'd found him in my bed, rather than taking my grandaunt home."

Niall strode toward her, towered over her, his eyes burning, his mouth tight.

"And you saw him no more, I take it." His voice was controlled, but barely.

"Why should I have?" her voice took on a suggestive tone. "I think, my dear, you know full well where I was last night."

Without warning he slammed his hand down on the delicate table next to her. It tipped, spilling the tray's contents. A large brown stain appeared on the pale green rug beneath it and Seana groaned, then stood up.

"I must see to things..." She fairly ran from the room.

Niall pulled Anne from her chair, his hand bruising her arm.

"Is that what you did, Madam, is that why you were so willing to take to my bed, distract me, to save your lover's life, and to betray Scotland in the doing?"

Beside her self with rage, she doubled up her free hand and hit him roundly on the jaw, and pulled back from him as he stood momentarily stunned.

"Yes, if you want to know, yes, I told him he was in danger. He was my friend! He came to Loch Laggan, he and Calum, and brought in crops, to stave off starvation of the crofters come winter. You and Grandfather had taken most of the men, with no thought about the survival of our people and the land. Yes, I told him to leave Edinburgh. I would not have him hung for a traitor for his love of me and of Scotland, and yes, of your daughter, whom you have barely noticed since her birth. He is not my lover, nor do I love him, though I sorely wish I did, for I would have run with him, and brought our daughter to live a better life than we'll all have after yon posturing popinjay and the silly folk who follow him bring hell to the Highlands."

She advanced on him, her face white with fury, her arms rigid at her side. "And I will tell you now, Niall MacGregor, I will not

■ 203 ■

Macgregor's Bargain

follow you into battle and bind your wounds. I will return to Loch Laggan and see to my own people, and may you burn in hell!"

He grabbed her again. "You are my wife. You will stay here until I tell you to go, and I will tell you to go when I am sure you will do no more damage to our cause. Hepburn probably knew little save plans for the next few days. But we will leave soon and when we do, you will be free to return to Loch Laggan." In spite of his anger, or because of it, she aroused him. He bent and kissed her, forcing her mouth open against his. "And besides, my sweet, you showed me again last night how very, ah, helpful, you can be to me. And, now, I will go and let you go on plotting against me. But I warn you, my dear, you will find yourself on a very short tether indeed from now on."

He pushed her from him and sauntered to the door. "And, Anne. You will pay proper attention to the popinjay and his men. You are my wife, and Loch Laggan and I might suffer if you cross the Prince. Popinjay he might be, but I have found he can be quite vicious to those who cross him, and should we win this war, we must be in a position to ask for favors from him."

He turned and grinned at her."Shall we meet again in my room tonight, sweet gentle Annie?"

"Bastard!" she spat as he shut the door.

Seana heard footsteps on the stairs and went into her sitting room to find her grandniece in tears, standing in the middle of the room

"Ah, my dear, what have you done?"

"What have I done? I have saved a friend from being hanged as a traitor. Is that so wrong, Aunt."

Seana gasped. "Jesu God-Hepburn?"

Anne nodded, wiping her red nose on the back of her hand. "I heard yesterday they suspected him, and he helped save Loch Laggan-could I let him die? I doubt he knew much about their plans, he's been with me these months past, he and Calum. And Niall accused me of taking him as my lover." The storm of tears broke again.

"Ah, my dear," Seana's own eyes filled, and she pulled her niece to sit beside her. "And you were not? You love him?"

▪ 204 ▪

Macgregor's Bargain

"Love Francis Hepburn? Oh, no, Aunt, I do not love him." Her breath came in hiccups. Seana patted her hand. "Aunt, I think it's much, much worse. I do love, but not Francis. " She raised her woeful face from her hands, and half-laughed, half -groaned. "I am afraid I've fallen in love with my husband."

"Dear God," said Seana.

The musicale was well attended, but seemed to lack a number of the men who were usually there. Wives shrugged but knew little. Fergus, always on the alert for news to pass on to Anne, slipped in and pulled her into an anteroom.

"They have left, Mistress. The MacGregor came back to the house and Calum was there, and Calum told him Cope was on the move, and Hamish packed their kits, and they were off, and Fiona's there weeping."

Anne felt her heart lurch. "Did you hear where they were off to?"

"Aye. I heard Musselburgh."

Anne motioned a servant and told her to fetch Seana.

"I must run, Aunt. I fear they will fight soon, and close to Edinburgh. Fergus said he heard them speak of Musselburgh. Fiona is home alone, and she's with child, so I must go to her."

Swiftly she kissed her speechless aunt and hurried after Fergus.

Chapter Twenty Four

Near Prestonpans, Niall, Alan and Calum stood aside from the others on Falside Hill, staring across a marsh at Cope's army.

"And how," said Niall to no one in particular, "do our leaders expect us to cross that??

They turned, hearing a shout from the west, and saw men returning from the direction of Tranent.

"Well, then, Murray's won. Those are the Cameron men O'Sullivan sent to guard near the kirk."

They waited, hearing angry voices raised, then Hamish emerged from the mob and sauntered toward them.

"There's a wee argument. First His Highness asked all and sundry how the men might act in battle. Then O'Sullivan sent yon men off to the west and Lord George Murray's fit to bust. Ker went out to see if the marsh is as bad as it looks, and reported it's far worse. And all are blaming Lord George for leading us up here without waiting for orders. And the Prince took it on himself to call Lord George an ass. By God, Niall, I think the only battle will be fought between Lord George and the Prince and his men." He spat and stared out over the morass in front of them.

Macgregor's Bargain

"Then Cameron of Lochiel came in, in a fury over men he'd lost at the kirk, and said he'd talked to a local who knew a path through the bog, so that's the way we'll go through. And the clans drew lots to see what their positions would be, and Camerons won the position on Prince Charlie's right. Och, the MacDonalds say they have to fight on the right, it's their privilege, and they don't hold to the drawing of lots. So they and the Camerons are at swords' point. We may be here till Hogmanay, and old Johnny Cope'll die of old age ere we're ready to fight."

Niall sighed, as the sounds of acrimonious voices reached him. "I do wonder what Johnny Cope thinks of all this." he squinted toward the west, where the sun lay near the hills.

"Get our men together, and we'll wait till we hear from Perth. Make sure they're fed, Calum, but no fires, and see if we're to spend the night here, or if all those grand decision makers have other plans for us."

He peered down at Cope's forces. "Poor bastards, they've moved their front four times, trying to figure out where we'll attack from. Mayhap that's the Prince's strategy, to wear them out before the battle."

Alan shook his head. "Ah, Niall, what is in store for us?"

When Calum returned, his ruddy face seemed to glow, whether with anger or with the afterglow of the sunset Niall was not at first sure.

"Now, then, Niall, what are we to do? Murray is in a fine temper, and let O'Sullivan have the side of his tongue. The Prince had his own fit, and now prepares for bed, with all his Irishmen around him, muttering that Murray's a traitor."

Niall took a deep breath, trying to swallow his misgivings. "Let's do likewise, and hope for the best."

He looked up to find Hugh Drummond coming toward him. As always, when talking to Niall, the younger man looked abashed. Niall could imagine what he was thinking, and grinned, which made Hugh stumble.

"Ah, I have a message from my brother. We're to be on the left, in the charge. We're to be ready at three in the morning and be through the bog and in place before the English."

Niall nodded. "We'll be ready, and my regards to your brother and my wife's grandfather."

Hugh blushed, and turned, running into Calum. He muttered an apology and hurried off.

Niall stood, hands on hips and stared after him."My dear wife does pick the oddest lovers."

"You speak, cousin, as if there had been more than one."

Niall looked at Calum. "The thought had crossed my mind there might be another."

Calum gave a short laugh. "Are you still going on about Hepburn?"

Alan said coldly, "Anne may as well be my sister. Watch, MacGregor, that I don't take offense at what you're suggesting."

Niall said, "Anne has a way of collecting defenders. I meant naught by it, only that after Hepburn escaped, I did wonder why she helped him."

"Helped him?" Alan stared at him.

"Ah, yes, you weren't privy to that final act. She admitted she did it-for friendship, for Loch Laggan, and because I'm a bastard."

"D'you think he took much information with him?"

Niall shrugged. "The Prince took him to his bosom, as a Protestant border lord who would follow him and raise others to come to the standards, so he was privy to much. But he had been at Loch Laggan with Calum these months, so mayhap he had little new to say. I only hope this is so. God knows if he were here now, he could take a pretty story to Cope."

"Does the Prince know?"

"I thought it best not to say aught yet. Let us see how tomorrow goes."

Niall spent the night wrapped in his plaid, sitting and staring at the English watch fires across the marsh. *More men there than here,* he thought. *And what news has Hepburn brought to his masters? What has he found out from our Prince and his cronies?*

And what of Anne? She had indeed changed. When he first met her, her thoughts were clear in her face and eyes. Now, there was a distance, a covering up, that seemed to break only when they made love. It was this more than any real evidence, that had made

Macgregor's Bargain

him sure Hepburn had become her lover. He rubbed the stubble on his cheeks and looked at the restless forms around him. His men, his responsibility, and he had so little power now. He had chosen to follow his Stuart king, and follow him he would, but could he throw his men into a battle when his own leaders seemed so inept? When they quarreled among themselves and questioned the courage of the men who followed them? His thoughts turned back to Anne, and her sharp words.

He thought that Anne was right, the babe had meant little to him, nor had Anne, at first. But she had been a good wife, a good keeper of Caorann Castle. Should Niall die, she would do well without him, and without that bastard grandfather.

He stood and moved among his men. Calum sat up and stared at him. Niall shook his head. "It's not yet time."

His cousin, his friend, pulled his plaid tighter and stood, and the two men moved away from the sleeping men.

"D'ye think it's a bad battle?"

"I don't know, Calum. We will fight as we're told, as we've done time and again, and we'll see each other after the battle, or not."

A runner came from the Prince's men. "Time, sir, will you warn your men to be quiet? We're to move east, and come at Cope from there."

Niall nodded, and motioned to Calum. "No fires, they're to eat cold bannock. Promise them strong drink after this is over and we're back in Edinburgh."

Calum grinned. "And women. Don't forget the women. I've not found one bonny enough to compare with yours, but I'll settle for less, after today."

Quietly, the army moved out, the MacDonalds leading the way into the pitch black of early morning, led by the Duke of Perth. Horses were left behind, but even so, Cope's men were alerted.

When the sun began to rise, Niall waited with his men behind the MacDonalds. He saw with dismay they had gone too far, that there was a gap in the Jacobite lines. Toward the Royalist army's lines, he could see massed red coats behind a bristling fence of cannon. He heard muttering beside him, and realized that Calum

■ 210 ■

Macgregor's Bargain

was muttering Hail Marys. There were so god damned many of them.

He heard bellows from the left flank, saw it advance, shooting, saw a few Royalist gunners run, heard the first bagpipes skirling the pibrochs, the war songs playing to rouse the men, found himself running forward, screaming, saw his men loose their plaids and run toward the cannon in their long saffron shirts, saw his own cousin James MacGregor, son of Rob Roy, fall, a surprised look on his face, his sword arm lying on the ground. Calum ran beside him into the midst of the red coats. Niall fired his pistol, flung it aside, reached for his broadsword and hacked his way through the throng, bagpipes urging him on. His sword became slippery with blood, and he found himself standing back to back with Calum, surrounded by four Royalists who had chosen to stand and fight. Like himself, Calum was so lost in his fury he seemed more berserker than disciplined soldier. They knew little of what went on outside their own small area until they saw the Prince riding toward them crying to his men to stop killing his father's subjects.

Niall, standing among the dead, dropped the point of his sword and stood, looking around the battlefield. Those who had not fled lay dying or sorely wounded, some trapped against a wall of Preston House. Others sprawled flat in that odd boneless manner of the dead. He drew a shuddering breath and he and Calum stared at each other.

The roar from the crowded streets preceded the returning army. They marched in from the east with their thousand prisoners and their prince on his white horse leading them.

Anne and Fiona looked at each other.

"'Tis over?" Fiona's face was white.

"I'll send Fergus out to see."

But there was no need, for she heard the lower door crash open and Fergus's high voice.

"They've won! They come in victory!"

The boy sprinted up the stairs toward them, his freckled face beaming. "I saw the prince, and your grandda riding just behind him."

"And...the others?"

"Och, aye, I did see the MacGregor, and Calum riding beside him, and Hamish behind. They were riding past Holyrood, so they'll be here soon. And Hamish had a great bloody bandage round his shoulder..."

He stopped, gaping, as his sister turned white and sat down abruptly.

Anne boxed his ears. "Stupid *nickum*! Did you have to be so happy about it? Your sister's husband has been wounded!"

Fergus looked penitent, and put his arm around Fiona. "Ah, dear girl, he was riding straight and tall, and smiling at the crowd. It couldna be a great wound." He was slapped again, and outraged at the way his sympathy was spurned, ran back down the stairs.

Anne sat down and drew a deep breath. "Fiona, let us have some food prepared, for I'm sure they'll be hungry. Will you talk to Cook, and tell her to heat a great deal of water, for they'll need baths."

Fiona, glad to be busy, nodded and ran off, looking in a mirror first to make sure Hamish would see her looking well. She peered into a looking glass and pinched her cheeks to bring color back to them.

Anne waited till Fiona left, then she too looked in the mirror, smoothing her hair under its lace cap. She could do nothing about the dark circles under her eyes. Her fears had kept her from sleeping these several nights, and now Niall was coming safely back she hoped he would be too preoccupied to notice her tiredness. Fiona had noticed, but she too had not slept well.

Anne heard footsteps on the stairs, and she hurried into the salon and picked up a book. Niall came into the room, dirty, tired lines framing his mouth, a stubble of red beard darkening his face. His filthy shirt was covered in rust colored stains. Her heart beat so loudly in her own ears that he must hear it.

"MacGregor, you have won a great battle, I hear. And now the town is celebrating. Everyone seems to have become Stuart supporters."

He said, "Victory does that."

She stood up. "Do you wish food or bath first?"

His grin broadened. "You are a cool one. Did you not worry a bitty about your husband?"

She moved past him to pull the bell cord. The sidelong look, the small smile. He caught her arm.

"First, I think..."

She pulled free. He smelled of gun smoke and grime and blood and days of sweat.

"First, I think, a bath and a whisky? And then Cook will have a massive meal for you and your men. Is Fiona with Hamish?"

"All white face and bravery and trying not to cry. He is not hurt badly, a ball tore past him and cut his shoulder a bit."

"And you, MacGregor, not a scratch to show from your heroic battle for your king?" She led him into his room, where a fire had been started and Fergus and another servant were filling the bathtub.

"I hope never to have to bleed for my king." He stripped off his shirt and trews, and stepped into the hot water, sinking down to cover his chest. His hair, cut short to wear under his wig, was as filthy as the rest of him.

Anne directed Fergus to bring him soap and a brush, and brought him a tumbler of whisky.

Niall sighed deeply and closed his eyes as he swallowed great gulps of whisky.

Anne leaned against a chair and watched him. When he opened his eyes they stared at each other for a moment, until she looked away.

"So, the battle went well?"

"It was a rout. It was over in 15 minutes. So many English dead, a great many captured, and Cope fled, his troops pell-mell behind him. The Prince was most noble. Some of our men were insane with blood lust, and he rode among them, beating them back, shouting that the English too were his people. He's treating the prisoners most humanely, and hopes to show them the error of their ways."

"And he thinks out of his generosity he'll convert the Sassenachs? He's gormless."

Macgregor's Bargain

His dark brows drew together, though his eyes remained shut. "He has shown he can be a good soldier, and his own men- and I- grow to respect him."

"And so what happens now?"

Niall sighed and took another drink. "We meet tomorrow morning at Holyrood. We'll probably refight the battle and make plans for the next one." He opened his eyes, his dark intense gaze on her. "And what of Hepburn?"

"I helped him escape. I know no more."

"Well, Mistress, he knows where Caorann Castle is, with the corn he helped reap, and the fat cattle and the good horses. Best hope he has gone south and not west."

"I have written to Iain, and warned him. He has written that Fort William is still in Royalist hands."

Niall kept his steady gaze on her. Then his lip curled. "Wee Hughie fought like a man, should you care. Poor lad, he couldna meet my eye. Mayhap I should have told him his lady love was proving false." His grin broadened as he sang,

"O waly, waly, love is pretty
A little while, while it is new,
But when it's old, it waxes cold,
And fades awa' like mornin' dew."

Her reaction startled him. The cool Anne who had greeted him faded too, her cheeks paled, and for a moment before she turned from him he caught the glint of tears in her eyes.

She stood abruptly, and muttered, "I'll see to your food."

Frowning, he leaned back. Could she love Hepburn so much?

He shook his head. He had noticed a certain moodiness during her monthlies; she was probably simply in a sulk.

He bellowed for Fergus, knowing full well that Fiona would have Hamish immobile, either nursing him or loving him.

Calum ate with Niall, and Anne silently sat beside them as Hamish and Fiona served them.

"Well, dear coz, can't you at least say that you're delighted the MacGregors came back of a piece? And there was a Clan MacGregor there. We're no longer proscribed!" His laughter brought a smile

■ 214 ■

Macgregor's Bargain

to Anne's lips. "Mayhap we'll become true gentry, and no longer, um, find our cattle."

Anne's laughter at her cousin's sally was genuine, and Niall felt a stirring of relief.

That night, she sent Fiona off to be with Hamish, and sat before her mirror. She brushed out her hair so it fell around her face and over her shoulders, and thought of the two of them and their love.

How good, how simple to be loved by your lover, and yet it must not happen so often, for all the songs written about such as she, who love and are not loved.

Unknowing, she began humming the tune Niall had sung earlier. She had not heard him enter, but he was there, lifting her hair from the back of her neck, brushing his lips just behind her ear. She leaned back against him, and as his raised his head their eyes met.

"Annie, what do you think when you look at me with your eyes all shadowed??

She swallowed, then forced a teasing grin. "MacGregor, you have taught me well. I was thinking exactly what you were thinking, if the great lump I'm leaning against means anything."

"Gentlemen," said His Royal Highness, "we must collect as much food as we can, and powder and balls and men to use them, and we must train those men. I have word from the South, and know with all my heart that we will gather more and more to our rightful cause. We will prevail, and the rout at Prestonpans will only be the beginning. We will prepare and we will march south within two months."

Niall kept his face still as he looked at the Prince's advisors: Murray and Perth, to whom he owed loyalty, and the Prince's own Irishman Sullivan, whom the Scots loathed.

Murray took a deep breath. "Into England, Highness?"

"All the way to London." Charles beamed. "The people will welcome me, and as we will receive more equipment from France, more men will rally to our cause."

He turned to Niall. "MacGregor, I do miss our witty Hepburn. Have you sent him to rally more people?"

Dia. Charles would never believe Hepburn would betray him. "Yes, Highness, even now he is probably far to the north, gathering men." Or the south, or west toward Loch Laggan.

"Do let me know what you hear." He turned his back in dismissal. Niall bowed his way out, and found Calum waiting for him in an anteroom.

"We go south soon."

"Och. I had thought so. And did he ask after our Lowland friend?"

"He did, but I put him off, told him Hepburn was out recruiting. I may announce his untimely death in Highland snows, if I were sure he wouldn't pop up firing at us during a battle."

"You have no choice, man. His Highness would not take kindly knowing there had been a spy close to him, or that you covered it for your wife's sake."

"If I thought that he would make a difference, I would tell the Prince. But it would be easy enough to tell him that the man simply was warned off, we know not by whom."

"Aye. 'Twould be a better course. I'd hate to see my sweet coz hanging on a gibbet."

"Your sweet coz ought to be hidden out at Loch Laggan, where she could do no more harm. But then of course, that is what she has wanted all along." Niall looked uncomfortable. "Calum?"

Calum stopped, arrested by the note in Niall's voice.

"Calum, this is for your ears alone. I tell you because I have no one so like my brother as you. It does not go well, Calum. This turns to madness, and to men's thoughts of themselves. His Highness will not tell the truth about our numbers, nor does Sheridan. And Murray will not trust him, nor the Irish. Our men are not ready for a long battle, and Prince Charles will not see that all men will not rise to aid us. He does not understand the Highlanders, and thinks them traitors if they leave to go back to their farms. He asks for their love, and gets it, and he's a brave man. They love him for that. But that is not enough alone to foster several thousand men 900 miles. Calum, when we go, I must go with him, as I have pledged so. But you are my kinsman, who has pledged nothing. If you wish you may stay with Anne at Loch Laggan."

Calum waved him away. "I go with you. Our men go. But Niall, do make Hamish stay behind. Someone, some MacGregor needs to be there, to call up our kin who are not fighting, to help Anne should she need it."

Niall nodded, then shook his head. "Aye, we'll do that, but who among us is brave enough to tell Hamish?"

"He's going to England? In spite of the lack of food? The men returning to their homes? The fact that the English do not want a Papist king? That *bumailer* is the greatest *cuif*! And those who follow him are greater *cuifs*!"

Amused, Niall watched Anne pace her sitting room, poor Bard standing to one side, watching her anxiously, his tail waving in a tentative movement. Niall had never seen Anne so angry, so furious that she could only bring up Gaelic words.

"Fools or no, Anne, we go. He's waiting for the French to send money and arms, and troops to be added to our own."

"And how many do you reckon you have now? With all the men leaving?"

"Where did you hear that?"

"'Tis common knowledge. At any market stall you hear. You hear too how the bonny Prince expected Highlanders to bury the English dead at Prestonpans. Highlanders! Expected to dig graves and carry loads! The man knows nothing of his people, and he wants them to march to London!"

Niall, sprawled in his chair, looked up at his wife. She was bonny. Her hair came loose from its pins, and her cheeks were bright red, her eyes hot.

"Anne, be calm, there is nothing to be done except prepare."

"That I will do, Niall MacGregor! I will not stay here, I will not curtsey one more time to that foppish fool!"

"And I say you will not leave."

Her eyes narrowed. Then she shrugged helplessly. "Of course. I promised, didn't I? And when you leave for England, I will go home."

Macgregor's Bargain

"Hamish will accompany you. He'll be most unhappy with me, but I'll explain."

"Explain?"

"That you may need more than Iain and boys. We do not know what will happen, Anne."

Her brows shot up, and her voice held an ironic note. "This does not sound like you, MacGregor. D'you fear something?"

How could she be so canny? What had given him away?

"I fear nothing, Annie, save for your tongue, which is sharp as ever I could hone a dirk. Now, Fergus tells me that we have nothing to do this evening. Why do we not sit like an old married pair, me with my whiskey, you playing your clarsach, with that great beast of yours guarding you?"

Chapter Twenty Five

Niall found in the siege of Carlisle more evidence that the army would never be an entity. He listened, too stunned to believe his ears, as Murray explained why he would not allow his men to relieve the Duke of Perth's people on the siege lines.

"I will not have my men endangered by lying in trenches within musket shot of the town!" he thundered. "Ye let Perth do as he will, I must care for my own. Already they're in lodging so poor they can't keep out of the rain!"

Charles, red of face, yelled back. "I am your Prince! I command here, not some jumped up little laird!"

Niall, disgusted, bowed his way from the Prince's quarters. Calum waited outside, holding his horse.

"Wade's not coming, cousin. A man slipped from the castle and threw himself on our mercy. Luckily one of ours found him. He's on his way to the Prince now. Seems Wade sent a message that since there was no earthly reason to capture Carlisle, we must not be wasting our time, and are on our way to Lancashire."

Niall grunted. "And well we should be. What we hope to accomplish here I do not know. But here we are, as Murray

• 219 •

Macgregor's Bargain

planned, and at least we're not sprinting toward London, as the Prince wished."

The white flag showed above the town next day, and after threats that it would be put to the torch if the castle did not surrender, Durand submitted to the Jacobites.

Niall looked over the men who followed him in the Prince's army, and wondered if they would have the strength to get back to Scotland. On the whole, townsfolk were not forthcoming with food or welcome. Pamphleteers and novelists like Henry Fielding had published broadsides telling of the savagery of the Highlanders, raping and killing, stealing and destroying innocent English folk and their possessions.

At Manchester on November 28, a local regiment joined them. But from a captured government spy they learned that William, Duke of Cumberland, second son of King George, had 10,000 men in his army. General Wade, with another 10,000, was headed toward Manchester.

Niall swore when James Drummond, Duke of Perth, brought the news to his men that the Jacobites, their followers, their herds of cattle, would continue south to Derby, with an army of less than 5,000. Some of the soldiers were boys of ten or twelve, hardly able to carry heavy shields.

By the time they had reached Derby, there had been few skirmishes to hearten the men, as the Loyalists bolted at the sight of the Jacobites. Word came that London was in a panic, sure that Charles' army would be able to capture the town, and that thousands of Jacobites prepared for him.

Niall, riding on reconnaissance toward Newcastle-under-Lyme, flushed a party of dragoons who galloped away, leaving an intelligence officer behind.

"My name is Weir, sir," the man answered Murray, when they had brought him back from headquarters. "I will tell you what I know about our troops, for your spies must surely know our numbers."

Murray paled at the figures Weir gave him. Niall, standing beside him, bent his head.

Macgregor's Bargain

At least three for every one of them, and the Royalists well fed, well armed. *Would that we had spies as good as theirs.*

At council, Murray bluntly put the numbers before the leaders, as Charles stared at him unbelieving.

"Sir, we cannot go on. We should have turned back at Manchester. Our only hope is to retreat, to meet John Drummond's army that's from France, and to go back to the north to fight on our own land."

"You, sir, you tell me, your Prince, that we cannot go on. We are within striking distance of London, there are rumors that Wales will rise up to join us, and you would flee like a frightened woman?"

Murray, face scarlet, grimly stared back. "I invoke the council's decision on this. We know of the strength of nearby armies, but not how many may come to aid the King."

"The King is my father!" Charles spat. "I am his heir! And you dare to question me, when I am able to grasp the throne in a few short days!" He pounded the table and screamed. "I, I am the heir. I will rule all Britain!"

The men eyed each other, and Perth stood up. "Sir, I pledge myself and my men to your cause. We will follow you to London."

But slowly, one by one, the others shook their heads.

Murray spoke up, though Charles scowled at him. "Your Highness, since we have word that Lord John Drummond is on his way from France with arms, money and men, why not head north and meet him, and then discuss what we can do next."

"Murray, we have time on our side! London is in a panic. Should we turn back now the men will be disheartened. We must not lose momentum."

Niall wondered, in this case, if Charles was not right.

But it was decided. The Jacobite army began its grim march back to Scotland. The men were underfed and food in midwinter hard to come by. After their cattle were butchered and stolen there was little left. Horses were stolen in order that the men would not be left behind. The townspeople were even more hostile, and often stragglers were found lying in ditches, their throats cut.

Prince Charles, who had marched cheerfully with the men on the way south, now was last up in the morning and surly most of

Macgregor's Bargain

the time, often drunk with his cohorts. He never missed a chance to voice his opinion of Murray's insistence on retreat.

Niall, riding with Calum, avoided all of them. His grandfather in law, riding with Perth, had denounced him for a coward for not siding strongly with Perth and the Prince. Since then the old man had taken every opportunity to tell him that he deserved the slut he had married.

Too, there were always government troops, never engaging them, but over every hill. Niall had sent one of the Manchester men, dressed in the uniform of a captured dragoon, to London with forged papers. The man, Henry Osbourne, returned with more bad news from his contact in London.

Osbourne would not meet Niall's eyes as he recounted what he had learned. "Your, ah, friend says that already the Hanovers are planning what to do after they win. Sir, one of your kin, John Mohr MacGregor was captured and has been a spy for the Hanovers for some time. He is giving them the names of all the Jacobite leaders, and has informed them that gold has been sent from France and hidden in the Highlands. He goes by the name of Pickle, from Smolett's book. I don't know how your friend found his real name, but he is sure he is correct." Osbourne drew a deep breath as Niall stared at him.

"No, it cannot be. A MacGregor, and Rob Roy's own son!" Niall looked form Osbourne to Calum. "Cousin, we are lost if we cannot persuade Prince Charles to retreat to the Highlands."

In Kendal, the Duke of Perth's servant was murdered by a mob, and no longer could Charles express his belief that all the people were for him. Finally, at Clifton there was a skirmish, Niall and Calum and their men in the midst of it. When it was over, two of their own, one Iain's son Lachlan, lay among the dead, with fifty loyalist dragoons.

Calum, a cut above his eye covering his face with blood, said to his cousin. "Ah, for a coward, you fight well."

"A good fight with sword and pistols is much better than listening to all those who hold our destiny fighting amongst themselves."

Macgregor's Bargain

At Carlisle, Charles stubbornly insisted that several regiments be left to defend it, though, as Murray and Perth pointed out, there was precious little chance it could be defended. After all, had they not taken it with ease?

But Charles prevailed, reassuring the men he would soon be back, to again go into England and claim the throne.

On December 20th, they crossed the flooded River Esk, and were back in Scotland. Charles used his horse as a barrier so the water would not sweep the men away.

That night, though, there was still very little for the men to eat, except in Prince Charles' tent, where he dined with Sheridan and O'Sullivan, there were bonfires to warm the men, and pipers.

Chapter Twenty Six

Fires burned high in Castle Caorann, and the cold wind carried so much snow that few ventured out save to tend to beasts. The snow had been heavy enough since early December to effectively cut them off from all but their nearest neighbors.

Anne had been surprised that Alan had returned to his home, his belief in the Prince gone before the army had left Edinburgh.

"Your grandfather told me never to come to his home again," he grinned, as he and Lucy sat before the library fire with Anne.

"You were a brave man to take a stand, Alan, and I know neither Niall nor Calum would say different. They went because they still hoped, and Iain and Hamish have never quit saying they should have gone."

She looked down at her daughter where she lay next to Bard on the hearthrug. Catriona, fat and rosy, her first fuzz of red hair quite gone, chewed on her fingers and grinned back, her other fist tangled in the fur of the long suffering Bard.

Anne sighed. "It is hard, hearing nothing. I hope the snow doesn't keep us from all news all winter."

And I hope, I hope, that as I feel, that my love lives.

Macgregor's Bargain

"'Twill be a small Hogmanay," Lucy said. "Will you come to our house? It isn't so far to come, unless we have another blizzard. Anne, you look as if you haven't slept. Is aught the matter?"

Anne looked apologetically at Alan.

"Promise you will not think the less of me and think me a victim of female vapors."

Alan laughed and stretched his legs toward the fire. "I never knew a lass less apt to have vapors. Come, dear friend, I'll hear and not sit as judge."

Anne sighed and leaned back in her chair, so that Lucy and Alan could see only her profile, lit by the fire.

"It's the dreams, you see. You know Morag has always said that I have the Sight, though it's only the past year and a bit more that I've had the dreams - them and the - the other things. I dream I am here, or in my room, and I do know that Niall is nearby, but I cannot hear him, or see him, I simply feel him near me. The dreams come often, so that I dread the night to come." She sighed, and bent to tickle Catriona. "And then there was the time, you know the wee glen up the mountain, Alan, that I have gone to since I was so small? But I went into it and it didn't welcome me. It was full of cold, and there were loud voices, so near that though I could see nothing, I could feel my fear. And then, in my own room, my own most private room one day I went in, and there was such a sadness that I wept, and do not know why."

Her profile was stern, and her voice could have been telling a story of someone else.

Lucy shivered. "But, dear, do you think it could be just being here so far from Niall..."She stopped realizing what she said, and looked guiltily at Alan. They had discussed this and agreed not to say anything to Anne.

"So far from Niall?" Now Anne was looking at them, her brows drawn together. "What has that to do with anything?"

Alan nodded to Lucy, and awkwardly he stood and stretched. "I think, Annie, I shall find Iain. We must needs talk of stores, for we will have to get food to the army."

Anne looked from Alan, as he left the room, to Lucy, who stared at her hands, her face flushed.

▪ 226 ▪

Macgregor's Bargain

"Perhaps I misspoke, Anne. You have proven a dear friend to us at a time when many folk refuse to see us because of Alan's decision. I do not want to cause you pain, for I love you more than I could love the dearest sister. But we know, Alan and I, because we know you well. We have seen your sadness and fear for Niall, and know you love him."

Anne leaned back in her chair again, and firelight caught the shine of tears slipping down her cheeks. Bard, ever sensing her mood, gently disengaged himself from Catriona and came to put his paw in her lap. She ran her fingers through his long rough coat, then laid her head down on his.

"Lucy, I shall probably regret this, but I will tell you what I plan. The dreams, you see, have led me to believe that Niall may..."she gulped, looking down, stroking Bard's head. "That Niall may die. I agreed before we all left Edinburgh that I would bring supplies and money to them when we heard from them. And before the last snow Iain's nephew came back to tell us the army was once again in Scotland, and that Lachlan had been killed. When the weather clears enough to take food to them, Iain and I will go with supplies, and from there I will find him, and tell him I love him. I have no thought that he loves me, but if he dies without knowing...."

Lucy shook her head. "Anne, 'tis hard enough for men to break through the passes in the winter. You would be foolhardy to do so."

Anne looked at her friend, tears still on her cheeks. "Have I not always been foolhardy? I made a vow with a man I didn't know, and have come to love him as I have come to know him." She stopped and sighed and smoothed Bard's head as it rested on her knee. "Did you know that Francis Hepburn was a spy, and that the night of the ball at Holyrood I helped him slip away? And did you know that though he believes above all else in the Cause, Niall did not report me, nor treat me, after his first anger, with any but the greatest respect? His only thought is to get the Stuarts on the throne, he has had no time for any other but the lightest dalliance, but he has, in his own lights, been honest with me, yet I have left him with the belief that it is Francis whom I love. Not, mind, that I said this, but the daft man cannot understand why else I would see

Hepburn safe." Now there was a tone of exasperation in her voice. "Men can always use loyalty to their fellows as a reason to behave in a certain way. They do not understand a woman who might also do so for her own reason."

Lucy came and perched on the arm of her chair. "Then, my dear, of course you must go. Alan cannot, of course, though he will help Iain and Hamish prepare, and we will insure that you are with them when they go."

In the first week of January General Henry Hawley reclaimed Edinburgh for the Royalist forces, and set up a gallows in the market square for any Jacobites who might be captured.

That same week, the Jacobites settled at Bannockburn to besiege Stirling. Although their forces had grown with Lord John Drummond's French troops, the exercise was futile, and Niall fumed as they waited for cannon. The town surrendered, but the castle was as impregnable as that of Edinburgh. There was nothing to do but wait.

Niall and Calum were left to cool their heels outside Stirling Castle with Perth's men when word was received that there had been a battle at Elphinstone, and the Jacobite battery was silenced.

"Worse and worse, coz." Although they were supposed to be keeping watch for the elusive cannon, some of which were still missing, Niall and Calum had retired in disgust to what seemed to be the one friendly tavern in Stirling, the other tavern owners having fought the Jacobites before the town surrendered.

"We will miss another stirring battle. The other troops move to Falkirk, and we rest our asses in a tavern, all for our great brave Prince."

A month ago, before the news of the terrible recapture of Carlisle, Niall would not have taken kindly to disparagement of the Prince. But word had come that the Jacobites who had tried to defend the castle had been brutally murdered, hanged, drawn and quartered, by the redcoats. Now, he thought bitterly, even Anne's condemnation seemed too mild.

Shortly after nightfall, when Niall and Calum had returned to camp, men started returning from Falkirk.

"They ran. The wee lobsters ran!" One delighted MacDonald yelled at Niall. "We ran alongside their horses and pulled them down!"

After the vanguard came wagons full of food, more than the Highlanders had seen for a long time, and better. Then there were wagons of mortars and balls and powder.

There was glee in the Jacobites' camp, but the Prince was not to be found.

Calum, who had mingled with officers and men as they returned, came grinning to Niall.

"Och, Murray has embarrassed our Prince once more. He chose to attack at Falkirk when the Prince ordered him to wait till morning."

"And where is the Prince now? I seem to be not part of the circle."

"Ah, now there's a story. Seems there is a young lady who is under the care of her uncle, and she dotes most devotedly on our Prince who, 'tis said, has a cold."

Niall grinned at this. "Now he is truly a Highlander. He has the itch, he has a cold. Next, perhaps, he'll lose that damnable accent."

Calum turned serious as he watched his cousin staring toward the east as if he would will the sun to rise. "Coz, I find it passing odd that our Prince's crown seems to be tarnishing in your eyes. What d'ye know? Is ought happening that I should know?"

"I, too hear things, Calum. I have no wish to desert our Cause, which I believe in with my whole self. But, Calum, Charles does not see things as they are, here, and he knows things abroad that we do not. I stepped into his rooms to see how he fared, and Sheridan was with him. They spoke of the King of France and his designs on England. They stopped, and the Prince sent me away." Niall scowled at the celebrating men.

"He was in a gey temper, and screamed at me. That, I think, has ended my usefulness to him. He trusts only his Irishmen and has seen me be friendly with Lord George Murray, who he sees as his enemy. He will not tell us, from now on, what he plans."

Calum whistled between his teeth. "Do we stay, Niall? The MacGregors are going north into Sutherland to try and find more men. Do we go with them? What do we owe to the Drummonds?"

Macgregor's Bargain

"I made a vow, Calum, I cannot go back on it. When I married Anne, I became by marriage a Drummond. If you choose to go with the MacGregors, I will not hold you. I have only poor expectations of what may happen with this army if we do not retreat to the Highlands."

Calum shook his head. "We're kinsmen, half Drummond, half MacGregor. We'll stay and see this together. Our men will stay with us, as they have pledged to you, as you have pledged to Perth."

Niall nodded. "Then so be it. Now, shall we find our way back to our tavern, and wait to find what morning brings?"

The morning brought a council of war.

Charles, horrified, listened to Murray and the clan chiefs insist that they must retreat to the north.

"We are Highlanders, Highness. We would not desert you. If you will only hear us out. We may yet win the day, but there are many desertions. Men wish to go home to see to their families. They are underfed, and the snows lie so deep that marches are terrible."

"Retreat! But do you not realize that with retreat, the men will lose their will? Tell him, Sheridan! Tell him we must not retreat!"

"We must have more men. We cannot have half our fighting force away to their lands."

Sheridan gazed haughtily at the Highlanders. "His Highness has shown the way. Will you not understand that he will be your king?"

Niall spoke softly to the Irishman. "Your Prince does not understand his men. As Murray has said, they are Highlanders. In the Highlands, they will fight, in the hills and the corries and the glens, none will defeat them. But they do not fight as others fight, following orders, marching and fighting in files. We cannot expect them to."

Charles turned blazing eyes toward him. "How dare you question me! You have been my man since I came to France, and now you speak as a traitor. These men followed me to England, and they will follow me to Hell, should I ask them."

The Duke of Perth and Alasdair Drummond stared at Niall as if they had never seen him.

Macgregor's Bargain

"Highness, I meant no insult to you. I have given my life to you and to your father and I will continue to do so. But Lord Murray is correct. We must think of the kind of warfare that will be fit for the men we have. They are suited to the hills. Should we go back into them, we will be able to defeat the English, with all their horses and cannon."

Charles's venomous look was directed at Murray. "Very well, I shall consider it. I will give my answer in the morning. Come Sheridan."

His coterie followed him from the small room, and Niall breathed a sigh of relief. The Drummonds once again viewed him favorably.

In the morning, the Highland army headed north, and when they reached Crieff, Murray and half the army headed for the east coast and Aberdeen, and the Prince led the clans toward Inverness.

Chapter Twenty Seven

Deep snow along the Great Glen slowed them, and the pack garrons had hard work wading through it with their heavy loads. Iain made sure the little horses were given food and rest, and they moved slowly. As the Drummonds went they collected food and money from supporters, and spent nights comfortably enough. To avoid Fort Augustus at the end of Loch Ness, they rode southward through steep terrain, for like Fort William the newly built fort was still in loyalist hands.

They found no house one night, nothing but a dun, the remains of a fort built before the oldest of their people, before legends. The rock walls were thick as the reach of Iain's arms, and as they crept inside, the half ruined roof protected them. Iain tethered the ponies near them, and he and Fergus, Hamish and Anne, drew close. Anne was bundled in her own plaid and an old one of Niall's. The men had managed to gather bracken in places where the wind had swept the snow away, and Hamish started a small fire. They ate dry oats, and Anne, smiling, drew from her skirts a small flask.

They grinned at her as she offered it round.

Macgregor's Bargain

One more day would take them to Inverness. They were unsure whether the army had turned south again, or was still at Stirling. Young Rab Drummond had fought through snow as he came straight north from Stirling. All he knew was that Niall had told him to find more men and supplies to add to the army. It was assumed that word of mouth would help them locate the Jacobites.

The small fire lit the old walls, and Anne leaned back, looking around. There was a feeling here, of beings who hovered just out of the firelight. She shivered and drew her plaid closer.

"Come closer to the fire, lass," Iain urged.

She leaned against him. "Iain, you and Morag have been so strong, with Lachlan gone. Yet you still wanted to come with me."

Iain said, "Lachlan was a gift to us, as are all our children. Yet I still have three sons with your granda, and they need food. I worry, though, about how your husband will look on my bringing you along."

They all knew they faced Niall's wrath in bringing her, but she would prevail.

The wind moaned a bit around the top of the dun, and Anne, nearly asleep, jerked upright and looked around wild-eyed.

"Easy, lass, it's only the wind."

"No, I think not, Iain. It's all those who came before us speaking in their own tongue."

"You do have wild fancies." He grinned into the firelight. "D'ye mind coming to me one day and asking me what the gray haired lady was doing in your grandfather's room? You said she was not dressed properly, you could see her legs, and when you asked her who she was, she walked through you. You made us all walk through all the castle looking for the lady, and never a hair did we find."

"No, Iain, I don't remember. How odd I must have been. What do you think I saw?"

"Well, you were but a wee thing, but you always had a bit of mischief about you, so we never knew if you did see something, or if you just wanted to affright the girls."

Anne laughed sleepily. "I recall nothing. Seems I should, if I had seen a specter."

Macgregor's Bargain

She sighed, and was asleep.

There was an inn, just south and west of Inverness, and there they stopped next day. Anne sent Hamish and Cailean into Inverness to collect what news they could, and to find if there were Loyalist troops around.

The host was delighted to have them, and professed his loyalty to the Prince, and made sure his grooms cared well for the ponies and their burdens. It was a small inn, but clean and warm. Anne, damp and chilled, stood with her hands held out before the great fire, still wrapped in her two plaids, one just slipping from her hair.

The outside door swung open, and she heard the thump of boots and loud male voices.

One voice, a familiar one, broke through. "By God, I do need some warmth, and look, coz, a lass to give us a bit."

She swung around, to see the stunned faces of her husband and his cousin.

Niall stood, staring at her, at her clothing steaming gently, her plaid slipping from her hair so it was lit red by the fire behind her.

She gulped and stared back at him.

He was first to recover.

"Well, Madam, have you come to join our forces to fight for our noble Prince??

"Dear Coz!" Calum strode forward and embraced her heartily. "Anne, you are foolhardy. But what have you brought us?"

Anne, in reaching down to pick up her plaid, had forgotten she was wearing trews.

Calum broke into laughter. "A fine looking lad we have here, though a bit broad in the hips." He spun her around. "A bit heavy in the chest, too."

Anne, laughing too, saw the set expression on Niall's face. "I fear, Calum, that your cousin is not as delighted to see me as you are."

"I believe Calum said the word 'foolhardy.' In truth, Anne, this time you have gone beyond being merely a nuisance. You could well have fallen into the hands of our enemies. They, too roam the Great Glen."

■ 235 ■

Fergus came in with a load of wood. "Aye, sir, we saw them with their lobster coats on. As we went round Fort Augustus we saw a patrol. We went into a corrie, and lay in the bracken, and they rode anear us!" His excitement did nothing to improve Niall's temper.

He drew in a deep breath. "Have you nothing more suitable to don, Anne? There are near twenty of us who'll be staying here, and although they're mostly my own MacGregors and some Drummonds who have at least heard of my wild wife, I would like you to be presentable."

Anne's cheeks flamed, and as she opened her mouth Calum signaled to Fergus to flee.

"I'll look to the men, Niall. Anne, do you have your belongings brought in?"

Neither heard him.

Anne strode toward Niall in her stockinged feet. "I brought you food and money for your godforsaken cause, you bastard. I went to every landowner who wasn't with you and your silly Prince, and if the man was away, I begged the womenfolk for all they could spare! How dare you speak to me in such a way! I knew I would have better luck in this than any man I could send. I have six pack garrons laden with oats for your men and fodder for their horses, and I have bags of gold and silver, and some women even gave me their jewelry to be melted down for the cause. And your only interest is that I may look outlandish! As soon as I have dried my clothing and rested, I will take my men back to Loch Laggan, and you may go on your way to hell!"

Niall looked down at her, bemused, then picked her up and headed for the stairs. Anne was too stunned at his action to protest, too excited by his nearness. Automatically her arms went around his neck and she leaned against him.

"You smell like a wet dog, MacGregor."

He sniffed the top of her head. There was just the familiar smell of his wife.

"I had looked forward to a hot bath here. Which is your room? Are you alone?"

She nodded and pointed.

Macgregor's Bargain

He set her on her feet and held her at arms' length. "It was a brave thing you did, Annie. Now I will thank you. But it was rash. We have seen crofts burned here and there, and women raped and murdered. I regret what I said. Now, do you really want me in hell, or shall I take a bath??"

Her answer was to open the door and pull him inside.

"I believe, MacGregor, there is another choice."

A big round tub appeared, showing Fergus's legs beneath it. Hamish followed him, and spared MacGregor a brief grin as he poured the first buckets of hot water into the tub. Niall was sitting up in bed, Anne sleeping at his side, little of her showing save for tousled hair.

After the tub had been filled, and Hamish found soap and sheets for drying themselves, Niall pulled back the quilt and kissed Anne on the shoulder.

She rolled on her back, yawning capaciously, stretching arms above her head.

"Will you take the bath first? Even after a week's travel, you smell bonny."

Later, bathed and clad in a simple, hoopless gown, rumpled from being wadded in a saddlebag, she pulled up white stockings and gartered them.

Niall said, "Here's my only clean shirt. It's the worst for wear, I fear."

"I brought you more, and another pair of trews. I wore your old plaid, to bring to you, but may I keep it for now? The way home will be cold."

He nodded as he pulled on a pair of breeches and then his boots.

"We'll be here for a week or more. We have passed word as we traveled that men could come to us. Murray is greatly afeard that now we're in the Highlands, we may lose many men who choose to go home. I told him we would collect what we can to fill in the ranks. You should stay for a while; 'twas a long cold trip and I'd not like you take a chill. The Prince is recovering from one."

Macgregor's Bargain

She rose and walked to the window, looking at the falling snow. "Mayhap I'll have no choice by the morrow. The flakes are big as goose feathers. Are your men warmly quartered?"

"Sleeping four to a bed, But that's still better than what we have done. How did you manage, the way from Loch Laggan?"

"Mostly we stayed with those I knew. But the last night we stayed at a dun above Fort Augustus. Twas strange and eerie. I thought I heard voices, but Iain laughed at my fancies. He reminded me that Morag thinks I have the Sight."

He said, "And can you see what we may have for a meal? I have not had much hot food these past days, nor, I suspect, have you."

He pulled her shawl around her and led her downstairs, where the guidwife had laid out meats and breads and big bowls of boiled carrots and cabbages.

"The men have the itch, and I've made them take as much cabbage as they'll eat, it seems to help."

Niall's men trooped in, Drummonds and MacGregors who grinned when they saw her, having heard of her exploit from Iain and Fergus and Cailean. Others, a few odd MacDonalds and Atholmen, eyed her with a mixture of horror and awe. They were used to their own strong woman, but a few murmured that they were glad she was the MacGregor's and not theirs.

Later, when they had withdrawn to drink their ale with their own fellows, Anne and Niall sat with Calum.

Niall poured her a mug of brandy and added hot water to it.

"Drink," he ordered.

"Now, tell me what you are doing here, and where you go?"

Calum spoke first. "Well, Coz, if you have not heard, we had a victory at Falkirk. It was a rout, and our spies tell us that General Hawley was quite put out and even hung some of his men on gallows in Edinburgh, that he'd put up to hang us!" Calum found this most amusing, grinning and shaking his head.

"Dear me, I do wonder how Aunt Seana is faring."

"Well, I would imagine, there seems to be no great retribution against townspeople."

"So, then where do you go from here??

■ 238 ■

Macgregor's Bargain

"Toward the east," Niall said. "Most MacGregors are heading north, into Sutherland, and Murray has already gone toward Aberdeen. But the plan is to met near Inverness to plan our campaign."

Calum, unable to avoid twitting Anne, said, "Now, then, Annie, ye must not pass this along to your light o' love."

Anne fought the urge to slap him soundly. She cast a sidewise glance at Niall and saw his jaw tightening.

"And how is your Galahad? D'ye see him?" In spite of himself, his words were sharp.

Irritated, Anne snapped, "Of course not, you gleikit man. I helped a friend, and I do hope he's back in the Borders, away from all this."

She flounced up. "I'm off to bed."

Niall stood, too and stretched, grinning at Calum. "Well, then, Calum, since your foolish words ended a pleasant evening, I'll leave you to your bedmates, and I'll go to mine."

His cousin threw his boot at him.

The wind rattled the small window, but the room was warm from the chimney coming from the downstairs fireplace. When Niall opened the door, Anne was once again at the window, clad only in her shift and shawl, her hair unbound.

He came behind her and lifted the curls behind her ear, and gently bit her neck. Her response was immediate as she turned to him, mouth reaching for his, arms circling his neck, fingers in his hair.

"Slowly, Annie, that first time today made me behave like a green lad. Let us taste first."

He bent his head and kissed her throat, and then her mouth, then the tops of her breasts. He led her to the bed, her shawl dropping to the floor. He pulled her chemise over her head, and she lay back on the bed, arms above her head, staring up at him.

Childbirth had been kind to her. Her breasts were a little softer, a bit fuller, the nipples more pronounced. Her flat belly had faint white lines on it. He bent to kiss them, running his tongue along them until she moaned with pleasure.

■ 239 ■

Macgregor's Bargain

He pulled off his own shirt and breeches and lay next to her, pulling her close to him, breathing in her smell. There had not been a woman in a very long time, and he realized that he had not wanted one. Till now.

Later, he held her and slept, and she lay on her side, back to him, tears running down onto her pillow.

There were the words, *mo cridhe.* Had he said them, or had she? My heart, my soul, my love.

The snow fell during the night, and the next day, and the day after, and then the wind blew fiercely, so the accumulated snow drifted up nearly to their window, and the men had to dig paths to the stables to care for the horses.

The innkeeper, his wife and the serving wench were kept busy preparing food and doing such cleaning as they did. Anne had brought her own sheets and pillows, of course, and was heartily glad for it. She had examined the quilts for lice.

During the day the men began vying for her attention, and at night, Niall had every part of her.

And yet she had been unable to find the words to tell him. After the first night, carried away by passion she might be, but she watched her tongue most carefully. And Niall, who did not watch his, spoke hoarsely in French and Gaelic and English. The Gaelic being her own language, she could, of course, understand. From that she could guess at the French, and knew his words said nothing of love and a great deal of lust.

They awoke a week later to a warm sun and blue skies.

"March is an evil month, and not to be trusted," Niall murmured as he pulled her to him. "We shall stay in bed a while, and see if it will turn to winter once again."

But it did not, or at least, the fiercest weather didn't return and there was a thaw, so snow began to melt in the stable yard, and the horses were brought out to stretch their legs.

"When will you go?"

"Soon. We must get these supplies and the money to our forces, and hope that more men will follow, A shipment of gold was sent from France, and more troops, but the seas are treacherous, and there have been many English ships between here and France."

Anne said, "And where will you go?"

"East. To find the Prince and Murray and their men. Murray has virtually taken over control of the Army and Charles and his coterie loathe him. I fear the greatest battle will be between the two of them."

"Niall, at Falkirk, were you there? Have you been hurt?"

He shook his head. "I was not at Falkirk. I was at Stirling. There have been skirmishes that I have been in, but no battle since Prestonpans. Even now, because our men and theirs are so spread out, I am sure there have been several skirmishes since we have been here, held safe by the snow. Anne, you too must go. I would like to see you go to Edinburgh, away from the fighting. I believe Loch Laggan will not be safe for you."

"And for my people there? I will not desert them. Niall, are you afraid that the war is lost?"

"Anne, I do fear that. It is more difficult every day for me to believe that Prince Charles can take even Scotland, let alone England too."

She sat down, looking at her hands clasped so tightly the knuckles were white.

"What will you do?"

His grin was ironic. "Why, I will fight by my Prince's side, should he choose to fight. And then I will come home to Loch Laggan to my wife and we will spend all our years together, with many bairns to raise. Mayhap we could invite Francis Hepburn to join us."

And mayhap you will die, and all the men who fought for that cause will die. And Scotland will be laid to waste by the victors.

But she merely grinned back at him, in such a way that made him think he must have her back on the bed, and said, "D'ye mean join us in bairning? After the third or fourth, would it matter who fathered it?"

There was a picture in his mind, for an instant, of Anne, abandoned as he had seen her in his own arms, in the arms of Francis Hepburn, and a white-hot flare burned. He picked her up and threw her on the bed, and took her, using none of his skillful wooing, willing that picture out of his mind.

Macgregor's Bargain

As he lay beside her, exhausted, he turned his head to find her staring at him, and realized that the violence in him had found a like feeling in her, and she had desired it as much as he.

"Do you suppose, MacGregor, that those folk who I heard at the dun did such as we just did, mating in violence?"

Gingerly he felt the marks on his shoulder where she had bitten him.

"I'm sure their women were fierce, Annie, but I wonder did the men approach their beds with caution, knowing what awaited them."

In the morning, as Anne went down the stairs, she heard Niall and Calum.

"Make sure there's enough fodder to see them home. The snow will be little enough at lower elevations along Loch Ness, that they'll have no trouble."

"Have you spoken to Anne yet?"

"I wait for her now. Have the men ready in the morning. We leave at daybreak."

She halted, frozen. She knew it must happen, and yet, so soon. She gulped and turned to go back up the stairs when Niall's voice halted her.

She stopped, not daring to turn around, feeling tears, hoping they would not spill over.

"Anne, you heard."

She nodded, not turning.

"I'll be down in a moment. I, uh, forgot my shawl."

She fled up the stairs and into her room, shutting the door behind her, leaning against it. He could not go. She took a deep breath and wiped her eyes with the back of her hand. Reaching for her shawl, pulling it around her, she made her way down to where Calum and Niall waited.

"So you go, then, MacGregor."

He nodded. "I'm having hell's own time making Hamish go back, but he will. The weather bodes fair for a day or so, that will set you on your way tomorrow."

"And so we go west and you east, to try and put an army together."

▪ 242 ▪

Macgregor's Bargain

"We will, Anne, we must try, at any rate."

She nodded, and turned her attention to her porridge, although she felt that every bite would choke her.

The day went too fast, with Niall and Calum preparing horses and packs, and Anne wondering if she would have the courage to speak to him as she had planned.

And when night fell, they made love fiercely, then gently, then Niall slept, and Anne watched him.

He woke to her crying. "Anne, what is it?"

She sat up, and put her face in her hands. "A dream. A dream."

"Tell me."

She shook her head. "It is too strange to tell. Do go back to sleep."

He pulled her into his arms, and they slept until they heard the rattle of harness in the stable yard.

Anne sat up and watched him dress. The shirt and breeks she had brought him, the vest and coat. She pulled on her own trews and sark and stockings, and went to her pack.

"This is for you. The women at Loch Laggan wove it for you."

The plaid was subdued, the colors that would blend with bracken and heather, green and gray and muted red.

"Go safely, MacGregor."

He nodded, and picked up his pack, grinning. "You'll not come below and give me one of your long hot kisses, that I may be the envy of all?"

She didn't smile back, this time. She simply stared somberly at him, and then she spoke.

"Niall, I love you more than I love my life. When you go, you will take my heart with you. *Mo cridh*, I cannot live without you."

He halted, already turned to go, and looked back at her. She stood, tall and straight in her plaid trews and stockings, her sark still loose about her hips. Her eyes were large, and there was a glimmer of tears in them. He had never seen her so, proud in the truth, giving herself to him. He felt the fear that he had felt after that dream at Loch Laggan.

And something inside him, something fighting that fear, hating it, made him speak.

■ 243 ■

Macgregor's Bargain

"Ah, but remember, my dear, should I fall, should our cause be lost, throw yourself on the tender mercies of Francis Hepburn."

He walked back to her, kissed her roughly, and left the room, not looking back at her.

She stood still for long moments, heard Calum's shout, "Farewell, dear Coz!"

And heard them ride away.

Chapter Twenty Eight

The snow lay deep in the Highlands, but along the lochs it was fairly easy to ride. With out the pack ponies, their journey was swift. Anne, stony faced, speaking to no one rode alone and spoke shortly to those companions who tried to engage in conversation. At night, she sat alone, and was brief with her news to people with whom they stayed. She insisted they ride by moonlight as they passed the smoking ruins of Fort Augustus, burned by the Jacobites.

Colonel Grant's forces, on their way to Fort William after their victory at Fort Augustus, offered them a hot meal and a secure resting place for a night, and a tent for Anne, for it was snowing again.

She curled into a ball in her plaid and watched the dance of firelight on the canvas wall of the tent. She heard the men's voices clearly. Runners had brought news to Grant, and he shared what he knew, as Iain passed around a flask of whisky.

Charles was now at Nairn, and the clans were all joining him there. There had been a few troops come over from France, but gold that had been sent had either been lost or fallen into enemy hands.

The Duke of Cumberland, the son of King George, was now leading the Royalists, and word was he was a fierce fighter.

The next morning, they bid farewell to Grant and his men, and turned south to Loch Laggan.

Bard bounded to meet Anne, making great leaps through the new fallen snow, dancing beside Vixen till the tired mare curveted and kicked at him.

They rode to the stable block and Iain helped Anne down. He held her for a moment, wondering what had happened that last morning. The glow he had seen in her during the days with Niall was more than the fulfillment of the nights, he knew.

He sighed as he watched her walk to the castle.

Och, weel, that's work for Morag, not a man.

His own Morag came toward him, arms outstretched. "My own lad, I am that glad to see you and Fergus home safe."

"How is Fiona?"

"Abloom, but gey worried about her man, of course. So Hamish did come back."

"Poor lad. He wanted there to be two of him, one to go with MacGregor, one to be home with Fiona. Morag?"

She looked up at him, her shawl pulled tight around her face. "Come inside, let me make you something hot. Why, what is it?"

"Something has happened to our Anne."

Startled, Morag looked toward Anne's retreating back, the dog Bard now walking sedately beside her.

"Ye must talk to her. She has not been herself since we left for home."

"You great lout, she loves MacGregor. She's sad and afraid."

"She loves him, aye, I thought as much. But there's more, I think."

She nodded. "I will see to her, but first, I'll get you into warm dry clothes and give you a warm drink. Anne will see to her daughter first, I've no doubt. Then I'll see to her."

But Anne was not forthcoming. She shook her head and refused to be drawn in.

Morag agreed with Iain, but here was little she could do. Anne played with her babe, spent long evenings alone, reading in the library, and sometimes Morag spied her walking on the battlements as she had done as a child.

She was polite, distant, and pleasant when Alan and Lucy came, but unreachable.

Lucy too became troubled and spoke to Fiona. "Is she bairning, Fiona? Is that why she is so unlike herself? Has she said ought to you?"

Fiona shook her head. "She has not been home long enough for me to know. I can tell you what Hamish told me. She and MacGregor spent most of their time together, and with Calum. She seemed content, even knowing the men would have to leave shortly. Then the morning they left, she didn't come to see them off, she stayed in her room until they were gone, though Calum called out to her. And when she came down, she looked neither angry nor sad, Hamish said. He said she looked like a, a statue, I think he said. And she wouldn't speak to anyone."

Lucy shook her head. "Mayhap what's best is to leave her until she is ready to talk of it. Our concern may hurt her the more."

And so they treated Anne as if they noticed nothing wrong, and she spent most of her time with Catriona, who alone seemed to be able to make her really smile. The baby, now six months old, seemed to be perpetually laughing and crooning to anyone who would stop and look at her. Even grim Jane became pleasant around Catriona.

And all the time, in Anne's mind, Niall's words repeated themselves. And all the nights, Anne saw death, and a field of blood in her dreams.

On the fourteenth of April, the Duke of Cumberland, the younger son of King George of Hanover, ruler of Great Britain, reached Nairn.

Prince Charles had occupied the last few weeks in and around Inverness, attending parties, hunting and fishing, drinking with his cronies. He finally settled in at Culloden House, to the dismay of its owner Lord President Duncan Forbes, who was attempting to stay neutral. Niall and Calum and their men had rejoined Perth's

Macgregor's Bargain

army and the scattered troops began to gather around the Prince, the grounds of Culloden House covered with tents.

Charles took command of the strategy meeting outside Culloden House that evening. "O'Sullivan has chosen the most propitious site for our coming battle, which I will lead."

Murray sat back at his chair. "Your Highness?"

Charles waved his hand. "I will be heard. You will not speak unless I tell you to. Now, O'Sullivan has chosen Culloden Moor, and there we will meet our enemy, the son of the usurper who now sits on the throne. And we will carry the day. God is on our side, and we will retreat no more."

He stood, motioned to O'Sullivan and his other friends, and led them in to dinner at Culloden House. They were quickly emptying the Lord President's wine cellar.

Niall, weary to the bone, so grim that Calum no longer tried to jest with him, inspected the small stores they had brought back, and found that there was very little else for the army to eat. Charles had announced that his hunting and fishing brought food for the men, but there was precious little, and no money to buy more.

Niall joined Lord George Murray as the Jacobite leader stood staring across bleak Culloden Moor at the troops being assembled in battle formation, facing eastwards.

Murray studied the landscape: open moor, suitable for a cavalry charge. "This is a poor place for us, and a very good one for Cumberland's troops. His horse will be able to maneuver well. And I like not those enclosures. They will not allow our men freedom to charge. I tried to move the lines to the higher ground, but O'Sullivan and the Prince would have none of it." Enclosures, large rock walls surrounded farm fields on either side of the moor.

Murray had asked Niall and Calum to reconnoiter back toward the River Spey, and the news they brought was not good.

"They are encamped near Nairn, sir," Niall said. "We had four men with us, and we tried to count their forces. There are over ten thousand of them, sir, and many horses and cannon. One of my men slipped close into their camp, and they are well set for supplies. The men look rested and well fed. They have a large herd of cattle with them, probably our own that we had to abandon."

"How far from us?"

"Less than eight miles, I'd say."

Murray drew in his breath. "I must speak to His Highness. Our own men have so little their rations are cut to nothing. O'Sullivan has not brought food down from Inverness, says he is too busy to be bothered, although that is his responsibility, and I've had to flog two of the poor starving devils for stealing."

"Sir, if I may speak?"

Murray nodded. Niall had grown to respect the crusty, highhanded man. Though at times he had disagreed with him, Murray was the best soldier they had, the one who seemed, even with his growing hatred of Charles, to see the situation most clearly.

"Sir, if they pull us into battle here, on a moor, we are lost. The moor will be better for Cumberland's men, fighting as they do. We must pull back to the hills where their cavalry cannot perform, where they cannot drag their cannon."

Murray nodded. "I agree, and that is why I plan to try again to change His Highness's mind. We need go no further than across the Nairn, where the ground is unfit for Cumberland's cavalry."

But Prince Charles would not see him.

At noon, when it was obvious that Cumberland's army would not fight that day, the tired men were called from the battle positions.

Murray, Perth and Niall returned to their men. Old Alasdair Drummond, so ill with pneumonia that he had been in bed all day, hobbled in to camp to ask what had taken place.

Niall's bitterness could not be contained. "The Prince will lead us into battle, colors flying, pipes playing, and our starving, itching, scabby Highlanders and a handful of foreigners will fight on a flat moor, against ten thousand well fed, well disciplined troops."

The old man bent over, coughing, leaning against his hound bitch that had followed him to England and back again. The he drew himself upright and glared at Niall. "Best not speak treason, MacGregor. Kin by marriage ye may be, but ye're still a MacGregor, and like all your lot, ye think ye're better than those that lead ye."

Macgregor's Bargain

Niall made an impatient gesture and turned to Murray. "I will ride out to the east. There may be a place where we will be able to watch for Cumberland unseen."

Murray agreed, staring across the bleak moor, and Niall rode off, Calum staying behind to count the number of troops they could depend on. Men were wandering in, but horses and troops showed a weariness from little rest and less food.

Niall looked northwest where gray clouds hid the Highlands. "If we could convince him to return to Inverness, to cross into the Highlands..." But he knew that it was hopeless, that they were doomed to be sacrificed to Charles' unworkable plan.

Now all he wanted was to spend some time alone. He nudged Iolair into a trot toward a thick grove of trees. They looked strange in this barren place, bent into grotesque shapes by the eternal wind.

Iolair shied suddenly as they approached the trees, and halted, ears twisting back and forth, snorting. Niall turned around, feeling as if someone was near, but saw nothing to account for his and his mount's uneasiness. He dismounted and, holding Iolair's reins, walked toward the trees. When the stallion balked, Niall tied him to a sturdy clump of heather and entered the grove.

In the deep silence, tall lichen covered gray stones stood among grass covered mounds. Other stones thrust up through the grass like bones. Still feeling as if he were being watched, Niall approached the nearest standing stone. It was covered not just with lichen, but with strange circles and deep round indentations. He pressed his hand against it. The old ones were here. He felt them around him. Suddenly so weary he couldn't stand, he slumped down, leaning his back against the stone, looking around at mounds like massive graves, the stones leaning toward him as if listening to him.

Anne entered his thoughts. She would have found comfort here, among the spirits that dwelled among these stones. He thought of the way he had left her, so frightened for their future, so angry at his own part in destroying it. He saw her face, chestnut hair tangled, her eyes reddened with crying after declaring her love, and his angry rejection of their future.

∎ 250 ∎

Would he see her again? And their daughter? He doubted it. Prince Charles' scant forces would face the Duke of Cumberland's disciplined army and lose. The Highland men, given permission, could melt away to the north and west and save themselves, but Charles, so sure of his God given right, would insist on this battle. Did leaders ever think that God *wasn't* on their side. Niall sighed and stood, looking around at the massive stones, drawing a certain serenity from them, from the trees, from the mounds that without doubt sheltered the bones of past warriors.

A note to Anne! He could at least send something to let her know he loved her, that he had lied out of fear.

Niall strode out to where Iolair stood nervously, whickering when he saw his master.

More bad news awaited him on his return to camp.

Calum said, "We have hundreds fewer than we thought. Some say some of them have gone to find food, for, Niall, in all truth, the poor men are starving. Some have gone home. And some say they will not stay to fight, for they have heard the Prince plans on making them fight on the moor. Lord Ruthven's men have not arrived, "

Niall and Calum, some MacGregors and a few Drummonds, left, unseen, to go to the west and find men who were able to stand and fight for Prince Charles.

They found men. Some had simply lain down and died of cold and starvation. Some could barely lift their heads as they begged for food.

They did what they could, carried some to the nearest houses, where food had been sold to the Royalists because the Jacobites had no money to pay. Protests were brushed aside, and Niall gave what money he had to insure the clansmen would be cared for.

He remembered the night before when the leaders of the clans quarreled over where they would stand in the battle lines, and wondered that they were not here, looking out for the men who had followed them because their kind had always followed their chief.

He remembered that the Duke of Perth had actually shot his own men who had refused to fight for Charles. As Niall and his

Macgregor's Bargain

men rode, they sometimes found men who had simply gone to find food, who were on their way back to battle. Some had gone home to check on families, and were returning. Some fled at the sight of them, determined, after they saw that moor, not to fight.

Niall and Calum returned to Culloden moor at dusk, sleet pelting them, to find preparations for a surprise attack on Cumberland was being planned.

Cumberland, it seemed, was celebrating his birthday, and according to scouts, was feeding his men well and giving them brandy so they could drink to his health. Prince Charles and O'Sullivan announced that, as the Royalists would be celebrating, the Jacobites might win in a sneak attack on Cumberland's troops. Charles ordered Murray to tell his men.

"But the men are exhausted, and so hungry they are dropping." Niall listened in disbelief to Murray's report. "And we still wait for the rest of our army; Lord Lovat, the Mackenzies, others are on their way."

"I do not want this, but it may be the only way. We can hope the Duke's men will be sleeping soundly after the food and drink he gave them." Murray sighed and looked over the men surrounding Culloden House. "Och, MacGregor, we could have taken back Scotland, but never, never, could we have taken England. And now we must try to save what we can. Besides, even if we are found out, we may retreat as far as Culcarick, which has better ground for us to fight on, than the moor."

Men began to wander off, looking for food, ignoring their officers, as their leaders continued to debate the wisdom of the night attack, but Charles was obdurate.

"Our men will fight and win. Cumberland's troops will be in a drunken sleep by the time we attack. Round up your men, promise them English meat when we win!"

Chapter Twenty Nine

At eight o'clock on the night of April 15, Murray and his men led the way toward Cumberland's camp, followed by Charles and the Duke of Perth. Niall rode with the Drummonds in the rear. Horses and men mired in bogs, and men too hungry to fight simply lay down and would not get up. By two o'clock they were still several miles from the enemy camp.

Knowing they couldn't reach it by daybreak, Murray sent back the order to turn around.

"It is Murray's fault," Prince Charles muttered to his advisors as they turned back to Culloden House. " He could not muster enough men. Had we four thousand rather than 1200 we could have taken their camp."

After a march of 12 miles in the dark, the exhausted Jacobites trooped back 12 miles to Culloden, reaching the moor after daybreak, and tired and unfed, waited again on Drummossie Moor.

Niall, in the tent he shared with Calum, lit a candle and began to write. Calum came in as he finished.

"Take this, Calum. Should we become separated and you cannot find me, take it to Anne."

Calum studied his cousin, started to say something, then nodded and held out his hand.

Murray was still arguing with O'Sullivan on the morning of April 16th. "We must take down the enclosures around the fields on our right, or we will be cornered."

"Nonsense." O'Sullivan seemed to shrink as he looked across the moor where the Royalist troops were lining up in rows, the black mouths of cannon facing the Jacobites. "There are bogs that will slow the horses. The redcoats will not go that way, they will charge straight at us."

"But if we cross the Nairn, set our troops on yon hill…"

"No. This is our plan," O'Sullivan glowered at Murray. "Our Prince has agreed on the site I have selected, and this is where we stand. The bogs will halt the horse troops and the cannon will be mired!" He turned on his heel and strode toward where Prince Charles sat his horse. He spoke, then both men turned and glowered at Murray.

Niall MacGregor, standing beside Murray, watched the redcoats, keeping his face still, despair cold in him. The Jacobites had lined up, though men were still wandering back as leaders urged them to the battle lines, and Lord Lovat and his men had not come, though a messenger had brought news they were near. Niall looked back to the second line where men of the Duke of Perth and Lord John Drummond stood, old Alastair among the men, holding the deerhound bitch. The old man was bent over, coughing. Near him stood the sons of Iain and Morag, all of them save young Fergus who had been furious at being left behind at Castle Caorann.

"Stay with me, MacGregor," Murray ordered. "I will be with the Atholl men. I am moving my men so they can get around the Leanach enclosure to our right."

Niall nodded. Hamish and Calum stood behind him, and he motioned to them to mount and follow Murray. He swung up on Iolair and went to the right side of the line.

"We are closer to Cumberland than the left flank, sir."

"I know. I am not sure what they are doing over there. We must wait until we get orders."

Macgregor's Bargain

"Yon Camerons are seething," Calum said softly."They are always on the right. It is tradition. The Prince put the Athollmen there. The Prince has not learned the way of things."

"Aye, well, it is too late now," Niall said grimly. "By the end of this day there won't be enough men to make one clan."

He saw Murray's back stiffen, but the man did not turn or reply. Niall knew that Murray, too, saw the battle already lost. He looked over his shoulder toward the middle of the third row of men, the mounted troops, where Charles sat his horse between Fitz-James' Horse and Balmerino's Life Guards, the Irish Piquets and Royal Ecosse from France far to the left . The big white animal was moving nervously. Niall was sure that it was reacting to the Prince's anxiety.

Beside the Prince, his men O'Sullivan and addlepated Sheridan sat their horses. Since the first days of the Prince's arrival Sheridan had seemed less and less aware of their circumstance. And O'Sullivan was responsible for so much that had happened; the loss of food the men needed, the battle plans that made no sense. Morosely, Niall stared across the moor. Somewhere he heard the calling of a moorhen, then he saw rooks gathering in the trees where he had found the standing stones. They would eat well soon.

Twice as many men as we have, so many more cannon...

The rain had turned to sleet, blowing toward the Jacobite lines, and men pulled their plaids close around them.

They waited. Iolair stamped impatiently and Niall spoke softly to him. The sleet stopped for the moment, although the cold wind still bit into his face. He looked up and saw a golden eagle soaring above him, and wondered what it all looked like from the bird's height.: The rows of men, the glittering of sabers, the rolling moor, and far off, beyond Moray Firth, the blue shapes of the Highlands. Niall felt his heart quicken and he swallowed. Was he going to die here, far from the wife he loved, the child he hardly knew?

The Royalist troops seem to multiply, the dragoons moving toward the enclosure nearest Murray and the Atholl men.

They will try to surround us.

While the Royalists were ordered from one place to another, the Highlanders waited for the order to charge.

■ 255 ■

Macgregor's Bargain

Clan chiefs continued to argue about their rights to certain positions along the battle lines.

Murray and Niall rode along behind the front lines: Glengarry at the east end, Atholl to the west, and stopped, looking at the high turf wall that would block the Athollmen. Murray clustered them to avoid the wall, and rode back along the second row of clans, to the Duke of Perth at the east end next to the French troops. Old Alasdair Drummond, his gray deerhound bitch at his side, glared at Niall. Murray motioned Perth's forces forward.

As if some dangerous minuet, the British army shifted in reaction to the changes made in the Jacobite lines as Murray, Niall, Calum and Hamish rode back to the Atholl men.

No order came. The Highlanders began to show restlessness, moving about, shouting, as the disciplined Royalist troops simply stood, staring back at their enemies. Niall wondered how many of those in the redcoat lines had been at Prestonpans and Falkirk, and now yearned for revenge at their losses.

The cawing of rooks from the trees increased. Niall's mouth was dry, his hands on the reins slippery with sweat. Iolair curvetted and Niall tightened the reins .

A shout went up and order had been given, and the Jacobite battery roared, round shot arcing over the first Royalist line.

"They're shooting for Cumberland," Murray murmured.

Then the 16 three pounders of the Royalists opened up. The round shot soared over the first line. Those cannons too were seeking out the enemy's leader. Niall looked back, saw hussars and their horses fall, screaming, but Charles still rode his nervous horse.

Niall looked at the men around him. Some crossed themselves. He saw one man grip the shoulder of the boy beside him. A child, Niall thought. Perhaps 12 or 13.The man had brought his son to fight with him. For a moment his surroundings seemed far away, the sounds of cannon and screaming dimming. He looked around, saw the open mouths of men as they yelled their war cries, the smoke of Royalist cannon, the sleet, the trees where the rooks waited, and he thought of the calm waters of Loch Laggan, the

Macgregor's Bargain

castle standing on the rocks, Anne walking in the rose garden, the baby in her arms.

Then round shot landed behind him, among the Ogilvies, and the sound roared around him again as Iolair reared and whinnied in fear, and his own heart thundered.

Thickening smoke hid most of the Royalist lines, and the Highlanders still waited impatiently for the cry of "Claymore!" Man after man fell in the steady rain of round shot. Jacobite cannon fell silent, the men continued to fall, and still Murray did not receive order a charge. Then a young man galloped his horse up to Murray.

"An earlier messenger was killed. You are to order a charge!" he shouted.

Murray screamed the battle cry. "Claymore!"

At last the pipes played the pibroch, the cry of "Claymore!" reverberated along the line of Highlanders. Men of Clan Chattan ran forward, yelling their war cries, pipes screaming the rant tripping over their own dead. An steady spray of grapeshot, pieces of old iron, nails and leaden balls, from the closest cannon tore men apart. Wounded and dying screamed, cannon roared. Stewarts and Camerons, Mackintoshes and MacGillivrays collided as they raced forward toward the Royalist lines, waving their swords, yelling their war cries. Other screaming clansmen drew their swords and ran at the English lines, breaking ranks, dropping muskets, some moving to their right around the Leanach enclosure, beating back the Royalist left. Some no longer had their targes, their shields. Bare legged, many barefooted, kilts pulled around their groins they ran to be met with a barricade of bayonets. Some drove through the Royalist lines and were killed before they could escape. The Jacobites blocked by turf and stone walls were killed, then more dead fell on them. They slipped in the blood of their clansmen and fell under grapeshot, the nails, balls and pieces of metal tearing them apart. In places, bodies piled three or four deep.

In the melee, Niall saw little, the smoke of the Royalist guns hiding Cumberland's lines. He drew his sword, and raced forward, Iolair leaping over bodies. A hussar galloped toward him and Niall swung his sword, and the hussar fell. Looking toward the

■ 257 ■

Macgregor's Bargain

Drummonds he realized that Murray's men were far ahead of those on the left: as he had feared, Drummond's and Perth's men were floundering through a bog. Then he felt Iolair stagger, and saw a bullet had grazed his horse's neck. They galloped forward, until Niall realized he was surrounded by Royalist cavalry. A redcoat swung his sword and Niall felt the blade's path along his leg. He pulled Iolair around and galloped back, the horse leaping over piles of dead and wounded Highlanders.

The Highlanders' right wing was caught in a vicious enfillade, as the Royalist Hussars attacked them from the side of the enclosure. Murray's horse bolted, taking him through the Royalist lines. Murray reined in his mount and careened through the Hanoverians and back to gather his men into ranks and take them off the field. Niall saw him yell, but could not hear over the crash of battle. Then Murray motioned him to retreat.

When Niall caught up with Murray, he looked around for Calum and Hamish, and saw them with Murray's Athollmen. They seemed unwounded. He looked down at his leg. A seam of blood ran down into his boot. Blood had dried on Iolair's neck; the wound seemed superficial. But the stallion's legs were covered in the battlefield's gore.

Murray, his wig gone, tears making runnels of gray in his smoke blackened face, screamed, "We must go. They have beaten us, and they will kill us all if we stay. We are to gather at Ruthven Barracks. Perth and Lord John Drummond are taking their men away now. I give you leave to go before the butchery begins. God keep you safe."

Clansmen broke and ran, chased by Cumberland's cavalry. Some escaped. The people who had come to watch the battle along the road to Culloden did not escape.

Prince Charles Stuart was led, crying, from the battleground.

Niall, Calum and Hamish rode the lines, looking for Alasdair Drummond and found his body and that of the deerhound lying near the torn, bloody bodies of the three sons of Iain and Morag. The volleys of grapeshot had ripped through them. The rest of the Drummonds and Perth's men were retreating, screams on the

Macgregor's Bargain

battlefield continued, and sleet was already showing white on the dead.

"We go to Loch Laggan. There is no more we can do here." Niall turned Iolair away, then bent over and vomited. Hamish and Calum, both weeping, followed him, all three wondering what they would find when they returned to Castle Caorann. As they rode away, they heard the screams of the dying, triumphant yells of the Royalists.

In less than an hour the battle was over, but the killing would go on and on.

Chapter Thirty

Loch Laggan lay under a light mist. The mountains had stopped the sleet and icy rain that had fallen on the battle at Culloden, and though it was only April there had been a thaw that turned the stable yard to mud. But the knowledge that spring was coming drew Anne out of doors.

There had been rumors of battles, but they had heard only by word of mouth, not to be trusted as truth. Anne knew that she would feel Niall's death; therefore she knew he was alive. The pain had lessened, and she was nearly what she had been before that morning at the inn.

There was something about the coming of the spring, no matter how far away it really was, that gave her hope. Her people had survived a winter; there was food enough for now. Catriona thrived, and Fiona bloomed with the child she was carrying. Hamish had resigned himself to his role, and helped Iain prepare for the spring planting. The road toward Fort William, was watched, and movement of British soldiers always caused alarm, but thus far they had not come as far as Loch Laggan.

Anne wandered into the stable yard where Iain and Hamish, taking advantage of the sunshine, were mending harness.

Macgregor's Bargain

"I'll ride today, Iain. Vixen is in sore need of exercise, as am I."

Iain, glad to see her near to being her old self, rather than the wraith of the past winter, grinned and went to saddle Vixen.

"Do you wish company?"Hamish looked up at her.

"No but thank you. Take Bard so he won't follow me."

Iain led Vixen out and helped Anne mount.

"Where will ye go?"

"Up into the glen, it's been a great while since I've been there."

"Are you better then?"

She laughed as she wheeled the mare. "Twas just a silly fancy. I'll not be long."

The mare pranced along the peninsula leading up to the hill, along the burn that ran into the loch. The breeze was chill, and Anne pulled Niall's old plaid around herself. It gave her comfort to wear it, and she fancied she could feel him and smell him. He would return, and although he had told her he did not love her, she had her people and her land, and perhaps it would be enough that she loved him.

The mare's ears pricked as she crossed the road that led to Fort William, and looking north, Anne saw, not a quarter of a mile away, a small troop of redcoats, and realized they had seen her, and were spurring their horses toward her.

Without thinking, knowing only that she must not ride back home, she urged Vixen up the hill. The mare was swift but the great cavalry horses gained on her.

There was a shout, a loud noise, as Anne reached the small glen, and she felt the mare begin to fall. Another noise, and she thought she heard someone scream "NO!" as she fell.

Francis Hepburn pulled his horse up, and jumped down before it had stopped.

There had been a moment when the figure had turned, and the plaid had slipped, and he caught a glimpse of bright hair and a profile he knew well, and he had screamed at his sergeant.

She lay where she had been thrown when the mare fell, her plaid now spread under her, her hair coming loose from her plait, curling round her face as he had seen it so often.

Macgregor's Bargain

She breathed, though each breath was labored.

His sergeant came up to him. "Another of the bastard savages down, eh, sir?"

Francis Hepburn drew a deep breath. He stared down at Anne, seeing a patch of blood seeping through her hair.

"You are to go back to Fort William and report that we found one woman, and she is dead. I know the castle yonder and I will take it for the crown,.."

The sergeant grinned. "Aye, sir, better you than me. Take care they do not knife you in your sleep. Do you want at least one of the men to come with you?"

"No. I will take care of this. Go on your way."

The sergeant signaled to the men, and they turned to head back to Fort William.

Hepburn waited till they were out of sight, bent his head, and looked at the face of the woman he loved. Then he gathered Anne in his arms, and leading his horse, made his way down to Caorann Castle.

Bard ran to meet him, tail between his legs, stopped, and howled.

The way home had been long, and Niall, who had gone into the last days of battle dressed as a gentleman, in plaid trews and green coat with silver trim, now was clad as any clansman, in a great kilt of the new plaid Anne's people had made for him.

From a distance, up steep mountainsides. Niall saw whole glens in flames, where crofting communities had been put to the torch by Royalists. He and his men had slept in the open, occasionally finding a crofter still fortunate to have a home who would put them up in his single room, the cattle in the byre next door giving them warmth through the night.

The people had little to share, but they did so for that was the way in the Highlands. They asked of lairds and chiefs, of sons and kin, and Niall and Calum and their men could offer them little. Niall and Calum heard of women and children swept away by gunfire as they fled up the mountains.

Always, in the long trek through the Monad Liath Mountains, they had to take to the heather, to lie still as Royalist troops moved

Macgregor's Bargain

around them. Gray Mountains they were called, and gray snow clouds clung to their summits like an omen. Granite scree and clumps of heather slowed them, and corries filled with snowmelt bent their route.

In the steepest of the mountains, at Corrieyairack Pass, near where, such a short time ago, Jacobites had routed Cope's soldiers, they saw a troop of Redcoats on the military road to Fort William. Lying shivering in the heather and snow, plaids protecting them, they watched the disciplined cavalry ride by below them. Calum, beside Niall, drew in a sharp breath. Leading them was Francis Hepburn.

That night they found a family crouched beside a spring, an ancient broch protecting them. A gaunt woman with haunted eyes looked up at them dully. Two bairns with thin faces and pot bellies clung to her. A girl of perhaps twelve sat at a distance, rocking, humming to herself, clinging to a rag doll.

"The laird came, and told my Angus he must fight for his clan, or lose his home, and so he went, and I thought I'd never see him more," the woman said in a dull monotone. "But Angus came back, and then the Sassenachs came, with Campbells who could speak the Gaelic, and they called him a traitor and killed him. And they took my lass... She's been like that since. I begged them to take me instead but they laughed and the Campbell said who would want a dried up dirty old woman like me. And they burned our house and took our cow and killed her."

As they lay in their plaids that night, Calum spoke softly to his cousin, voicing Niall's own fears. "Loch Laggan is so close to Fort William. If Cumberland is giving no quarter, if the Sassenachs are killing even those who didn't fight..."

They walked, leading their tired horses, down the last glen and saw Loch Laggan below them, the castle and the buildings still standing, and Niall leaned his head down that his men would not see his tears.

It was surprising that no one challenged them as they came.

Niall opened the great door, and Jane came toward him. Her face had grown gaunt, and there were deep lines in it now.

"Sir. You have come home. I am glad."

Niall stared at her. "Where are they all?"

She motioned. "In the library. Sir, I am most heartily sorry."

"You are sorry? Jane, what has happened??"

Jane repeated, "They are in the library." She paused. "Himself? Drummond?"

Niall shook his head.

Jane turned away, her head bowed.

Francis Hepburn stepped into the hall. "You have come in time."

"What are you doing here? Where is my wife?"

Niall strode toward him, reaching for his dirk.

Then Hamish stopped him. "No. He has saved us."

Morag came from behind Hepburn and reached for Niall's hand. "Come, Sir."

Knowing, yet not believing, he let her lead him into the library. He heard a babe's loud demanding cries. Catriona. Fiona was so great in her bairning that she waddled as she walked toward him with his daughter. He reached for both of them, and held them, until Catriona screamed indignantly at being crushed.

"Where is Anne?" His voice sounded faint in his own ears.

"She is in her room. Lucy is with her."

Niall waited to hear no more. He raced up the stairs and stopped at the door to Anne's tower room. It was ajar and he gently pushed it open and not daring to breathe, stepped inside.

Bard lay as he so often had, on a rug beside the bed. He raised his head and looked at Niall, then went back to his vigil.

The form on the bed was very still and he walked toward it. Then Lucy rose from her chair on the far side of the bed and came toward him. She, like Fiona, was in the last months of her pregnancy.

"Niall, thank God. We have been hoping."

Niall tried to clear his throat, then said hoarsely, "Is she dead?"

"No, my dear. But she won't waken. It's been two days."

Niall went to stand by the bed. Anne's face was swollen, there were bruises around her eyes, and a bandage on her forehead. Her breathing was steady. He bent and kissed her.

Macgregor's Bargain

Mo cridhe.

"Look, Lucy, her eyelids move."

"Yes, they do, often, as if she dreams. Sometimes she moans, and when Catriona is brought in, she seems to know it. But, Niall, she won't wake up." Lucy's voice quavered at the last words.

Niall put his arms around her and stared over her head at his wife, so still, caught in some other world. *Anne, wherever you are now, come back to me. I know I cannot live without you. Mo cridhe, mo beatha.* My heart, my life.

Lucy pulled away. "I will leave you with her for a few moments." She opened the door and went out, pulling it closed behind her.

Niall went around the bed and sat in the chair Lucy had occupied. From his sporran he pulled out the letter he had written the night before the battle. Bard came to sit beside him, still staring at Anne. The thick paper rustled. He reached for her hand, lying cool and limp on the coverlet, and curled his fingers around it, then began to read.

"My Beloved Wife,

Tomorrow evening might find me among the dead and I cannot rest until I tell you that I love you. At the inn, when you opened your heart to me, in my cowardice and fear of what might come, I could not find the bravery to tell you goodbye, and at the same time send you back to an unknown fate at Loch Laggan, and myself to the surety of death on the battlefield. I had felt a great fear that one of us must die, and it would be better that it be me. I have come to love you more than the cause I fight for, more that my life, and if I am wrong, and I live, I will cherish you and our child more than Scotland itself.

Then Niall folded the letter and put it in her hand. He got up from the chair and Bard went back to lie beside the bed, staring at Anne. As Niall opened the door Lucy slipped in and sat again. Pulling the door shut behind him, Nial leaned against the wall, his head bowed, looking over the balcony into the minstrel's gallery, where shadows moved.

Hamish waited with Fiona at the bottom of the stairs by the library. "Hear Hepburn out. He's been here since. We hear word of all the Highlands going up in flames at Butcher Cumberland's command, and he has saved her-your- people."

Niall nodded, taking Catriona and walking past Calum, standing white faced by the door.

Hepburn stood by the fire in the library, a deerhound pup worrying at his boot. The two men stared at each other, then both looked away.

Hepburn cleared his throat and spoke, his voice unsteady. "I would have given my life for her. She loved only you."

"What happened?"

"Two days ago, I was leading a troop, they saw her and gave chase before I could stop them. They did not see a woman. They saw only a Highlander in a plaid. Your old plaid, Fiona tells me, that she wore all the time. I had no time to stop them before they fired. Her horse was killed and fell on her. She hit her head. I could only protect what she loved-after."

Niall nodded, too numb to hate him or to thank him. Catriona, quiet now, stared at her father.

Hepburn walked to the door. "I have said the castle and lands are under my control. My commanding officer agrees. I will live at Fort William, and I have promised the commander I will bring grain and beef from these lands. I'll insure your lands won't be confiscated. I hope someday, Niall MacGregor, to meet you again in peace." He left, closing the door behind him.

Niall slumped into a chair, Catriona on his lap. She looked up at him and grinned, an endearing gap between two front teeth, her eyes the color of his, the shape of Anne's. She turned her head to stare at the fire.

Anne, mo cridh.

As if she heard his thoughts, Catriona looked back at him.

Niall kissed the soft curls. "Catriona, mo cridhe," he said.

Up in the tower room Bard suddenly stood, tail wagging and laid his head on the coverlet. Anne's hand moved, then tightened around the letter.

Author Bio

Rowena Williamson lives on an island in Puget Sound, where she is a member of RWA, SCBWI, PNWA, The Northwest Institute of Literary Arts, and The Historical Novel Society. She has attended the NILA MFA Residency and is a senior reader for literary agent Andrea Hearst. Williamson has done extensive research on the Battle of Culloden and Scottish history, both in the United States and in Scotland. *MacGregor's Bargain,* under the title *The Road to Culloden,* was a finalist in the Historical Novel Category at the 2010 PNWA Conference. Her short stories have appeared in a number of anthologies.

Made in the USA
Charleston, SC
17 December 2012